THE UNIQUE MAGAZINE
Spring 1990

ISSN 0898-5073
Art by Janet Aulisio

Weird Tales® is published quarterly by the Terminus Publishing Company, Inc., P.O. Box 13418, Philadelphia PA 19101-3418. (4426 Lar-
chwood Ave., Philadelphia, PA 19104-3916). Second class postage paid at Philadelphia PA and additional mailing offices. Single copies,
$4.00 (plus $1.00 postage if ordered by mail). Subscription rates: Eighteen months (6 issues) for $18.00 in the United States and its
possessions, for $24.00 in Canada, and for $27.00 elsewhere. The publishers are not responsible for the loss of manuscripts, although
reasonable care will be taken of such material while in their possession. Copyright© 1989 by the Terminus Publishing Company, Inc.;
all rights reserved. Reproduction prohibited without prior permission. *Weird Tales*® is a registered trade mark owned by Weird Tales,
Limited. Typeset, printed, and bound in the United States of America.

THE EYRIE

Once more into the breach, dear friends, once more — Welcome to the *seventh* issue of our revived, as opposed to exhumed, *Weird Tales®*.

The chief order of business this Eyrie continues to be a reminder about subscriptions. If your subscription has expired, or is about to, please renew at once, so that you don't miss any issues. Remember that while we do have back issues available (any issue from #290 to the present postpaid for $5.00), supplies are limited, and the issues will not be reprinted. Subscriptions are, in any case, the lifeblood of the magazine. We need you. *Weird Tales®* has been, for almost a year now, the sole professional magazine of fantasy and horror in the United States. Short horror fiction continues to flourish in the small press, and in assorted (mostly invitational) anthologies, while less-than-novel-length sword and sorcery and imaginary-scene fantasy seem to be in a sharp decline. If a new Lovecraft or Robert E. Howard or C. L. Moore is going to be found, he (or she) is probably going to turn up here, in the pages of *Weird Tales®*.

For that we need continuing subscriber support.

Also, we'd like to congratulate author Brian Lumley, whose novelette "Fruiting Bodies" (originally published in *Weird Tales®* 291, Summer 1988) has won the British Fantasy Award. Brian's *Necroscope* placed second in the novel category.

Reader **Jim Clar** of Rochester, New York,

sent us a clipping from a newspaper which suggests that maybe "Fruiting Bodies" isn't entirely fiction, by the way. It reads:

MYSTERIOUS SUBSTANCE EATS FAMILY OUT OF ITS HOME

Dayton, Ohio — A mysterious substance that erodes clothing and furniture has forced a family to flee their home and has baffled hazardous-materials investigators, officials said yesterday.

"Yesterday, the furniture started falling apart, and their clothing started falling off their body [sic]*," said Ray Hughes of the Dayton Fire Department.*

Now, if only these journalists and officials had been reading *Weird Tales®*, everything would have been much clearer to them. The headline puzzles us, though. Does the "its" refer back to "substance," meaning that this nasty family of humans moved into a house owned by the Slime before it drove them out, purely in self-defense?

This isn't the book-review section of the magazine, but let us recommend a book to you anyway: *The World Beyond the Hill* (subtitled *Science Fiction and the Quest for Transcendence*) by Alexei and Cory Panshin (Jeremy P. Tarcher, Inc. $29.95), which is not merely a history of science fiction (and a good choice for next year's non-fiction

Hugo-winner), but a study of the development of SF as *myth*. The function of science fiction in literature, say the Panshins, has been the restoration of the plausibly miraculous or transcendent. At the end of the 17th century, the Age of Reason set in, and Western intellectuals could no longer take seriously the old world of *spirit*, magic, ghosts, gods, and the like, which had been supplying the element of wonder since the beginning of writing at least. The last great works of the old world were *Hamlet* and *Paradise Lost*. The first of the new was *Frankenstein*. In between there was virtually no fantastic literature written in Europe. Then science fiction was gradually invented, we are told, and it alone could be a *complete myth*, an imaginative extension "beyond the hill" (that is, beyond the world of mundane experience) which could possibly be *true*. It gives us a mental picture of the universe we live in, and where we are going, even as the works of Homer gave such a picture to the classical Greeks, or the Old Testament to the Hebrews.

Why are we bringing this up in *Weird Tales®*, you may ask. Well, what's stirred up the dust in our eldritch crypt is the Panshins' corollary statement that *fantasy* (including, presumably, horror fiction), like mundane fiction, is only imperfectly mythic and somehow less compelling, less important, less *true*.

We immediately wonder why fantasy and horror are selling better than ever. You'd think that if they'd lost their edge, they'd become at best curios, like the Lost Race novel or the metrical romance. Obviously they haven't.

It can't be that people literally *believe* in the fantastic elements in the stories: in magic swords, curses, divination, reanimated corpses, spirit-possession, and the like. There are indeed many people in our society who *do* believe in all these things and more, but if we seriously thought that *Weird Tales®* merely encouraged superstition, we would have considerable qualms of conscience about publishing it. We're not here to contribute to social malaise. We don't want to aid and abet — to use Chet Williamson's wonderful phrase — New Age bozos who haven't made any intellectual progress since the Paleolithic. This is a serious matter, and would make a good topic

Editors & Publishers:
John Betancourt
George H. Scithers
Darrell Schweitzer
Assistant Editors:
Leslie Smith
Dainis Bisenieks
Vincent Evangelisti
Diane Weinman
Marc Jones
Circulation Manager:
Richard Kabakjian
Computer Consultant:
David J. Williams III
Of Counsel:
Yale F. Edeiken
Art Consultant:
Joseph Fleischmann III
Photographer:
Advanced Litho, Inc.
Typesetters:
The Twin Company, Inc.
Campus Copy Center
Printer:
Malloy Lithographing, Inc.
Hard-cover Binder
Hoster Bindery, Inc.

SUBMISSIONS?

Like most editors, we get unsolicited manuscripts, *lots* of them. We survive, as do other editors, only by imposing Rules.

Yes, we read unsolicited manuscripts — *if* they are in proper manuscript format. Each must arrive with a self-addressed, stamped return envelope big enough to take that manuscript back to you, or with a stamped, addressed, business-letter-sized envelope *and* instructions to dispose of the manuscript if not bought. And no, we will not read manuscripts in unacceptable format.

This proper format is described in numerous reference works. One of them is *On Writing Science Fiction: The Editors Strike Back!*, by George H. Scithers, Darrell Schweitzer, and John M. Ford — which also goes into the whole art and practice of writing and selling fantastic literature. *On Writing* is available for $19.50, postpaid, from Owlswick Press, PO Box 8243, Philadelphia, PA 19101 (if you live in Pennsylvania, add $1.17 for sales tax).

for another editorial someday: the human race is living in perilous times. The environment is in danger. Species are going extinct as fast as they can be counted. We have the capacity to completely sterilize the planet. Therefore we must be in firm touch with reality. We must learn how to maintain the Spaceship Earth correctly, and not just wish our problems away. In short, in such circumstances, anything which makes us stupid might well kill us.

But credulity doesn't explain why people read (or write) supernatural fantasy. The Panshins give us the correct answer, but they let it drop. On page 126 they are discussing Lord Dunsany (whom you will be reading in the pages of *Weird Tales*® before long, by the way):

What makes Dunsany special . . . is that while there is no apparent modern human science in his fantasy stories, nevertheless they are steeped in the new scientific philosophy. More than any other imaginative fiction of their time, they are built on the firm foundation of unyielding despair. . . . Dunsany was a mocker of idols — and the Edwardian exaltation of Man was an idol. Holding onto the belief in the innate specialness and the superiority of humanity was a form of self-flattery, an easy way out of the dilemmas posed by the new scientific universe.

That's it. The old superstitions, newly revived, warmed-over, and offered with higher price tags by the New Agers, offer *comfort.* They hearken back to the medieval universe in which all things were in neat order, Mankind was the center of attention, and there were all manner of spirits and powers ready to help us out of difficulties. Nowadays, for a stiff price, there are any number of magical charms, protective spirit-entities, or reassuring past-lives available to the gullible.

Modern fantasy — good modern fantasy, for grownups — doesn't comfort. One of the first truly modern horror writers, Lovecraft (who was modern in his thematic material, if not in his technique), never offered comfort. His monsters, even the objects of sorcery in his stories (such as the dead men raised from their "essential salts" in *The Case of Charles Dexter Ward*), embody the

(then) new scientific universe of Einstein and Hubble and Heisenberg, in which Man is but a speck floating on a mote of dust in an endless void, with no particular purpose or meaning other than what he can give to himself. The monsters are symbols of chaos, of the uncontrolled forces beyond our tiny planetary domain and our feeble senses.

Similarly, few modern horror stories offer comfort. When was the last time, outside of certain specialized genres aimed at believers, you saw the hero of a story rescued by his guardian angel, or by friendly, magical forces which just happen to be all around us? The characters in, for example, a Ramsey Campbell story encounter *chaos*, the wild and frightening unknown, and there is no one to hold their hand or help them out. No one is watching. They prevail on their own, or they don't survive. (There have been a few helping-hands in Stephen King's work. But how many readers felt cheated when *The Stand* was resolved by the sudden and literal appearance of the Hand of God? It was only the strength of King's storytelling, and the intense feelings he'd aroused for his characters, that prevented most of us from chucking the book across the room at that point. That ending is not one of King's more brilliant strokes.)

Good fantasy, even when it *does* involve gods and angels and spirits, doesn't offer any easy outs either. The spirits there are symbols of the unknown and possibly (at least to most of the characters involved) unknowable.

In fantasy, these symbols embody both wishes and fears. In horror, they are strictly fears. Even the variously-masked slashers of the cheap "slice & dice" films are symbols of fear. It's something in the air, very contemporary; something which may also be found in the novels of Peter Straub (*Koko*), David Schow (*The Kill Riff*), Rex Miller (*Slob*), and numerous others. We fear chaos, uncontrolled violence, and, much more distinctly, serial killers with knives or other implements. (As this is written, Calcutta is being stalked by the "*Stone Man*," a serial killer who drops fifty-pound slabs of rock on the heads of people sleeping on the sidewalks. It's sufficiently bizarre that a novel will inevitably result.)

Fantasy and horror still have the power of complete myths, but their language is not

that of science fiction. They work in symbol rather than idea. But the myths they have to offer are contemporary ones, still valid, and the difference in approach, in the long run, hardly matters.

Peni R. Griffin writes:

The quality of the whole issue [294] was palpably high, but "Courting Disasters" was so good I can't even remember what else was in it until I think. When I do think, I find that "Why Miracles Don't Happen Anymore" (though I'm sure God could still find a prophet among the same class of people he drew on for the original ones, it is effective as satire) and "Florian" follow.

I thought when I began it that "Upstairs" was going to be high on the list, but it was a crashing disappointment. How could anyone who writes so well bear to write such a silly story? The whole situation is unbelievable from a human point of view. The father chops his kid up at Thanksgiving dinner, nobody in the gathered family interferes, and then he collects the bits and lugs them back up to the room? People just don't act this way — no, not even insane people. I thought for a while we might be getting the mad child's hallucination here, but the last line was too clearly meant as physical reality. Even the state of the body is simply ridiculous. It is easy to talk about chopping people up, but in fact dismembering is a major undertaking. Bone is resistant stuff, and does not give at the first blow. If you'll examine the scene-of-the-crime pictures of, say, the most famous axe-murder of all, you'll find that the bodies of the Bordens are largely still intact. When corpses are found reduced to component parts, they have (in every case with which I am familiar) been cut up after death to facilitate disposal and/or confound identification. It is clearly asinine to do this with a body your family saw you kill; and to take it back upstairs instead of burying it under the floorboards, using it for kindling, or strewing it in remote parts of the county heaps idiocy upon idiocy.

You ever notice how people will talk on and on about things they don't like, and dismiss things they like with a word or two? Sorry to run on — but it makes me angry, because John Accursi is clearly a talented stylist, and seeing all that beautiful prose lavished on such tripe is as painful as if, say, Sir Laurence Olivier had been in a Friday the Umpteenth *movie.*

Another rude letter from an unprofessional, I see (Bret Berman). Is there something about Weird Tales® *that attracts these, or do all magazines get letters like this, and y'all are just the only ones that print them?*

In our experience, from working on both *Amazing* and *Isaac Asimov's Science Fiction Magazine,* all magazines get such letters. We are perhaps a bit more candid about printing them; but we do so only when it will be instructive, rather than just out of spite; although we have to admit that sometimes there *is* a strong temptation to hang someone out to dry. There is a famous saying, "Never argue with the man who buys ink by the barrel." That is, if you write a nasty and stupid letter to a magazine publisher, he might retaliate in the most fiendish manner possible — by printing the letter.

Tim Norman of Garland, Texas, writes:

Recently two things occurred that distress me. I had a subscription to Twilight Zone Magazine *almost from the beginning, which I enjoyed thoroughly, and now* TZ *has ceased publication. I also subscribe to* Castle Rock, The Stephen King Newsletter, *and recently the editor informed its readers that it will cease publishing in December. Could the editors of* Weird Tales® *help me find an appropriate replacement for these publications and what they offer? I wonder if you would find it within the realms of your publication to include information on the latest events concerning the world's most read author in the horror genre.*

The last issue I wish to address is regarding manuscript format. I have read in On Writing Science Fiction: The Editors Strike Back *and in other sources that editors don't like to read manuscripts done on dot-matrix printers. In recent times, however, a lot has been done to improve the quality of dot-matrix printers. My printer has a "Near Letter Quality" mode that I think is very good. Could you address this matter?*

Gladly. Editors live by their eyes. Therefore they don't want to see the products of bad dot-matrix printers, in which the text looks like existential gray fog. A NLQ mode which produces print which is solid and **black** is fine. If you can see space between the individual dots, or if the underlining cuts off the bottoms of letters like 'g' and 'p,' that is not good enough. The basic standard is that someone must be able to tell, distinctly, what every letter and mark of punctuation is *on a second-generation photocopy*. Why? Because the custom often is that the editor copies the story and puts the copy in a file. The original is then given to a typesetter. If that original is lost, the editor has to make a copy of the copy, and the typesetter still has to be able to tell a period from a comma.

As for news and the like, there are *still* more sources of this kind of information than we can even keep track of. New small-press magazines keep popping up like toadstools. A promising new one is *Scream Factory*. Another, longer established, is *Midnight Graffiti*. The most basic source of publishing news and gossip is the science-fiction news magazine, *Locus*. So our feeling is that *Weird Tales®* should not try to compete in this area. You can order most of these small magazines from Robert Weinberg, whose address appears in all our issues.

Luke O'Grady has kind words for Robert Sampson:

I just got my first two issues of Weird Tales®, *numbers 293 and 294, and I'm glad I did. It's fantastic!*

Unfortunately, I've never read the original Weird Tales®, *so I can't compare the two, but I know what I like.*

I have heard a lot about the old Weird Tales®, *and I bet they would have loved Robert Sampson's "Magician in the Dark." I'd love to see more by this guy; the story was completely satisfying in every way.*

I liked being introduced to Avram Davidson as well. I found his style awkward at first, but by the third story I was beginning to really enjoy it. His use of humor is unique and refreshing.

That, of course is the whole purpose of a magazine like ours, to introduce readers to writers they haven't previously encountered. The title *Weird Tales®* draws interested readers. Then we can publish even authors who have never appeared anywhere before. That's why newcomers usually break into print in magazines before they publish books.

Robert Sampson is a relatively new writer.

For a brief moment we thought we'd discovered him, but then we found his name in *New Black Mask* and elsewhere. Avram Davidson, of course, has been around for many years. If you truly never have read anything of his before, let us recommend his short-story collections, starting with, say, *The Best of Avram Davidson,* and then such novels as *The Phoenix and the Mirror* and *The Island Under the Earth.* Owlswick Press (the publishing company owned by Editorial Horde member George Scithers) will soon publish a massive Davidson volume, *The Adventures of Dr. Eszterhazy.*

R.P. Newson of Felixstowe, Suffolk, England, begins his letter with what we admit is a great opening line:

As a professional gravedigger, I have particular interest in your magazine.

When I heard that Weird Tales® *was being revived I was somewhat uneasy, but when I saw the first New issue I was amazed — it was as if you had never been away, and so far you have really lived up to my expectations.*

In the past I have collected a few of the original Weird Tales® *at Comic Conventions in London and I am always looking for more.*

I remember reading somewhere in one of my reference books on Weird Tales® *that in the days of the artists like Bok, Finlay, Freas, and Dolgov, and the great Margaret Brundage, fans of* Weird Tales® *could buy a piece of artwork from the magazine for a reasonable price. Is there any chance of this happening again? If so I would be very interested, as I cannot obtain any artwork on this subject in England.*

Quite probably you can. There are numerous conventions in Britain, the annual Fantasy Convention being the most obvious, where surely you will be able to find a good deal. Further, if you are serious about buying original art, you can write to the artists, either directly, or through this magazine. As for the price being "reasonable," these days, well, in the 1930s artists worked for a pittance, and the magazine bought everything — the original art, and all rights to it. Nowadays we think it "reasonable" that artists should be able to make a living, so we buy only the right to reproduce the drawing or painting in an issue of the magazine and we return the originals.

The artists then make sometimes substantial amounts from sale of the originals, as indeed they should.

We doubt many people bought original Brundage work, at whatever the price, by the way. Her work was done in chalk pastels, and was much too fragile to send through the mail.

Why do you speak of Kelly Freas as if he were a figure of the remote past? He's still very much around, and illustrating a future issue for us.

Donald Franson of North Hollywood, California inquires:
Did anyone ever discover how Weird Tales® *got its name? I recently bought a copy of* The Moon Terror, *the 1927 anthology of stories from* Weird Tales®, *all published in 1923, the first year of the magazine. I was just reading "Ooze" by Anthony M. Rud, and a few paragraphs from the beginning I came upon this sentence:*
"It seemed then that only through filtration and condensation of their dozens of weird tales regarding 'Daid House' could I arrive at understanding of the mystery and weight of horror hanging about the place."
Since this story appeared in the very first issue, and was available in manuscript when the magazine was being put together, could the idea for the title have come to the editor from this source?

Probably not. Most likely the publishers put out market reports soliciting material, with the title *Weird Tales®* already in place, before they had received any manuscripts. According to the best sources, the title was suggested to the publisher, J.C. Henneberger, by lines from Edgar Allan Poe's "Dreamland":
From a weird wild clime that lieth, sublime
Out of Space — out of Time.
Those lines also supplied Clark Ashton Smith with the title of his first Arkham House book, *Out of Space and Time.*

Melissa Singer of Tor Books remarks, editorially:
Flipping through the Fall 1989 issue of Weird Tales®, *I found myself most delighted by Mark S. Painter, Sr.'s "Why Miracles Don't Happen Anymore," which caused more than one chuckle.*

But I found myself wondering why Painter had avoided what seemed to me to be the perfect punchline to the story: After God's tried everyone else, he comes to the Jews. I can just see the fellow he approaches, listening to the speech, then saying,
"So. You're back again. Every time You get turned down by all those other religions, who do You come back to, looking for help? The Chosen People, right? Haven't we given enough? We gave you Noah. We gave you Abraham. We gave you Moses. Every time You need a prophet, You tap some Jew. And the last time — we're still having trouble from last time! That poor carpenter's son . . . what You did to him shouldn't happen to a dog! . . ."
At which point, of course, God abandons the attempt.
Sorry. It's not my story, of course. And it's a good story as it is. (I am Jewish myself, which may be why I noticed the lack.)
Thanks for another good issue.

Daniel Wright, a long-time reader of this magazine, takes us to task for an off-hand remark a couple issues back:
The last letter I wrote to Weird Tales® *was a little over forty years ago. It was in praise of Jules de Grandin. This letter is in his defense.*
You do us all a grave injustice by referring to Seabury Quinn's work as "inadvertently funny." You refer to his stories as pastiches, although that implies an open imitation of another's work. Whatever influences shaped Quinn's tales, this word does not apply. You suggest his fans might find the stories "campy fun." I assure you, those who would find them so are not his fans.
These are good, solid stories that will outlive us both. Their ability to extend the imagination lies undiminished and of course they will forever belong to the history of horrific fiction.
I find your attitude extremely cavalier. I do not suggest that reprints be a part of your editorial policy, but I do suggest that even if the Jules de Grandin tales hold no thrills for you, that you exercise respect and discretion concerning them.

We suspect, with all due respect, that there are very few true fans of Seabury Quinn's celebrated "Mercurial Frenchman" left alive. It is to the history of the field that we turn in defense of our own views. The intervening decades seem to have borne us out: Quinn's position in the horror field remains a lowly one. No major critic or reference work has ever suggested that the de Grandin stories were anything more than formula hackwork. It's clear that even the more sophisticated readers of the time didn't take them seriously. Lovecraft said it best, when he suggested that there was so much good material wasted in Quinn's work that someone should get permission to go back and *write the stories*. Pastiches? Well, Quinn was hardly an innovative writer. His French detective and sidekick are basically warmed-over Holmes and Watson, with a dash of Poe's M. Dupin, save that Quinn didn't know as much French. Otherwise the de Grandin stories are conventional exercises in the "psychic detective" mode pioneered by Algernon Blackwood and William Hope Hodgson.

There are three ways of judging importance in literature: critical consensus, influence, and lasting popularity. Quinn seems to have struck out on all three. He influenced no one. His work now seems to be entirely out of print, so this entire discussion must seem pretty esoteric to many of our readers, who otherwise would be able to read Quinn and make up their own minds.

While we admire and respect the past tradition of this magazine, there are, we have to admit, some things in it we cannot bring ourselves to regard as any more than quaint period pieces: *The Moon Terror* by A.G. Birch, the various serial novels of Otis Adelbert Kline, and, yes, the Jules de Grandin series. Sorry.

The Most Popular Story

Opinions on issue 294 ran to extremes, but, despite one reader intensely loathing Karl Edward Wagner's "At First Just Ghostly," that story is the clear winner. Second place goes to "The Pit-Yakker" by Brian Lumley, and third to "Courting Disasters" by Nina Kiriki Hoffman, with enough favorable opinions to constitute an honorable mention for R. Garcia y Robertson's "Three Heads for the High King." J.K. Potter's unique photographic artwork was also controversial, but more liked than disliked.

He is, in our perception, the single most popular artist in the horror field, particularly in small-press book publishing. So we were especially glad to have him.

We'd like to thank the readers who voted. There were more votes last time than ever before. ⊗

BACK ISSUES STILL AVAILABLE!
$5.00 Each
(postage included)

#290 (spring 1988 — our special 65th Anniversary Issue, with Gene Wolfe as Featured Author and George Barr as Featured Artist. Plus F. Paul Wilson, Ramsey Campbell, T.E.D. Klein, Tanith Lee, and more!

#291 (Summer 198) — Special Tanith Lee/Stephen Fabian Issue. Plus Brian Lumley ("Fruiting Bodies" — winner of the British Fantasy Award), Morgan Llywelyn, Harry Turtledove, Nancy Springer, and more.

#292 (Fall 1988) — Special Keith Taylor/Carl Lundgren Issue. Stories by Alan Rodgers, W.T. Quick, Tad Williams, and more.

#293 (Winter 1988/89) — Special Avram Davidson/Hank Jankus Issue. Plus Robert Sheckley, Keith Roberts, Carl Jacobi, Ian Watson, and more.

#295 (Winter 1989/90) — Special Brian Lumley/Vincent DiFate Issue. Plus Phyllis Ann Karr, Keith Taylor, Robert Sheckley, and more.

WEIRD TALES® IN HARDCOVER
You can also get The Unique Magazine in a high-quality hardcover edition. All issues are available in the trade hardcover format ($20.00 per copy; 4 or more issues for $12.00 per copy). The signed/limited 100-copy edition is still available at $50.00 per copy for issues #291–#295. (Sorry, #290 is *sold out!*)

Order from:
Weird Tales®
PO Box 13418, Dept. B
Philadelphia, PA 19101

THE DEN

by John Gregory Betancourt

This Den is being written in that curious lull in the convention schedule — just after the exhausting World Science Fiction Convention, Noreascon III, which was held in Boston this year; and right before the World Fantasy Convention, to be held in Seattle in just a matter of days. Two days, as a matter of fact.

I like to start each column with a brief essay of some kind. Nothing is really *new* in the field; the various book publishers keep putting things out as per their schedules, and all *New! Exciting!* developments will probably come at World Fantasy.

So it's a dull time. But still very hectic. I got married two days ago (thank you, thank you), and will be honeymooning at World Fantasy and then in San Francisco (earthquake? what earthquake?).

My wife (Kim) suggests I put on my Harlan Ellison hat and make this a diatribe against the New Jersey Division of Motor Vehicles and its bureaucracy, which refuses to let her change the name on her driver's license to Betancourt. But I'm feeling too happy at the moment for polemics, so . . . to the books!

Songs of a Dead Dreamer, by Thomas Ligotti
Robinson Publishing, 275 pp., £5.99 (trade pb)

Ligotti is one of the best-kept secrets in the fantasy and horror field — his strange stories (some of which are coming up in *Weird Tales*®) are striking, innovative, de-

lightfully crafted, and at times as chilling as anything being written today.

Songs of a Dead Dreamer contains an even 20 tales, subdivided into "Dreams for Sleepwalkers," "Dreams for Insomniacs," and "Dreams for the Dead." Topics range from pursuit of the living by the dead ("The Christmas Eves of Aunt Elise") to visitations by demonic beings ("Eye of the Lynx") to strange experiments in occultism ("The Chymist").

Unfortunately, this edition (an expanded and much revised version of a small-press book that is now long out-of-print) is British, and sure to be hard to find . . . but any major specialty book dealer should have copies. If you can't locate it at a science-fiction convention, you might try ordering through Weinberg Books (PO Box 423, Oak Forest, IL 60452 — & ask for a catalog while you're at it, since they have the largest mail-order business in the field, just about).

Death Song, by Douglas Borton
Onyx Books, 287 pp., $3.95

Similar in title to *Songs of a Dead Dreamer*, but completely different in every way except for its high level of suspense, is Douglas Borton's second novel, *Death Song*.

The future bodes well for Borton — and if you're not already familiar with his name, you're really missing something. It's not everyone who gets a rave quote from Stephen King ("Scary, vivid, exciting, and authentically creepy . . . Borton is very, very good!") . . . and from what I've read of Borton's work (the above, plus the first third of *Manstopper* so far), Borton fully lives up to that praise.

It's not so much the subject matter of *Death Song* that makes it memorable: an ages-old religious cult has been waiting for the return of its dark god — that return to be heralded by a Death Song, which will open gateways, etc., etc., etc. What's different is Borton's sure hand at characterization. He makes these people live, makes the reader care about poor Billie Lee Kidd, country & western singer who accidentally performs the Death Song during one of her concerts.

Borton's prose is clear and crisp, his action well-paced and believable. All in all, *Death Song* is one of the finest modern-scene horror novels I've read in a long time. Recommended.

Farewell Horizontal, by K.W. Jeter
Signet Books, 237 pp., $3.95

This is one of those rare books whose main science-fictional innovation is its setting: in this case, the Cylinder, a huge building so vast and so old that the residents of its upper floors have lost all sense of where they really are. Indeed, to them the world is divided into the Horizontal (those who live within) and the Vertical (those who live on the outside walls). The Cylinder is further divided by superstition: the people who live in the walled-off center of the Cylinder (the Dead Centers) are monsters; below the level of clouds — many hundreds of kilometers below — is some sort of hell.

There are vague references to some long-past war, and there are evidences of bio-engineering floating (literally) about. But most of the world remains unexplained; there's enough material yet unmined that I hope Jeter *does* come back and write more about the Cylinder and its people.

As for plot: Ny Axxter, an artist whose canvases are people and whose medium is biofoil (aluminum foil on which pictures can be projected) is your typical down-and-out artist just scraping by on the Vertical. His main clients are just-starting-out bands of punks and warriors who want to look fierce in combat. But when he stumbles into a Cylinder-shaking conspiracy involving the true power-mongers in his society, he suddenly finds himself running for his life.

The prose is a bit murky at first, but it's well worth staying along for the ride. Jeter's usual anti-authoritarian politics are a pleasant change from the usual militant flag-waving in so much SF these days.

The Fortress of the Pearl, by Michael Moorcock
Ace Books, 162 pp., $16.95 (hc)

I was hooked on the Elric Saga as a teenager, when I came across a copy of *Stormbringer* in Greece. It was rich in imagery, full of adventure and derring-do in a fantasy world like nothing I had ever encountered before. I therefore have a soft spot in my heart for both Moorcock's writing, and the albino mage-warrior Elric in particular. (And judging from the success of the series both in the U.S. and abroad, I'm not the only one.) Any new installment in the series is to be greeted with open arms and much trumpeting of horns.

After a slow start, *The Fortress of the Pearl* really gets moving, back in the classic sword & sorcery mold: rescued from certain death in a magical desert, Elric is forced to undertake a quest: to recover the Pearl from the Heart of the World — which isn't even on this plane of existence. Little is known of this Pearl, except that it will confer great power upon its owner — and everyone else who has sought it has died on gone insane.

But Elric is uniquely suited for this quest. His sorcery, his personal code of honor, and his runesword — what more could he need to accomplish his quest?

Of course there are complications. And here is where the book's real trouble starts: when Elric is the guiding force behind the action, it all works. But as he takes on a guide through the various other planes, his powers are useless, and he even leaves his soul-drinking runesword behind. He becomes little more than a tourist in a strange land, looking but not acting. Nor does introducing Jerry Cornelius in one of his guises give the book any more credibility . . . rather, it detracts from the storytelling by making the book reflexive, or even metafictional. . . by making the reader aware that this is a patented Moorcock Book, subject to the same conventions of all the others. Anytime you drag the reader out of storytime, you're not doing him any favors.

For all the otherworldly flavor, for all the

strange sights and sounds of Quarzhasaat, the city of the Sighing Desert, *The Fortress of the Pearl* is certainly more than able; but when the quest gets underway (the last half of the book), the story's power fades, and you know this isn't Moorcock at his best.

This Immortal, by Roger Zelazny
Baen Books, 216 pp., $3.95

This Immortal won a Hugo Award in 1967 in a tie with *Dune* — but somehow, I missed reading it, though I've had a copy for years.

I'm pleased to say I just finished it, and it's terrific. It hasn't dated in any way. For those who *haven't* read it, this situation is simple: after a nuclear war and then contact with aliens, most of Earth's population has left for the stars, leaving a few die-hards and historians behind.

Conrad Nimikos, Minister of Culture, Arts, and Monuments, is suddenly saddled with personally escorting a Vegan through many of the historical sites on Earth. It is a task he dislikes — he wants to laze through the years, since he's grown tired of struggling. As the book progresses, Conrad turns out to be more than he seems — he is immortal, and had been guiding the Earth through an attempted repopulation and revitalization for many generations. When that revitalization failed — who would want to return to the Earth, anyway? — he contented himself with keeping Earth from being a tourist park for wealthy Vegans out for thrills.

But his Vegan tourist is more than he seems, too, and the fate of humanity hangs in the balance.

Zelazny was certainly one of the best SF writers of the 1960s. In a time which produced many classics, it's good to see that one of his still holds up.

Pornucopia, by Piers Anthony

Tafford, 187 pp., $19.95 (hc)

One of the oddest items to appear of late is a pornographic novel by Piers Anthony. Originally written in 1967 for Essex House, it languished unpublished after that company folded. Now it's out and available for the interested (adult) reader.

Yes, it really *is* pornography . . . set in a fast-moving future where fantasy creatures (satyrs and demons and vampires) are real. Anthony probably should have retitled it; it sounds like a *Xanth* book, but it's certainly not.

Whether the book is any good or not as science fiction seems a moot point (it's okay — amusing at times, but far from brilliant); it's more a novelty item, something odd and very much off-the-wall.

Because the "book contains explicit sexual references which may be objectionable to some readers" (according to the publisher), you must be at least 21 to order it. Address: Tafford Publishing, Inc., PO Box 271804, Houston, TX 77277. Include $2.00 for postage and handling.

Of Note.

Signet has republished Kirby McCauley's groundbreaking horror anthology, *Dark Forces*, in a nifty new edition. It's a real eye-catcher, and any horror aficionado who missed it the first time should certainly pick it up. Stephen King's novelette, "The Mist," is probably King's best short work, and worth the price of admission all by itself.

Janet Fox's *Scavenger's Newsletter*, "a marketing co-op for SF/fantasy/horror writers/artists interested in the small press," continues to delight me. It's got news, reviews, market tips and information, and some useful articles, suitable for anyone interested in the small press. Order a sample copy for $1.50 from: Janet Fox, 519 Ellinwood, Osage City, KS 66523. ⊗

CORRECTION

According to R. Dixon Smith, editor of Carl Jacobi's short story collection *East of Samarinda*, correct price on that tome is $33.95 (hardcover) and $16.95 (paperback). This is better than the $25.00 the review slip listed, and which John Betancourt used in his review last issue.

PROFILE: DAVID J. SCHOW

by Craig Spector, John Skipp, R.S. Hadji, and Joe R. Lansdale

It's my experience that you can count the best friends one accumulates in a lifetime on the fingers of both hands; the true blood brothers can fit comfortably on one, and still leave a pinkie free for demitasse. David J. Schow has been one of mine, practically from the moment we met. Guess which finger.

He's one of the bad boys, and he's one of the best. He says he's a splatterpunk, and he should know. Read anything by David Schow and know what that moniker *truly* means. Dave's writing is one of life's finer things: heartbreakingly knowing, lethal in its precision, possessed of incendiary acuity and more sheer bang-per-byte *fun* than anything written by anyone, anywhere. Dave loves his work. He has a right to.

Come up against it and you'd best have your battlements in place. Dave's perimeter is secure, his ego-armor formidable, and he takes no prisoners. But if you have no fear of the frontal assault, and are willing to put yourself at risk, and can take the hits, you can penetrate the labyrinth around Dave's heart. I go there every chance I get.

It's worth the trip.

The walls are intricate, inscribed with cuneiforms meticulous and exact, an archive of startling insights and observation at once jagged as broken glass embedded in raw concrete, cool as carved planes of polished marble that glisten like living skin. Elegant *grotesques* brood in the shadows, bask unrepentant in the light. There is danger in the journey, a sure sense that this one's for real, and for keeps. You can be hurt. You can be transported. You *will* be transformed.

But if you can take the hits and wear the scars of such dangerous knowledge well, you'll arrive at a door, battle-scarred and banded. The door is heavy, but never locked.

Nothing bars its entry save the strength of the one who dares knock. Open it if you can. Enter at your own risk.

And be amazed.

There is a garden there, exquisite, lush beyond belief, and the beauty of what grows inside those walls will steal your breath away.

There is a table for two in the center of the garden. He'll be waiting for you there, with glass raised high and the devil in his eyes. Have a seat. Kick back, relax. Get ready for it.

If you're nice, Uncle Dave will tell you a story.

And you'll be glad you came.

— **Craig Spector**

I'm wondering if the April '84 issue of *Twilight Zone* magazine has become a collector's item yet.

That was where I got my first major Schow-buzz. If was a story called "Coming Soon to a Theatre Near You," and reading it was like getting a Post-It note from God saying, *You are not alone.* Altogether a breathtaking experience. From the Last Gasp Eco-Funnies layout by Marcus Nickerson (heavily under the Davoid influence, as I later discovered) to the You-Are-There killer palpability of the prose, Jack Daniel Stoner's night at the Omicron laid waste to the rest of the magazine and, frankly, to just about anything I'd ever read.

First came the fact that it was *my* culture he was describing. It was six months before we sold *The Light at the End,* and the streets had become my frame of reference. The fried-out human effluvium he described, the sticky grindhouse floors and gray concrete they adorned, were the stuff of my daily life.

14

Until that point, I hadn't realized that Manhattan and Hollywood shared that much in common.

But it was more than what he saw; it was *how* he saw it, and how he chose to express it. This was a writer who cared enough to make sure you knew *exactly* what he meant: no dicking around with oblique obfuscations; none of this "Pay No Attention To The Man Behind The Curtain" shit. The story just *sang* with utter confidence and total honesty, and I was blown away.

So I rang up T.E.D. Klein [then *TZ*'s editor] and demanded to know everything about this incredible, heretofore-unheard-of talent.

Who, I needed to know, *is* this Oliver Lowenbruck guy?

Which brings me to one of the things I hate most about Schow: his fucking pseudonyms. I don't know how many he has, but they're certainly enough to keep me from ferreting out all his little lame puppies from the formative years. Plus it creates the illusion that there are *several* people writing fiction of that caliber today, when in fact there's only one.

Sorry, Chan. I think that's morally wrong. And it pisses me off, besides.

He lets me call him Davey, but I wouldn't advise that you try it. He's also the only person I know who'll admit to a fondness for Tobe Hooper's *Lifeforce*, just in case you were thinking he was infallible or something. I've been waiting nearly six years for the world to catch up and recognize how goddam brilliant and important he is.

It appears that the world is getting warmer.

About fuckin' time, sez I.

— John Skipp

When asked to contribute an appreciation of Dave Schow's writing, two qualities came immediately to mind as indicative of the whole. The first, being the most obvious, is a protean diversity enfolding multiferous literary forms and, specific to the fiction, demonstrating startling variations of style, texture, and mood. I might add that Schow's commitment to excellence is such that it at once belies any notion this range merely indicates the hungry gadding of a hack. Protean he may be, but no chameleon. The second quality, namely integrity, constantly affirms this distinction by an adamant refusal to compromise the material, or the reader. This is *serious* horror fiction. Schow always delivers, and never cheats.

His short fiction illustrates the above, casting a dark eye over deceptively familiar terrain mined with nasty surprises. The same Dave Schow that proffered the muted unsentimental nostalgia of "One For the Horrors" and "Lonesome Cowboy Blues" can crank up the buzz-saw for exuberant gross-outs like "Blood Rape of the Lust Ghouls" and "Jerry's Kids Meet Wormboy." His, too, is the cold urgent whisper of "The Woman's Version," rising to screaming bloody murder. His spare prose is hard as a bullet, penetrating directly through the meat to the bone. These shorter pieces are notably cool to the touch, deeply felt yet truly *chilling*. Latterly, the novellas present a smoother surface, the proverbial still waters through which we glimpse ominous stirrings in the depths. "Red Light" and "Pamela's Get" explore adumbrations of psychological terror with an increasingly sensitive and mature artistry, the imagery by turns fragile and forceful. Quiet horror, but not gentle.

Two ingredients of the "cultural mulch" that informs contemporary consciousness assume distinctive significance in Schow's work: rock 'n roll and Hollywood. The former affects the writing in every aspect, from the sonority of the prose to the rhythm of the pacing. Like the man says: "When horror succeeds, when rock 'n roll succeeds, they're dangerous." Unsafe at any speed. Schow's attitude toward Hollywood is at once intense and ambivalent, a true love of film tempered by a cynical awareness of the process manufacturing the illusion. That, and of the ways the illusion itself undermines the structure of reality for many who succumb to the glamour.

A part of this milieu, yet apart, Schow gets us where he lives, "in the heart of the beast," the Hollywood that never rests and is always hungry. This is a glaring pitiless world, where the only compassion to be found is that discernible in the author's tone. Schow speaks for a generation of young horror writers when he says: "We've developed a more cynical coping mechanism. It's got a real brutal edge to it, an almost defiant vision."

His personal vision finds its fullest expression to date in *The Kill Riff*, a complex yet accessible work that resists classification. A suspenseful *noir* thriller, it is also a horrifying study of sociopathic rage, and its relation to a rock milieu that feeds the beast. *The Kill Riff* integrates its many parts into a compact whole, loaded with momentum and menace. Shockingly brutal, consistently humane, this is an easy read but a hard book, its ferocity shaped by such virtuosity that I could scarcely believe this was a first novel. It serves notice that Schow will be a major horror writer for the coming decade.

If, that is, he chooses to define himself as such, for he could as soon be acclaimed as a suspense writer. Or a film scenarist. Why not all the above, and more? Considering the talent, no limits seems less a posture than a modest proposal, not to seek out gratuitous excess, but rather to explore the possibilities inherent in pushing back the edges. An edge is like a horizon; always receding beyond reach, but the approach covers such interesting terrain. Dave Schow is determined to keep hunting for hybrids out past artificial genre/media barriers, and judging by the results thus far, I look forward to the pleasure of their disturbance.

— **R.S. Hadji**

I met David Schow at a World Fantasy Convention in Tucson and knew immediately that here was a special kind of guy. I liked his stories already, but I liked the man even better.

He looks like a Heavy Metal Horror writer, and though I suppose you could say he has written Heavy Metal Horror (*The Kill Riff* comes immediately to mind), he's also written a lot of stories that fall well outside of that view. But to look at him — dressed in leather, his black hair tied back in a pony tail, wearing gloves with no finger sheaths — he looks like someone who might eat cats. Raw. (Only bad kitties, of course.)

Well, he looks that way at first. More you look at him, sweeter he looks. And in fact, he is sweet. A lot more sensitive than he likes to believe, I'm sure. Spoils his Splatterpunk persona. He's the kind of guy that remembers birthdays and anniversaries, trips you're going on. He sends cards or flowers or toys. He's got a great, if goofy, sense of humor. And instead of eating kitties, he's more likely to take one in and raise it until it's ready to go off to college.

You look at his apartment and it's like a warped Santa's workshop. All sorts of demented things. Windup toys. Drawings. Photographs of friends. It's a busy place. And it comes closer than anything — outside of his actions — to identifying the inner man.

And David is a busy man. Look at all the work he's turned out in the last few years. He's a novelist, short-story writer, film critic, screenplay and teleplay writer, and the best friend you could possibly have. And he even finds time to sit up to ungodly hours and argue about everything in the world. Pleasantly and intelligently, of course. (When I think of David talking, I always think of a radio announcer. He has that kind of voice.)

I admire David. He's made himself what he is by sheer tenacity and hard work. And what he is is a remarkably talented writer. One of the major horror writers working today.

I love him like family. I just wish I knew why he wears those leather gloves without finger sheaths. It is perplexing.

— **Joe R. Lansdale**

⊗

MOVING?

Don't leave *Weird Tales*® behind! Send us your old address *(don't forget the zip code)* and your new one. We'll make sure you receive each issue without delay. Not a subscriber yet? Turn to the inside back cover for more information.

WEIRD TALES TALKS WITH

DAVID J. SCHOW

by Bill Warren

Weird Tales: You dropped out of college, and walked away. Why?

David J. Schow: I thought I could make a living running science-fiction conventions. I had gotten involved in running several conventions on the University of Arizona campus in Tucson. Simultaneously, I became a dealer at conventions, running a dealers table and selling stuff. I kept myself afloat. I was out of college and working at a bookstore, possibly the closest thing I've ever had to a legitimate job in my life. I only did that for nine months. I worked in the bookstore and my library grew. What can I say?

WT: How did you get from working in a bookstore to writing those series novels?

Schow: While I was in Tucson, I started writing movie reviews and features for the local paper, what was then called an alternative paper, which is now a safe, vaguely rock paper, like the *L.A. Weekly*. I began writing fiction, manuscript fiction, about the time I stopped going to the university. It was directed toward science-fiction digest-size magazines. I went down to a newsstand, bought a couple of them, and thought, "I could do this."

I got fired from my bookstore job. I floated for a year by working conventions and stuff. At the same time, I started going back and forth from Tucson to L.A., because I had a lot of friends here. Everybody else in the group was working in a theater on the Boulevard, so we could go see all of the movies on the Boulevard for free. This started about the time *Dawn of the Dead* came out. [1979] We wound up living in the basement of the Holly Cinema for three days, while we were switching apartments a couple of years later. We had to live on the left-over concession-stand hot dogs — *if there were any*. These things had been going around on a rotisserie for hours, and they were *green*. That isn't as bad as it got, but that's a good example.

A magazine bought a novelette that I wrote. This was Charlie Ryan at *Galileo*. At first, they failed to believe that it was a first sale, but we agreed on what he would pay me for it, it was like $225, something like that. I thought this was wonderful. I remember getting the check and making a trip to California, and very purposefully leaving the check at home. So that if California imploded I could go home and I would have this $225 check sitting there, that I could cash in.

I got a job in Chicago for six months. During that entire time, I had an apartment in Tucson, that I came back to when I left Chicago.

I was in Collectors' Bookstore on Hollywood Boulevard, looking at the magazine rack and thinking, "The next issue of this magazine is going to have my story in it." I picked it up, and flipped it to the back. And there was a thing saying "Coming next month, a

17

story by . . ." I groaned, I couldn't quite bring myself to buy that magazine just because it had that little box on the last page. So I put it back on the rack, walked around to the other side of the rack, and there was the *new* issue, sitting there, already. I bought it, ran to a Howard Johnson's, and sat there drinking coffee and reading my story over and over. I'd get to the end and go back to the first page. I sat there five hours, reading my own story. When I got tired of reading the story, I'd go back to the bio page which had my *photograph* on it, God help me. I thought, "This is it. I can get an agent and I can get contracts and Hollywood will be beating at my door." Needless to say, a whole lot of nothing happened for a while.

In 1980, I was writing a book for Jeff Rovin. One of the first gigs I got was a rewrite of a science-fiction film book, for which he paid me a thousand bucks. I diligently worked on it for a month, and sent it in and got paid. I rode on that and a couple of other gigs. For instance, I wrote a script for, I swear, robots at a shopping mall. A guy named Bill Price had these little radio-controlled robots. He had built a cyclorama, and a spaceship that shot CO_2 smoke out. He hired me to write 12 pages of dialog for these robots, while they were doing a little presentation in the shopping mall.

Then Jeff Rovin said, "Listen, my agent is working on a series, give him a call. Maybe he can get something for you." He'd been seeing my stuff all along, for a period of about two years. I went over, as described in the story "Pulpmeister," to a closed Lucky's supermarket on a Friday morning, made the call to New York from a pay phone, and billed it to a First National Bank office I knew was closed. He said he'd get in touch with the people at the publisher, and "I'll send you a bible."

I whacked out six two-page story outlines, using every television cliché imaginable, everything. Literally like one-sentence descriptions fleshed out into two pages of excelsior that looked like plot. I sent them to New York, and they paid $250 for each one of these things. $1,500 for twelve typed pages. I was like sucking wind, I couldn't believe this. I had to use a friend's phone to call the publisher; I felt that I had to make all this important editorial contact. I talked to this wonderful editor there who said, "Yeah, we like them, just write some good books." That was it.

I started writing those books about '81. I went from zero to ninety. I was used to getting a couple of hundred bucks for an article or a story; I had never achieved a pay scale like this before; I had plenty of money. And that was no longer a concern. You go from being an urban survivalist to realizing, "I have the money to do this." I wrote the first Eviscerator novel in a month, then I wrote a novel a month for the next two months, then I wrote two more in the next three months. They came very fast and furious, literally out of the typewriter and off to the publisher.

WT: You refer to these as the "Eviscerator" novels, but don't reveal what the real series was. Why not?

Schow: It's because it's ancient history. It's because it's my first novel-length thing. I don't want to sign one of them, basically. Every so often I'll go into a used bookstore and see them on a shelf, and say to myself, "Now, *that's* immortality. No one will ever buy this book!"

WT: How did you make the transition from Eviscerator novels to novelizations of "Miami Vice" and other shows?

Schow: I started doing novelizations in 1982. I went to Universal Studios; I wanted to do movie novelizations, and at this time *Streets of Fire, Halloween III* and *Videodrome* were all in production. I thought — "*Streets of Fire,* Walter Hill; *Videodrome,* David Cronenberg

— I would like to novelize movies by these guys." So I went in with my Eviscerator novels, plunked them on the desk, and said, "I can do this." They said, "That's great, we don't have anything for you." I started to bug them; everytime I had anything published, an article, a short story, I would send them copies. One day they called — instead of me calling them, they called me — and said "We don't have anything for you like that, but can you do this?" I said, "Well, I don't know; my schedule . . ." I had $40 in the bank at the time. I wound up doing eleven or twelve books for them over a period of about two years. Which paid the bills and got me up to speed, and also bought the time for me to write my first novel, the infamous novel that no one ever sees, that was going to change everything. It's in a drawer, right over there. It was my Jack the Ripper novel.

Flash back to 1981. The moment I saw *Twilight Zone* magazine, I thought "I gotta have a story in *Twilight Zone* magazine." I wound up having something in *Twilight Zone,* starting in 1982, every year, until the magazine expired. There had been a piece on old TV shows in *Twilight Zone* magazine. I said, "This all wrong," and gradually talked Ted Klein into doing an article — one — on *The Outer Limits.* When he got the article, it was compressed, and presumed a prior encyclopedic knowledge of the show. He said, "Why don't we let this breathe a little bit, and rewrite as a two-parter?" When he got the two-parter, he wanted to make it a four-parter; when he got the four-parter, he wanted to make it an eight-parter, and add an episode guide. When three of the installments were in print, that was enough to convince Berkley to buy it as a book project. Then [Jeffrey] Frentzen and I set out to make it into an actual book, which turned out to be three times the work we expected. The basic research, the gathering of

photos, all of the phone calls, all of the travel, was shared out about equally. But when the time came to write the book, for various reasons Jeff just couldn't do it. The manuscript that was turned in was written by me; the revision that was turned in was cut, condensed, added to and revised by me, by myself. Although there is not a page in that book that is not touched in some way by the work that he did. Our problem was compounded by the fact that by the time we got the deal to do the book, Jeff was on the East Coast, somewhere in the wilds of Connecticut.

WT: How did you change this trajectory from science fiction to horror?

Schow: I was always there to begin with; although I sold my first story to a science-fiction magazine, about conventions, but it was more about Lovecraft, Poe, and Fritz Leiber than it was about anything science-fictional. In fact, I've never written anything science fictional, except for a couple of novelizations, which were vaguely science fictional. The one time that I really tried to do it resulted in a story which is my most rejected story, ever. But that was the closest I came to science fiction, ever. There were a couple of other unfinished and/or unpublished stories that have elements of that in them.

I always tended to like horror movies better than science-fiction movies, if that has anything to do with it. It's kind of like *The Outer Limits,* which is nominally a science-fiction show, but was really more a Gothic-horror show than science-fiction.

WT: Of the books that have been published under your own name so far, none is a horror novel. *The Kill Riff* is nominally a horror novel, as *Red Dragon* is a horror novel.

Schow: Or *Psycho.* It's a thriller, a suspense novel. The book that I'm struggling to finish as we sit here — I gotta finish this book in ten days, folks — *The Shaft,* has bona fide supernatural stuff in it, but it's still more about dope dealers and sexual politics than it is about the monsters in it. So it may just be a fringe thing at best. I don't feel like writing a full-blown, old-dark-house clichéd monster thing. I want to approach it from another direction, if that makes sense. It wasn't a conscious decision to do that, but when you get the paper in the machine and working on it, to fall back on the traditional way of doing it, is like falling back on the worst TV cliché in the world to get through another five pages in a novelization. I want to find *my* way of doing it.

I'm working on a concept — not an outline, because I don't use outlines — for what will turn out to be a big suspense novel. No supernatural elements. And I have a novel that started out as a horror novel, but has become what they quaintly call a "psychological horror novel," which is about monsters in the Arctic. Now it's about people going crazy in the Arctic.

WT: Are you turning away from fiction now, and more toward screenwriting?

Schow: No. I've only been doing screenplays since December. I did one episode of one TV show, and two drafts of a feature. As soon as I finished the second draft of the feature, I went back to this novel, which has been on hold since last July. When I finish this novel, and the next polish of the feature, I now have lined up about six or seven short story gigs for various anthologies. That all need to have new stories written for them, because I don't have a back stock. Everything I've completed that I thought was worthy of publication, at this point is spoken for.

WT: Where do you see your career going?

Schow: I have three projects. I wrote an episode of *Freddy's Nightmares,* which more or less got me the gig to write *Leatherface,* or *Texas Chainsaw*

Massacre 3. When they saw the script for *Leatherface,* New Line Cinema started bringing me other projects that they were having trouble with, the first being a script called *Witchhunt,* which I did not want to rewrite. The second being *Nightmare on Elm Street 5,* which they wanted a dialog revision on, which was rich indeed, because I couldn't get the gig to write the screenplay originally. The head of the company saw my dialog, and it was exactly what they wanted. But fortunately, New Line is developing a couple of projects that they wanted me in on, such as the new version of *Village of the Damned.* I'm developing a feature with Mike DeLuca, which exists now as a two-page outline — we're back to two-page outlines! Arrgghh!

WT: Do you see yourself pingponging between books and scripts?

Schow: Absolutely. Last year, I agreed to write a comic book, something I never thought I'd wind up doing. It's all different; I don't want to not try any form of writing.

I found something really weird when I sat down to work on this novel, *The Shaft,* and I came to the realization that I am not a novel-a-year person. Ten novels in ten years? I don't think I could do it. I just put too much into the novels, as books, I really move into them and live with them. The first draft of *The Kill Riff* I wrote in six weeks, but the first draft is what sold and got me the money to go back and *fix* the first draft.

The Kill Riff was almost a novel twice before — Pinnacle Books almost bought it. I'm so glad they didn't, because it would have been for pauper's wages. Bill Thompson was going to buy *The Kill Riff* for Arbor House as a hardback. I got this letter back from him, and I said, "Bill Thompson? Bill Thompson? Bill Thompson is the guy who bought *Carrie*! Oh my God!" So I thought I would listen to what this guy had to say about this novel. And I made some big changes in it that derived directly from suggestions by Bill Thompson. Bill Thompson got drummed out by the accountants at Arbor House, and that whole plan went down the tubes. Then Tor bought it, about the time the dust from *The Outer Limits* book was just settling, one reason being that the editor who bought it for Tor was my editor on *The Outer Limits* book at Berkley, Melissa Singer.

WT: The other book you had your name on is *Silver Scream,* of which you are the editor. And this came together at a World Fantasy Convention?

Schow: World Fantasy Con, Providence, Rhode Island. I had written a bunch of stories, like "One for the Horrors," which is about movie theaters, "Coming Soon to a Theater Near You," which is about the Gordon, actually, in its heyday. And "Blood Rape of the Lust Ghouls," which is about a guy who goes to the World Theater to get away from his wife. And so at this luncheon, someone said, "Why don't you do a book of these?" Cinema-oriented horror stories. That's how that got born. The deal was made over a lunch, and Chet Williamson came up with the title.

WT: Most people tend to view these editorial jobs lightly.

Schow: I took it real personally, for one thing. One thing that I wanted to do was redress things that I thought other editors did wrong. I set up a bank account for this book, I did progress reports on this book, so every writer knew what was going on, I gave everybody little weird writer perks, like chattering skulls with the name of the anthology on them, and arranged for a decent copy detail, two copies of any and every edition, minimum.

Silver Scream took a lot out of me, and as you probably know, editing stuff is not very remunerative. All of that took a lot of time. And I'm not real anxious to do it again, although people like *Silver Scream* so much, that it's real

tempting. I told people at the time that maybe five years from now, I'll feel different, I'll probably edit another anthology if anybody wants me to.

WT: Why do people read the stuff and watch the stuff in the first place?

Schow: That's a good question, and one of the answers usually is this kind of "death rehearsal." I don't really buy that. I think it's life affirmation rather than death rehearsal. I'm absolutely convinced that I'm going to die, sometime. Maybe it boils down to the Nietzschean thing of "that which does not destroy me makes me stronger." How much can you take before the end? What can you survive?

It's also a forum that allows you to kind of acid-test these human values that we're always talking about hewing to when nobody's ever at risk. Like matters of personal honor and loyalty and fidelity to whatever concepts you follow. Writing stuff like this, especially in *The Shaft,* provides an excellent test scenario for the stuff people *say* they believe in. Then you put them in a situation where they have to stick to that doctrine, not doctrine or dogma, but their own personal codes. One of things about a horror novel is that sometimes it doesn't matter if you die or not. What matters is whether you die with your honor intact. Have they passed the test that the whole nihilistic scenario is? In terms of their own personal agenda.

WT: Why have a book with such a downbeat ending that the reader might as well not have begun the trip?

Schow: Because every time you sit down to write a story or novel, you're exploring a different path. You're trying a different angle of attack on the topic. That's why I find it frequently helps if a reader has read more than just one of your things, because you tend to be typed according to what the reader gets to first. Then you have other people who started at a different place in your timeline. "You know, I thought it was tremendously sensitive, and moving" — and then they get to "Blood Rape of the Lust Ghouls" and they come unhinged and spin out and hit the wall.

WT: Is graphic gore a crutch, a way of trying to avoid making things more subtly scary?

Schow: I think graphic gore is a crutch for people who can't write, or who need to get that novelization done in a hurry. It's a device, but every device didn't start off as a device; someone had to invent it. It's expedient to fall back on it in films; you're showing everything, and if you're losing the audience, you show a little more, you might get the audience back. But especially in written fiction, it's not only like good punctuation, it's useful. When people die certain ways, or when certain things happen to people, it *is* pretty revolting. There are cases where holding that back doesn't serve the story; there are cases where holding it back *does* serve the story. It's this kind of blind use of it, imprudence, that I think is the problem, and not the gore itself. It's that theory that if a bucket of blood is good, then two buckets will be even better. It's not necessarily so. It's all based on what the individual story needs. My very good pal Craig Spector summed it up best. He agrees that "Sometimes less is more. But sometimes *more* is more."

WT: Is there anything other than a trend in interest that explains the fall and rise and fall of horror?

Schow: When horror has boom periods, a lot of people get psyched up to do novels and movies and things. When the novels turn out not so great, and the movies turn out not so great, it tapers off. And anybody that's good at it tends to rise and persevere. When you experience the tapering off, what you're seeing is the seasonal pruning of the disposable stuff.

WT: What is bad horror writing?

Schow: Bad horror writing is writing that will fall back on elements like gore for lack of anything better, like story or character. What sums up bad horror writing is either constant repetition of a theme, or deriving your theme from other writers. Specifically, there are now a lot of writers doing books and stories whose entire education in horror has been Stephen King and nothing else. Maybe a little Clive Barker and certainly a lot of movies. Or falling back on those traditional bromides of the haunted New England town, and the sinister, malignant children, or the Old Ones coming back again. I think the laziest form of horror writing is Biblical horror. You wave a cross at it, it goes away, you say a prayer, you're okay; that's pretty established methodology for dealing with anything that scares you. It can't be horrifying, can it? In the way that cockroaches can't terrify you if you have Raid. You already have in your hands the thing to get rid of it.

WT: Who does bad horror writing?

Schow: Frankly, I don't read that much horror. I read the guys I like. Of the old school guys, I'm the world's biggest Bob Bloch fan, and I like Fritz Leiber when he's writing horror. I think John Farris is at the top of the field; as far as horror writers go, there's nobody better working now, among our still-living horror writers. I place him above King without a moment's hesitation, because he's a lot more adult writer, for one thing. And he doesn't write to reassure as much as King seems to. He seems to be that King-like family man, but with a much, much darker edge to his stuff.

WT: Do you think horror is currently evolving, or is it folding upon itself? Or is it a shakedown period?

Schow: Yeah, it is, we're going into one of the valleys right now, we have these peaks and valleys, a whole mountain range. There are periods when it's very popular, and a lot of people get signed on to books and films and stuff. Then you hit saturation. In this case, the saturation is partly due to the fact that Zebra and Leisure Books have been publishing a lot of horror novels, which they've been picking up incredibly cheap, and flooding rack space with. You go in and think, "Gee, these books have always been here," and it turns out it's not the same book on all the racks, but twenty different ones with similar covers. Gerund titles, "The Gnoshing." When enough of these things get out, there's that period when the chaff settles, and you're left in the field with the people who have any staying power. The people who have the staying power attract back to the field the readership that was possibly driven away by all the bad books, and the cycle starts over again.

WT: You said you wrote the Eviscerator novels in a month, but also that you recently realized you are not a novel-a-year man; now granted these are different levels of endeavor, but why the enormous change in pace?

Schow: Probably because the novels that are causing me so much trouble are Dave Schow novels, and not pseudonym novels. In fact, I recommended to a couple of other writers who are blocked that a way to flush their pipes, to blow the carbons out of the carburetor, as it were, would be to do a pseudonymous novel where their primary concern was not "How good is the writing?" but "How fast can I get it done?" It removes the onus of the stuff going out under your own name, and constantly worrying about whether it's good or not.

I found that in the case of the stories that I choose to turn into my own novel, they haven't been quick and easy propositions, partially due to the fact that when you get involved with the publishing industry on that kind of level, everything takes forever to happen. A

year delay is nothing in the publishing industry. Translate that to the movie industry, when they talk about something being on the shelf for a year, it's like a nightmare to them. Or in television, where the turnaround is so fast that you can write something in January and see it on the air in April, finished. That kind of delay in the book industry is nothing. A lot of the time factor is built in.

WT: How can you tell, when you get an idea, whether it's a novel idea or a short story idea?

Schow: I can't. The novel I was originally going to do for Tor was an expansion of a novella I had already written, and the book that I'm now finishing started out as a short story. And *The Kill Riff* started out as a novel. With *The Shaft*, at first I started to pad it out, to see if it could go off life-support at the longer length and breathe by itself. Then, while you're in the process of seeing whether this works, it occurs to you that you could put a whole 'nother level on this narrative, and you go back and you add that. And now you're going through another draft of the whole book with several coordinated levels of what this narrative is about going on in your head. And the thing grows by itself at that point.

It's not more incidents per se, to me, it's more interior stuff and more character. Because when you begin to expand what those characters are about, that's the point at which they start telling you what this is about, and it helps it become a book. You write a character, and the character says to you, "Now wait a minute, I wouldn't do that, and here's why." You know you're on the right track, because you at least know what you're *not* going to write about.

WT: And now about splatterpunk . . .

Schow: I guess that was inevitable. Kind of like a train wreck.

WT: What does the word "punk"

mean in all these subgenre movements?

Schow: When Punk music came in in the late '70s, it was kind of noisy and anti-melodic and anarchistic, basically, and that was to differentiate it from the traditional way that music was being done. It was loud and noisy and in your face.

Splatterpunk was a label, a big noise that certain of us could make to draw attention toward the writing. Then the writing could stand or fall on its own merit. It was an attempt to address an audience of something other than the type of tweedy academics who teach writing workshops and seek collegiate legitimacy for a field — horror — that's already legitimate.

There's this whole perception of horror being a genre ghetto. Mostly it's the perception of writers who came out of science fiction and brought that prejudice with them, as a sort of prefabricated cause to fight for. The fact is that horror has never been the second-class literature that science fiction started out as, and in some ways, still is. There are a number of shall we say journeymen horror writers who can remain big fish only so long as horror is a small pond. So they conveniently christen horror a ghetto field that requires their ministrations to save it. They need to form tea societies and elect officers and write reviews and give away trophies and complain about gettin' no respect. They preach to the converted. They are *very traditional.*

And here come those nasty old Splatterpunks, their hair is strange, their clothes are weird, their fiction is often noisy, and they do things like cross over to films, to music, to a whole audience uninterested in haunted New England towns besieged by the Old Ones and malignant, demonic children coming through the doorway to Hell and making deals with the Devil.

WT: It seems to me, then, that splatterpunk occupies a position — certainly not in content or style — similar to that of the science fiction "new wave" of the 1960s, in terms of its impact on the field.

Schow: Yes. It's like that in that it's a threat to the big turd in the small bowl theory. People like Charlie Grant, people like Dean Koontz, are making very loud, defensive noises against splatterpunk — and they haven't been attacked!

I see it as a broadening of horror, basically. Not broadening in any way it hasn't gone before, but opening a door that's been shut for a long time. There are people who will always see broadening the field as a threat. I think the point of it addressing a different audience is true, too, because people who are not horror fans but who may be fans of horror movie or something like that are now reading stuff where they wouldn't pick up something with a certain colophon on it — they're reading this stuff, because it relates to their position, or to the music they listen to, something like that.

I quote Oscar Wilde: "No artist is ever morbid; the artist can express everything. Diversity of opinion about a work of art shows that the work is new, complex and vital." But since we came up with this name ourselves, and as Spector says, it was our own preemptive strike, we named ourselves before somebody else could name us, it makes us more like the Pre-Raphaelites than the Impressionists, I guess. But you can't send it fifty cents for an official manifesto; we haven't printed them up yet. We do have t-shirts, though.

I got a letter from Bob Hadji. He goes as R.S. Hadji, but I call him Bob 'cause I know him. Bob, who runs a bookstore up in Canada, and ran until it died a magazine called *Borderland,* is one of the two or three most well-read people I know on this continent. And a person to whom the label of "critic" is in no way derogatory, because he really knows what he's talking about. He wrote to me, and he said, at the end of the letter (a letter full of praise for my stuff, so take this with a grain of salt), "Hopefully the artificial Old Guard/New Blood division will crumble beneath its own absurdity before long. There is no right or wrong way to write horror fiction save in a purely technical sense. You're a perfect example of a writer who can have it both ways, gentle or gross according to the needs of the story at hand. These are aesthetic questions; the entire spectrum of horror fiction is free to address the moral positions. The feud is a non-issue in a non-event." That kind of sums it up.

⊗

COMING IN OUR SUMMER 1990 ISSUE!

Our Special *Nancy Springer* Tribute

— *featuring* —

3 Outstanding new Stories by
One of America's Leading Fantasists!

— *plus* —

Stunning Artwork by Classic *Weird Tales*® Artist
Frank Kelly Freas

— and —

Eerie New Fiction by

John Brunner   **Thomas Ligotti**
("The Pronounced Effect")   ("The Lost Art of Twilight")

Susan Shwartz
("Swans' Lake")

Don't risk missing an issue!
Turn to the inside back cover and subscribe today!

NIGHT BLOOMER

by David J. Schow

Steven Keller hated all the bitches at Calex.

When not weathering their stupidity as marginally attractive cogs in Calex's corporate high-rise, he resented the living foldout girls flaunting it in the commercials for Calex Petroleum products that clogged up prime time television. He had pulled far too few consummated dates out of the female staff on the twenty-second floor to suit him; sometimes he went more than a week without getting laid, and that fouled his optimum performance workwise. At home he was perpetually short on clean socks. Most of his dress shirts did too much duty, and had gained skid-tracks of grime on the inner collars.

This was not Steven Keller's idea of the joys of upwardly mobile middle management.

That fat old bastard Bigelow had elevatored down this afternoon just to ramrod him. Business as usual. The cost estimates that had sputtered from Steve's printer had displeased Bigelow. That was the word the old lardball had used — *displeased*. As though he was not one vice president among many, but a demigod, an Academy Award on the hoof, a fairytale king who demanded *per diem* groveling in exchange for meager boons.

Displeased. Steve had watched his manila folder slap the desktop and skid to a stop between his elbows. Before he could lift it or even react, Bigelow had wheeled his toad bulk a full one-eighty and repaired to his eyrie on the thirtieth floor. Steve's own office was illusory. A work area partitioned off from twenty others exactly like it by dividers covered in tasteful brown fabric. His MA in Business Administration hung on a wall that was not a wall, but a reminder that he was just one more rat dressed for success inside the Calex Skinner Box. *Displeased* meant his

Thursday was history. The nine-to-five running lights on the twenty-second floor were dark now, and because of the change in illumination levels Steve could get a different perspective on his slanted reflection in the screen of his word processor. He laboriously reworked the quote sheets on his own time. He looked, he thought, ghostly and haggard. Used.

He punched a key and the revised lists rolled up. Bitches. Bastards. You could say those words on TV nowadays and nobody blinked. Their potency as invective had been bled away by time, and time scared the shit out of Steve. At thirty-five his time was running out. He had passed the point in his life where failure could be easily amortized.

He had spent his life living the introduction to his life. So far it had been all setup and no payoff. It had been a search that at times grew frantic; a dull joke with a foregone punchline. As he watched the printer razz and burp and spit up the new tabulated columnar lists — pleasing, now — he reviewed his existence as a similar readout. As an index of significant events it ran depressingly thin.

Apart from his degree there had been two wives, one at twenty-one and another at twenty-nine. Both were a matter of record now. To Nikki, Steve had suggested what was now called a summary dissolution; the cut-rate legal beavers at Jacoby & Meyers had split them for about two hundred bucks plus tax. With Margaret, the roles had been reversed. She never suggested anything. She simply sought out more sophisticated counsel, and did for Steve's assets what Bigelow's nightly shots of Kaopectate did for the old fart's Sisyphian regularity.

Calex recruitment had been the goal of his entire college career. The dream had been first class; the reality, a budget tour, via steerage.

The face on the screen did not yet require glasses. He supposed that was something. Apart from beaning the class bully with a softball during Phys Ed, at twelve, he could recall no other little victories. He would always remember the sound the ball had made when it bounced off the bigger kid's anthropoid skull — **twock!** Like a rolling pin breaking a thick candle in half. Steve Kelowicz, school shrimp, did not suspect the full savor of this victory until a week later. The lunchtime poundings ceased. The berserker had shifted his tyranny to less reactive targets. No vengeance ever came.

Steve's growth was undistinguished, and while his objectives matured, his satisfactions remained childish. He sought those things expected of his station — corporate achievement, the accumulation of possessions, the company of the correct women. As soon as it became legally feasible he Americanized the mistake that had been his last name. A Kelowicz might be a fruit vendor. *Keller* was a name that begged imprintation on a door panel of plastic veneer, assuredly a proper name for a Calex executive.

As the printer shut down he realized that Bigelow was just a grown-up version of the school bully — older, shrewder, more scarred, warier, like a veteran tomcat. Bigelow the Big just might need an unanticipated line drive to depose him from his nest on the thirtieth floor. A home run. It was a miracle that Steve could not force, though he felt entitled to a coup that would end Bigelow's taunts about his being an aging college punk.

Bigelow was just another threat, plumper, more streetwise. But still a bastard, and beatable. Steve's image on the video screen did not supply a very convincing affirmative, but at least he felt a bit better.

And what of all the bitches?

Once in Bigelow's extra-wide chair, Steve could order around the entire executive steno pool, and take his pick. His prime advantage over most of the denizens of the thirtieth floor was that he was a decade younger (and, he hoped, infinitely more potent) than the bulk of the veepee staff. The hierarchy inside the corporate headquarters of Calex was supremely feudal and caste-conscious. The peons working on the floors below you were more than literally beneath you. Steve's best sexual conquests so far had been career secretaries entrenched on his own level, women like Rachel Downey, captainess of the copy room, whom he had "dated" twice. He had discovered the hard way that Rachel the Red dyed her hair. Since their tryst had fizzled, he was finding it difficult to get Xerox work sent back to him on time . . . so thanks to her, he was yet again in the frypan with Bigelow through calculated, long-distance sabotage.

He shut down his machines and piled his work into his briefcase, the leather job with the blunt corners. On his way to the elevators he reviewed his mental checklist of local watering holes for "suits" like himself and came up with a few why-nots. Century City, alive with night-light, blazed in through the windows of the twenty-second floor and tried to diminish him. Just as his finger touched the heat-sensitive button, he noticed the car was crawling downward on its own, and he counted along with the orange digits: **28, 27, 26** . . .

The brushed steel doors parted. Bigelow was not inside, lurking in ambush, as he had feared. The only passenger at this time of night was a woman.

He would remember her amber pendant until the moment of his death.

"You look like a man bearing a burden," she said, in the kind of throaty voice that might have conferred an amusing secret to a lover.

"Oh yeah," he said mechanically, stepping in. Then his eyes tarried.

She was barely inside of a clinging, silky-red dress featuring a pattern of black oval dots and scalloped, shortie sleeves. The front of the dress divided neatly over her breasts — not Body Shop silicone nightmares, but a warm swell that was the real, proportionate item. Broad, shiny black belt — real leather — black hose, black heels, large clunky bracelet in enameled ebony, matching the pendulant onyx drop earrings. The face between those earrings was cheeky and feline, with elliptical sea-green eyes, a sharp, patrician nose, and neat small teeth. Her weight was on one leg, the other inclined to an unconscious model's pose. Her hands held before her a large, flat-brimmed sunhat of woven black fibers and a petite clutch-brief of papers. Her hair was unbound, strong coffee black-brown, and lots of it. Her expression, which at first had been neutral, now seemed one of avid but cautious curiosity; she examined him with a quizzical, cocked-head attitude.

The doors guillotined shut behind Steve with slow, inexorable Nazi efficiency. **Thunk.**

"I'm working late again," he said with a shrug, and was suddenly astounded at the bilge his mouth was capable of spewing. He checked her out again, and regretted not spiffing up before quitting the twenty-second floor.

"I'm overtime on behalf of the great god Bigelow." Her pendant, a rough-cut chunk of translucent yellow stone, dallied on a foxtail chain of gold near the hollow of her throat.

The orange floor digits winked from twenty-two to twenty-one and Steve's gonads finally kicked into brain override. *She spoke first,* the mechanism said. *You've got twenty floors to fast-talk this muffin into having a martini with you.* Chat footholds were already abundant — Bigelow, Calex, their mutual late oil-burning — but he faltered in response, as though the sheer pheromone outflow from this woman was stupefying him. "Uh Bigelow?" *Wake up, you moron!* Nineteen lit up as one more floor of time ran out.

"Mm. You look like another of his bond-slaves." Her eyes appraised him. "Nice to find a kindred spirit."

"Well, you know, we ought to be thankful that he takes the burden of credit off our lowly shoulders."

Her melodic laugh was as pleasing as her voice. She asked him his position, and he told her; she fingered her pendant (it caught even the soft light in the elevator, like a diamond sucking up the colors of the spectrum) and asked point-blank why he did not have Bigelow's job. He said something offhanded and ironic in response, and instantly felt self-consciously glib. She saved him again by speaking before he had time to think his unthinking words into a real *gaffe.*

"You'd fit one of those thirtieth-floor suites just fine. And I'd much prefer working under someone from my own generation."

His brain was afloat with possibilities. "There aren't many clean ways to erase a vice president." At once he began to fear that this woman, who seemed all too eager to be picked up, might be some sort of planted Bigelow spy.

"Oh, I've got a way," she smiled. "What I've always needed is a man willing to do it."

By now, there was no man in recorded history more willing to do it than Steven Keller.

Not too much later, when they were sweating and short of breath, Vivia told him about the seed.

"I can't see it." He disentangled himself from her hair.

"Just shy of the center." She broke the chain from around her neck and handed him the pendant. "Look at it while I go thrash out the ultimate martini, hm?" With that, she was up and striding across his bedroom, hips switching liquidly. Naked she was smooth of flank, balletically graceful; Steve's notice did not turn to the pendant until she was out of sight.

When he held it to the candle flame a tiny silhouette appeared, a dark bead trapped fast in the honey-colored amber. It was boring.

Vivia placed the martini shaker, frosty with condensation, on the nightstand within easy reach. The vermouth had given the ice the barest kiss; the drink was cold, and as she had promised, flawless, as perfect as her body was sleek, as her eyes were hypnotic.

Now Steve's brain was really rocking and rolling, and an imp voice said Vivia, Vivia *Keller*, not too shabby . . . but before he could polish off his drink she was tugging him down, wrapping her thoroughbred legs around him, engulfing him in her cascade of hair. Sometime before dawn she touched the empty shaker, and asked if he wanted more.

Not knowing what she was talking about, Steve nodded.

* * *

It seemed poetic that the perfect martini yielded what could only be called the perfect hangover — murderous, battering, as perfect as bamboo shoots or electroshock. The blatting of Steve's alarm did not penetrate his cognizance until 8:45, and the first thing he heard on the clock-radio was an advertisement for a perfume called Objet D'Art. Which, he knew, was manufactured by Michelle Dante Cosmetics, which had been co-opted by Calex Corporation in 1976. It was as though Calex itself had come home to invade his bedroom and whack him on the head with the guilt stick.

The revised cost estimate sheets waited in his briefcase while he at-

©JANET AULISIO 1989.

tempted to shower, dress and drive to work with only five minutes available for each task. He finger-combed his hair in the blurry reflection afforded by the elevator doors and straightened his tie by touch, praying that the shitty coffee on the twenty-second floor would at least deaden his breath to neutral. His eyes itched. In his haste he had climbed into his trousers without underwear, and now felt vulnerably askew below-decks. The trip up seemed unjustly quick in comparison to the deliciously slow descent he'd taken in the same car a scant thirteen hours previously. When the elevator disgorged him, he won few pitying looks. From the copy room, Rachel Downey saw him vanish into the brown-fabricked maze . . . and ignored him.

He found Bigelow seated on his desk, waiting. The bounceback of the ceiling fluorescents from the older man's harsh gold wire-rims gifted Steve with an instant migraine. No human pupils were to be seen behind those thick, black-hole lenses, merely multiple white rectangles of pain-giving light.

"It's nine fifteen and twenty seconds, Keller, did you know that? Your eyes are stubbornly red." Bigelow's voice was sepulchral and resonant, the bellows-basso of a vast, fat man.

Steve was weary beyond even snideness. "Yes sir. I've brought the revised estimates you asked for on the —"

Upon seeing the proffered sheaf of pages, Bigelow's expression rivalled that of a man whose pet cat has proudly sauntered through the kitchen door with half an eviscerated snake in its jaws. He dropped the sheets into Steve's own roundfile. They fluttered helplessly on the way down. "When you did not deliver these figures to my desk at nine o'clock this morning, I had young Cavanaugh revise them. Good morning, Keller." He slid off the desk, leaving a large buffed area, and trundled out without a backward glance.

Drained and hopeless, Steve just stood there. Cavanaugh did not drink. Cavanaugh was married. Cavanaugh had just neatly eroded another inch off Steve's toehold on the thirtieth floor. Should Bigelow die right this moment, he thought he might lock onto the vice presidency through simple corporate momentum . . . but not if Cavanaugh kept punching away, infiltrating his projects.

Vivia had been long gone by the time he opened his eyes, leaving neither last name nor current phone number. He stayed in a zombiatic funk through lunchtime, not eating, but his depression eased when he thought of accessing the Calex Building's personnel listings through one of the computer terminals on the twenty-second floor. With his eighth mug of silty company coffee in hand, he waded through the rollups searching for the first initial **V**.

Vinces and Valeries formed an entire platoon by themselves, with Victors, Vickies and Veras as the runners-up. Two Vondas, one Vianne, and no Vivia by the time he reached the last-name letter **M**.

God, what if her last name was Zamperini?

He'd risked all the computer time he dared, and decided to do **M** through **Z** on Monday, even though he'd hoped for a weekend tryst. As it turned out, Bigelow was not finished with him for this Friday, either.

No bulk blocked his doorway; this time Steve got his scorching over the phone: "It has just come to my attention, Keller, that you've been frittering valuable computer time in the pursuit of non-Calex —"

He squeezed his eyes shut as slivers of pain aligned themselves along his temples. Knowing full well that Rachel and some of the other bitches on the twenty-second floor were most likely eavesdropping, he held the receiver to his ear and went through the dance, not really giving a damn as Bigelow tiraded onward in his fat-cat drone, the sound of the axle of corporate doom pounding a few more dents into his sinecure at Calex. It had probably been a decade or more since the fat old bastard had last screwed his starched and reedy wife, and maybe sexual frustration was what gave Bigelow the stamina, at his age and with his rotten, cholesterol-gummed clock of a heart, to jump on Steve's head with both heels every time he made the slightest little . . .

Yes sir, he said robotically. *No sir. Yes sir.* And as with the best forms of torture, there at least came a hiatus.

The elevator doors slid back, revealing an empty car. Once again the twenty-second floor was mostly dark, and Steve stepped in, alone. Going down.

He felt like he was drowning.

"Your door was open."

His heart began to jitterbug with an accelerated thudding so sudden and intense he momentarily feared an internal fuckup. Vivia waited on his sofa, smothered inside of his brown plush bathrobe. The martini shaker waited on the glass-topped coffee table. It was very likely he had forgotten to lock his door while dashing out that morning; he locked it now, and as he did she stood up to greet him. The robe stayed on the couch.

Deep into the night, she mentioned the seed again, and Bigelow, and a solution to Steve's problem that sounded quite insane.

"It's simple, really, so it doesn't matter if what I say is crazy." She spoke past him, stroking his hair. "Just consider it a gesture. A contract, like marriage. If you'll do this tiny thing for me, I'm all yours. Desperate men have done crazier things for less return. You're shrewd, Steve — indulge me. I promise you it'll be worth it."

She demonstrated how. If he was not convinced, he was certainly intrigued.

Logy, he said, "So this is what you want me for," half-jokingly. Out of habit he'd been waiting for the catch to the whole deal; the condition she'd put to him that would render her down to the low rank of all the other Calex women he'd known, the words that would make her cease to be something special. Yes?

What came instead was a shiver of horror that *he* might never become more special than she deemed him at this moment, that he might never move up-market, as they said in jolly old Great B. That fancy triggered another, spurred by his notion that Vivia was of foreign origin, (thus her trace accent, thus her exotic manner) — not of Calex, not of L.A., but somewhere else. Somewhere else was where he needed to go; did he dare risk losing her, after she'd explained her plan bluntly, just because that plan didn't conform to linear corporate logic? *This is what you must do to have me,* she had said. No tricks.

That was when he decided to do what she asked, and not fake it. This woman would know if her rules were fudged.

He rose to begin dressing. When she rose on one elbow in the bed to watch, and told him how she needed him, he nodded, his blood hot and racing. He left to perform his task, his gesture, before the sun could announce Saturday morning.

Bigelow lived in a fashionably appointed ranch house in Brentwood, on the far side of UCLA. The drive took time even though traffic was sparse — cabbies, police, battleship-sized garbage trucks, and the occasional renegade night person.

Breaking Vivia's amber had proven simple; he'd used a cocktail hammer, and the pendant scattered apart into crushed-ice chips of see-through gold. The seed was tiny, no larger than a watermelon pit, flat and glossy like a

33

legless bug. It was in his pants pocket, inside a plastic box that had once held a mineral tie-tack.

Also in the pocket was his Swiss Army knife, and the full moon was reflected in the car's windshield — two more of Vivia's odd conditions fulfilled. It had to be done by the full moon, she'd said, so that they might both reap by the next full moon. Steve purposefully put her other instructions on hold while he drove; he wanted nothing to make him feel foolish enough to turn back. He thought of Vivia instead, of gaining her strange trust, of having her body for a long time. Longer than any of the bitches, since she could be many women for him — none of whom mucked about with excuses or mood-killing delays in the name of messy human givens like menstrual periods or birth control. She was admirably void of what to him was standard-issue female bellyaching. Instead she was very no-nonsense, a delicious riddle, perhaps beguiling. He judged her perfect for his needs, and wasted no time thinking of himself as selfish, or, as Rachel the Red had called him, a usurer. Rachel read too goddamned many gothic romances.

Bigelow's home occupied the terminus of a paved and winding drive that isolated it from the main road. Steve caught a flicker of a low-wattage all-nighter bulb glowing in a front kitchen window as he cruised the area. He parked around a corner a block and a half away and began his stealthy approach, thankful that the drive was not graveled.

The fat old bastard had once made bragging mention of his bedroom's western exposure, and Steve soon located the window above a precisely clipped hedge of rosebushes.

"You mustn't dig a hole," she had insisted. "You must uproot a *living* plant, and place the seed in the hole that results from the death of that plant." Luckily for Vivia's instructions, the

Bigelow grounds had abundant flora.

He threaded into the tangle of sharp leaves and spiked branches and hefted gently, fighting not to stir up a commotion. A thorn sank into the palm of his hand and he grimaced, but the pain made the contest with the bush personal. For making him bleed, it would die.

He thought of Neanderthal men ripping each other's entrails out, of grappling with Bigelow and wrapping his fingers around his fat, wheezy windpipe. The bush rattled a bit but was no match for him. When it came up, clods of deep-brown dirt hung from its freed roots.

There was no reaction or notice from within the house. Of course, if Bigelow suspected a prowler he would take no direct action — for that function there was a little steel sign at the head of the driveway. Every home in Brentwood had one, and Bigelow's read CONROY SECURITY SYSTEMS / ARMED RESPONSE. The threat implied by that little hexagonal sign compelled Steve to finish up quickly.

There was no need for the pocket-knife, since his palm was already slathered with fresh blood. He dabbed the black seed; "consecrating it" was the term Vivia had used. Somewhere in the darkness right in front of him, beyond the window, the impotent Bigelow snored on, hoglike, lying in state next to his frigid cow of a wife. Maybe they lolled in separate beds, genuflecting to that grand old era of Beaver Cleaver, when sex equalled pornography, when nice girls didn't. Steve grinned. Then he groped his way back to the gout in the earth and tamped dirt over the seed with his fingers.

It was in. As Vivia had wanted.

He lugged the rousted bush out with him so that it might not be discovered and replanted by whatever minority Bigelow engaged to manicure his grounds. Walking heel-to-toe in burglar doubletime, palm stinging and wet, Steve felt absurdly victorious, as though he'd just bounced a homer off Bigelow's noggin instead of merely vandalizing a hedge. He had come through for Vivia, and thus gained a kind of control over her, too. In a single day he had galloped the gamut of rough emotions. By the time dawn began to tint the sky, he felt renewed — exhausted yet charged, back in the running, a success in the making, confirmed executive fodder. Definitely up-market.

He ditched the murdered rosebush in a supermarket trash dumpster on his way home.

According to the adage that defines *sanity* as the first twenty minutes following orgasm, what Casey (Steve's most recent non-Calex blonde) had told him not so long ago was sane, reasoned.

"I don't think you *like* women very much. Present company excluded, of course."

"Of course." He stroked her thigh, his lungs burning with immediate umbrage at her remark. Who in hell was this vacant twinkie to pass judgement? They had swapped climax for climax, shared a smoke, and now she was gearing up to pry into his psyche. It always began around the fourth fuck or so, these sloppy digressions into his private feelings. He'd given her a good technical orgasm and this was how she responded. They were past the stage where he could joke off such an accusation, as more tentatively acquainted people can. His fingers traced upward knowingly, commencing an automatic process guaranteed to shut her up.

Further, it was Casey's opinion that some woman had done vast damage to Steve in the past. That he had been avenging that hurt on every woman he'd touched since, trying to distill away the poison inside him. That things could change at last, now that she had arrived on the scene.

In that moment Steve's judgement on Casey banged down like a slamming cell door. Things did *change*, and quickly. He brought the prying bitch off hard, with some pain. While she was still moist he slammed into her as though driving nails. The next morning he subtracted her from his Rolodex, hoping she was sore for a long time.

That was lost in the past now.

Now, Steve lay next to Vivia, recalling Casey's words and wondering if they might have been true . . . and whether Vivia might not be the turnaround he didn't even know he had been seeking for most of his adult life.

The past four weeks had been a whirlwind of input for him. When not assimilating and processing the swelling workload dumping downward from Bigelow's office, he was wrapped up in Vivia, who had taken a fervently singleminded interest in his sexual wellbeing. Bigelow had called in sick in the middle of the first week, and Steve had marveled frankly and quietly. The fat old bastard finally lumbered into the office late on Thursday, and botched everything he touched. By Friday — exactly one week after Steve had been carpet-called for using the computer on the sly — Bigelow had mazed his way back to Steve's cubicle in person again . . . but this time, it had been to thank him.

Oh, how he had savored that moment!

"You've performed admirably, Keller," he'd croaked, red-faced and dappled with fever-sweat. "You've risen to the occasion and saved my callused old butt; I was beginning to think you didn't have that kind of dedication. I appreciate all your help, and the extra hours you've put in during this . . . uh, time." Steve had said *yes sir* at the appropriate lulls in the rally-round-the-company spiel, invoking his new prerogative as victor not to rub Bigelow's veiny nose in the events of the past.

35

When the old man finished, he had shuffled out, slump-shouldered. He didn't make another appearance in the office until the following Wednesday.

That was when the thought of just what might be growing, unobtrusively, amid the rosebushes in Brentwood, began to gnaw at Steve.

"Why my blood, anyway?" he asked Vivia. "Why not his? I mean, he's the object — the victim, right?"

Whenever he brought up the subject of the seed, she seemed to answer by rote. "Whose blood is used for the consecration isn't important. It's who the plant grows nearest to. It leaches away the life essence, thrives on it. As it grows larger, it needs more. Those asleep near it are especially susceptible. It reaches maturity in one month, from one full moon to the next." She draped one of her fine white legs over his. "Then it dies."

"The blood is just to prime the pump? Get it started?"

"Mm." Her hands were upon him. Getting him started.

"Just what is it you've got against Bigelow? You know, I tried to find your company employee index number on the computer and came up with zilch." She had since given him a last name, but that had not dissipated the mystery.

"What is it you have against him?" she countered, with a trace of irritation. "And what does it matter? You're not the only person privileged to hate him for the things he's done!"

He thought she was sidestepping; then he caught on. Bigelow's blue-rinsed wife lent perspective to the supposition of a squirt of randiness somewhere in his boss's recent past. Promises, perhaps, traded for a bit of extra-marital hoop-de-doo with a Calex functionary who had just happened to be Vivia. Unfulfilled promises, naturally — the office rule was that verbal contracts weren't worth the paper they weren't

36

written on. So Vivia had lain back and devised her retaliation. For Steve to bring this matter up in bed, he now saw, was deeply counterproductive.

She did not let him pursue it further, at any rate. "It'll be done soon now, darling, don't worry it." She poured them both another of her stinging-cold, perfect martinis. "And we'll both get what we want."

He was surely getting what *he* wanted. Vivia seemed satisfied, too. He had long since given her a door key; he usually found her awaiting his pleasure, and he liked that.

"Give me what I want," he said, and she rolled onto him. He thought he was happy.

During the final week, Bigelow did not appear in the Calex Building at all. The scuttlebutt was that he'd suffered a minor stroke.

"I took a stack of escalation briefs out to his house, y'know?" It was Cavanaugh, Steve's former competitor, spreading the news. "Steve, he looked like *hell;* I mean, pallid, trembling. His eyes were yellow and bloodshot, the works. I was afraid to breathe air in the same room with him, y'know? It's like he got the plague or something!"

Steve nodded, appearing interested. He was learning the executive trait of letting subordinates do most of the talking. With open hands of sympathy he said, "Well, in the old man's absence I'm stuck with twice the work, and it's time I got back into it."

Cavanaugh was dismissed. That was something else new, and Steve was getting better at it. It made him feel peachy.

While he had made no effort to see what had blossomed at Bigelow's, his desire to know had germinated and grown at a healthy pace. Vivia had said the plant would die with the coming of the next full moon, its task complete. It all sounded like a shovelful of occult hoodoo, as vague as a syndicated horoscope. A thriving plant shouldn't keel over due to a timetable, he thought, horticultural genius that he was. Since the technique appeared to be working and producing results, simple Calex procedure dictated no need to scrutinize the hows and whys. You didn't have to know how a television set worked to enjoy it; how Objet D'Art functioned, to appreciate its scent on women.

Time was running short. Time for Bigelow, time to see what had sprung from the black seed.

"You don't really need to see it," Vivia had agreed. "That would be . . . superficial."

Again he nodded. Her words were reassuring and correct. Once she drowsed off, he went out driving in the wee hours one more time.

He duplicated his original route and found the Brentwood streets unchanged. A blue and white Conroy security car hissed past in the opposite lane. That was the last Steve saw of the local minions of armed response.

Two curious sights awaited him at the bedroom window. The first was Bigelow, tossing about in his bed, sheets askew. He was in the grip of some nightmare, or spasm. His flesh shone greenly under a ghostly-soft nightlight, by which Steve saw the bedstand, littered with medications. The old man's movements were enfeebled and retarded by fitful sleep; the thrashing of a suffocating fish.

Then there was the plant. Against the all-weather white of the ranch house's siding, it was quite visible.

It was confused among the rosebush branches, and resembled a squat tangle of blacksnakes, diverging wildly as though the shoots wanted nothing to do with each other. Like the chitinous hardness of the seed, the branches were armored in a kind of exoskeleton of deep, lacquered black. The small leaves that had sprouted at the ends of each branch were dead ebony, dull and waxy to the touch, with spade shapes and serrated edges. He leaned closer, to touch, and felt a papercut pain in the tip of his finger that caused him to jerk back his hand and bite his lip in the dark.

Kneeling, he unclipped a penlight from his pocket, oblivious to the risk of being spotted, and saw that the skin of the plant was inlaid with downy white fibers, like extremely fine hair. They were patterned directionally, in the manner of scales on a viper; to stroke them one way would be to feel a humid softness, while the opposite direction would fill the finger with barbs like slivers of glass. Steve tried to tweezer the tiny quill out with his teeth.

The black plant exuded no odor whatsoever, he noticed. He found that to be the most unsettling aspect of all, since all plants smelled like something, from the whore's perfume of night-blooming jasmine to the clean-laundry scent of carnations. This had all the olfactory presence of a bowl of plastic grapes.

He heard a strangled cough through the window panes, and saw Bigelow stir weakly in his bed. The moon was ninety percent full. Tomorrow night it would be perfect.

Watching his superior whittled down in this way, Steve realized that now it wasn't necessary that the old man actually die. Ever since his conjecture about Bigelow's dalliance with Vivia, he'd begun to feel an inexplicable fraternal sympathy for the old goat. Would Steve care to come to such a finish, merely because he'd chased a bit of tail in his declining years? Vivia sure was enthusiastic enough about jumping *his* bones to get her revenge on Bigelow. And Steve's future with Calex seemed locked without the nastiness of a death to blot it . . . didn't it?

Was he starting to feel sorry for the fat old bastard?

Inside the house, Bigelow let out a congested moan, and the sound put ice into Steve's lungs.

Impulsively he gathered the black plant into two fists and hoisted it upward, hoping to tear loose the roots. The rosebushes rattled furiously, shifting about like pedestrians witnessing an ugly car crash, but the plant remained solidly anchored, unnaturally so. Yanking a mailbox out of a concrete sidewalk would have been easier. Steve's hand skinned upward along the glossy stalks and collected splinter quills all the way up. This time he did scream.

Bigelow stopped flailing. Now he was awake, and staring at the window.

Tears doubling his vision, blood dripping freely from his tightly clenched fists, Steve fled into the night.

Shortly after lunch on Friday, Cavanaugh wandered into Steve's office wearing a hangdog H.P. Lovecraft face, broadcasting woe. His eyebrows arched at the sight of Steve's bandaged hands, but the younger man was determined to maintain the proper, respectful air of gloom and tragedy.

"I got the phone call ten minutes ago," he said, nearly whispering. "I don't know if you've heard. But, uh —"

"Bigelow?" Steve was mostly guessing.

Cavanaugh closed his eyes and nodded. "Sometime last night. His wife said he saw a prowler. He was reaching for the phone when his heart —"

"Stopped." Steve folded his hands on the desk. The old man had probably hit the deck like a sledgehammered steer.

Cavanaugh stood fast, fidgeting. "Um, Blakely will probably be asking you up to his office on Monday for a meeting . . . you know." Blakely was Bigelow's superior.

Heavy on the *was,* Steve thought as his line buzzed. He excused himself to speak with Blakely's busty girl Friday, who was calling from the thirtieth floor regarding the meeting that Cavanaugh had just mentioned. And, incidentally,

was Mr. Keller possibly free for cocktails after work? Was today too soon? Her name was Connie, and of course he already had her extension. Polite laugh.

At the flick of the wrist, Cavanaugh faded into the background. That was the last Steve ever saw of him.

Waiting for him at home were Vivia, the martini shaker — perfect — and a toast to success.

It took both his hands to navigate the first glass to his mouth, since both were immobilized into semi-functional scoops by the bandages. The more he drank, the more efficient he became at zeroing in on his face, and to his chagrin the anesthetizing effect of the alcohol permitted some of the last night's bitterness to peek out, and beeline for Vivia.

"Here's to us, to us," he said mostly to his glass. He was on the sofa, and Vivia sat cross-legged, sunk into a leather recliner across from him. His shoes were cockeyed on the floor between them. "Methinks I've just hooked and crooked my merry way into a higher tax bracket, thank you very much to my . . . odd little concubine . . . and her odd little plant. Perhaps we should consider incorporating. Corporeally speaking, that is." His sightline flew to the bedroom door and back.

Vivia raised her glass to him. She was wearing an Oriental print thing far too skimpy and diaphanous to qualify as a robe.

"So now, as — ahem! — partners in non-crime," he said as she refilled their glasses, "you have to fill me in on the plant. Where the hell did you come across something like that? You don't buy that sort of thing down at the Vigoro plant shop. How come people aren't using them to . . . Christ, to bump off everybody?"

She finished off her drink before he was halfway through his, and stretched languorously, purring. "This tastes like pure nectar," she said.

"Stick to the subject, wench."

She cocked her head in the peculiar way he'd become so familiar with, and mulled her story over before saying, "I had the only seed." That was it.

He remembered the amber, and nodded. So far, so logical. "Where'd you get it?"

"I've had it quite a long time. Since birth, in fact." She ran her tongue around the rim of her glass, then recharged it by half from the shaker.

"An heirloom?"

"Mm."

She was preparing to lead him off to the sack again, and he fully intended to bed her, but not before he could hurdle her coy non-replies and clear his conscience. "Tell me what happened between you and Bigelow." Instinct had told him to shift gears, and he expected a harsh look.

"I've never really seen the man."

The office coffee was starting to have an unlovely reaction to the quickly gulped booze, and he burped quietly. "Wait a minute." He waved his free hand to make her go back and explain. The surrender-flag whiteness of the bandages hurt his eyes in the room's dim light. "You two had some kind of . . . assignation, or something. You wanted vengeance on him."

"Hm." The corners of her generous mouth twitched upward, then dropped back to neutral, as though she was still learning how to make a smile. "In point of fact, Steven, I never said I wanted vengeance on anything. Perhaps you thought it."

Now this definitely registered sourly. For a crazed, out-of-sync moment he thought she was going to add, *no, I wanted vengeance on YOU!* like some daffy twist in a 1940s murder mystery. But she just sat there, hugging her knees to her chin, distracting him with her body. Waiting.

"Oh, I get it — you just help a total stranger, out of the blue, to do in his

© JANET AULISIO 1989.

boss, whom you've never met, with the last special black plant seed in the entire universe." The sarcasm was back in his tone.

"I was interested in you, Steven. No other."

"Why?" **Urrrrp**, again, stronger this time.

"Except for one thing you've been perfect for me. You were . . . what is the word? Fertile. You were ripe."

"Where'd I slip up?" Now his head was throbbing, and he feared he might have to interrupt his fact-finding sortie by sicking up on the shag carpeting.

She gave him her quizzical little shrug. "You were supposed to go uproot the plant tonight, you sneak. During the full moon. Not last night, though I don't suppose it'll matter." She rose; her legs flashed in and out of the wispy garment as she approached. "Let me give you a refill. This is a celebration, you know, and I'm ahead of you."

"Ugh, no — wait," he muttered, his brains sloshing around in his skull-pan like dirty dishwater. "No more for me." He put out one of his mitts to arrest the progress of the shaker toward the glass and blundered it out of Vivia's grasp. He was reminded of the time he had tried to keep a coffeeshop waitress from freshening up his cup by putting his hand over the cup to indicate no more . . . and gotten his fingers scalded.

The shaker bounced on the rug without breaking. Its lid rolled away and ice cubes tumbled out, clicking like rolling dice. Mingled with the ice were several limp, wet, dead-black leaves. Gin droplets glistened on them. They were spade-shaped, with serrated edges.

Steve gaped at them numbly. "Oh my God . . ." Poisoned! Unable to grab, he swung at Vivia, who easily danced out of range. He gasped, his voice dropping an octave into huskiness as he felt a shot of pain in his diaphragm. He understood that his body needed to vomit and expel the toxin.

But he wanted to get Vivia first.

He launched himself off the sofa and succeeded only in falling across the coffee table, cleaning it off and landing in a drunken sprawl on non-responsive mannequin limbs. The feeling in his fingers and toes was gone.

"Oh, Steven, not poison," he heard her say. "What a silly thing to think, darling. I wouldn't do that. I need you. Isn't that what you always wanted — a woman who truly needed you? I mean *truly*? Not in all the petty ways you so despise?"

His tongue went dead. His throat fought to contract and seal off his airway. If he could force himself to throw up, he might suffocate . . . or save his life. He was incapable of snaring Vivia now, but he sure as hell could use two fingers to chock down his tongue. He saw the expression on her face as he did it.

She watched intently, almost lovingly, with that unusual cocked-head attitude he remembered from their first meeting in the elevator. It reminded him of a cocker spaniel hearing a high-frequency whistle, or a hungry insect inspecting food with its antennae. It was an attitude characteristic of another species.

He heaved mightily. Nothing came up but bubbly saliva.

A tiny, hard object shot up from his gullet to click against the obverse of his front teeth. Its ejection eased his trachea open. While he spit and sucked wind, Vivia stepped eagerly forward with a cry of excitement identical to the sounds she had made in bed with him.

She picked up the wet black seed and held it between her thumb and forefinger. She tried to gain his attention while he retched. "This is the one I'll keep always, darling. You may not be aware, but amber takes *ages* to solidify properly."

He struggled to speak, to ask irrational questions, but could only continue what had begun. Another of the wicked little seeds chucked out with enough force to make a painful dent in the roof of his mouth. It bounced off his dry tongue and escaped. He did not feel it hit. It was chased by fifteen more . . . which were pushed forward and out by a torrent of several hundred.

The last thing Steve did was contract to a fetal ball, hugging his rippling stomach. His breath was totally dammed by the floodtide of beaded black shapes that had clogged up his system and now sought the quickest way out.

"I loved you, Steven, and needed you more than anyone ever has. How many people get that in their lifetimes?"

Then he could hear nothing beyond the rainstorm patter of the seeds, gushing forth by the thousands as his body caved in and evacuated everything, a full moon's worth. In the end, he was potent beyond his most grotesque sexual aspirations.

Vivia held the first seed of the harvest, and watched. The sight fulfilled her as a female.

⊗

ENCOUNTER

"What is it in the winter night
that swings in an icy breeze?"
(It's only a broken branch, my child,
caught up in some willow trees.)

"What is it staring at the moon
with eyes like whitened glass?"
(It's only a vagrant owl, my love,
watching the clouds that pass.)

"What is it high above the ground
walking on the wind it seems."
(It's only a drunken reveler
caught up in his whisky dreams.)

"What is it that swings with open mouth
while not a sound comes out?"
(It's only a mute from the village, dear,
a climbing but clumsy lout.)

"What is it in the winter night
that glitters as the frost comes down?"
(It's just reflected light, my child,
and we must hurry into town!)

— **Joseph Payne Brennan**

41

Weirdisms

"The Corpse Who Dances."

During the Tibetan **rolang** ceremony, the sorcerer must restrain the magically re-animated corpse until dawn . . . when he bites off its tongue.

The tongue becomes a powerful talisman and a magical weapon.

GET WITH CHILD A MANDRAKE

by Mary A. Turzillo

"The folk of the parish hold that I am imprisoned here," she said. Nicholas stood on the cold stones of the castle's floor with his mouth open. He, the sweetheart of the parish, and with nothing to say.

She looked at him for a long time with her glass-grey eyes. His soul wandered lost in them. Finally she blinked, and he remembered they were both alive.

"What would you have with me?" she finally asked. Her voice was husky for a girl who looked perhaps seventeen.

Nicholas swallowed. "I seek to learn dragonlore. The arts of witchcraft." Night sounds echoed in his ears.

"That may well be. But it shall be at a cost," she said. His eyes slid, again and again, to her body. It reminded him of a green snake, narrow-hipped (he liked broad hips) and delicate-bosomed (he liked small breasts).

"At what cost, lady? Pray keep in mind, I am only a poor scholar. My purse was never lined with sovereigns."

She had a thin, very red mouth. She smiled in a way that meant she had thought on something he knew nothing of. Maidens did not often smile at Nicholas that way.

"My father was a poor scholar," she said. "Poor soul."

"But at what cost, then?" he heard himself say. He thought he heard the dragon stir below. To ward off that dragon, he had taught himself a spell from the books he had stolen. He wondered how long that spell would hold.

"Cost? Not a jot more than your life," she said.

Nicholas shivered. He had foreseen something of this kind, back when he fancied, in his innocence, that he would rescue the mysterious maiden of the keep and learn the secrets of the wizard who, in the guise of a dragon, transformed by witchery, kept her in thrall in the great ruined castle.

"Cold?" she asked, raising her delicately shaped eyebrows. "Pray let me light the fire." Nicholas watched as she uncoiled herself and went over to the hearth. With boneless elegance she knelt and, with her back to him, set the kindling on the hearth ablaze. By his troth he would have sworn she but breathed on the tinder. "We do not often light the fire in June," she said.

"We? You and the dragon?"

"Mother and I."

"Your mother dwells here? But I had thought . . ."

"The folk of the parish hold that I am imprisoned here. Yet, indeed, this is my house and also my home."

Nicholas looked about him in wonderment. "What do you here all the day long?" He could well believe she did not keep house all the day long. But for a few joint-bones on greasy trenchers, there was no relic of cookery in this great hall.

"We keep our family's treasure." She smiled of a sudden. Her tongue, it seemed to Nicholas, flicked out of her mouth as she laughed.

"Treasure?"

"Surely, you have heard of treasure in this old hall, Nicholas, have you not?

43

And yet think not that it shall be yours for the asking, nor yet for the taking. The dragon will see that you get of it not a groat."

"Where is this treasure?"

"Under the earth. Or upon my finger, a ring of it. Sometimes of a holy day, I will wear gold chains, strung with pearl and coral, or cunningly-wrought brooches, or red and green baubles, as it pleases me. Today, as it chances, I wear none."

"But do you spend none of this treasure, then? For surely I have never seen the like of you at market buying victuals."

"Game, well-hung, is our most frequent meat." She shook loose her hair of its green-broidered cap. And her hair was a smoky yellow color, not the ghastly greenish grey it had seemed when first he encountered her outside the castle portals in moonlight.

"Mayhap," he said, "your learning is too dear for my poor scholar's purse."

"Well, let that be. I shall weigh your purse in good time."

"Shall not the dragon make trial of me?"

"I shall make trial of you," she answered, almost to herself. "Yes, the time is at hand. You, of all the parish and the lands around, will do. Now, what sorcery would you learn?"

Chivalry swelled, out of all season, in Nicholas's heart. "Any that my lady would care to teach."

Again she smiled, her teeth small and gapped, like a vixen's. "I shall teach you all. But come, first your bond."

Nicholas shivered. "My soul, is it? My immortal soul?"

"By Saint Margaret and Saint George, no! Your hand rather." She extended hers. He looked at that long, narrow hand, and at her solemn grey eyes, firelight dancing in them. He slowly held out his own chapped, ruddy hand.

She urged, "Come! Your hand, and

then your bond!"

"My lady, what do I swear?"

"That you will grant me my will within this fortnight, and thereafter if it be my will."

"And what does my lady swear?"

She sighed. "That I will do your body nor your soul no harm. That I will teach you as much of sorcery as ever I and my mother know. That you shall have your pleasure of me."

Nicholas quaked in his heart. In his mind's eye, he saw every jolly wench in the parish. Then must he forswear them all for this strange lady, with the body of a maid-child and the voice of an old widow?

He touched her hand. He fell in love.

Without further words, he staggered and knelt.

"Pledge me your bond," she said in a low voice full of power.

"That I will wed you?"

She flicked a lock of flaxen hair out of her face. "It may not come to that. Only pledge that you will do my will if my will be so."

Nicholas had read many romances, borrowed books and stolen. He had read of bargains such as this, and the knight (it was always a knight, never a young coxcomb of a scholar like himself) sometimes came to vast great fortune, and sometimes lost both life and soul.

"Swear you won't slay me?"

She pulled her skirts away from him. "So I *have* pledged."

"And that you won't slay my immortal soul?"

"If you had taken heed of your immortal soul, young . . . what are you called?"

"Nicholas."

"Nicholas, if you had cared a pin for your soul, you would not be here. You and your stolen books of necromancy, and your whoring ways with the parish wives. What would you say to Father John the priest if he came here now?"

"Then my soul must fly at fortune?"

"Your soul has already flown at fortune. I shall not be the one to damn it."

Nicholas sat on his heels and looked up at her as the dying rabbit looks at the vixen.

She drew back her hand. "Will you pledge me or no, moon-calf?" Her dress, he saw now, was of the strangest sempstering. Or mayhap there was no sempstering to it. The sleeves and bodice seemed of the sheerest gauze, while the waist and skirt seemed broidered like brocade all over with the same green silk. Yet there was no seam betwixt the two materials. Nicholas held himself a judge of fine dress, and was held in the parish a proper judge of beauty also. The lady's attire fascinated him like a snake's scales.

"Nicholas," she murmured, suddenly soft, "speed thee and pledge." She undid her laces and loosened the green gauze on her breast.

Of a sudden, Nicholas was nauseated with desire. He did not know if this lady was fair or loathely, with her thin lips, hollow loins, and maidenly breasts, but he knew he wanted to bury himself in her skirts, in her.

He swallowed the pool of saliva that had gathered in his mouth. "What shall I say?"

"Say, 'I pledge you, Alisoun, to do your will when a fortnight passes.'"

He said it. His first, miserable love had been named Alisoun. She had married another. How could this lady have the same name?

Alisoun knelt. "I pledge you, Nicholas, to teach you all I know of dragonlore, and to harm you neither in body nor in soul." She rose. "Come up the stairs with me."

Dazed, he pulled himself upright. The world had assumed a kind of penumbra darkening everything but lust.

"Giddy?" she asked. "Then I must lead you." The stone stairs were narrow and cold. At the landing, she bent and lit the candle there. He was right; she could light things with her breath alone.

"Will you teach me to do that?"

"Your child will do that," said Alisoun.

"I will get a son?"

"A maid-child, if good spirits will it. No son of yours could have a mortal maid to wife, for he must needs get his young on her, and she could not bear the heritage of my blood."

Nicholas stopped.

"I came here to learn dragonlore, not to be father to wizards and witches."

Alisoun looked back at him. Her face was sweet and sad in the dim light. "Ah, Nicholas, Nicholas! How can you know why you came here?"

Later, when he had seen how it was to be, and resigned himself, and got over the wonder of her, she told him the terms of their bargain.

"Nicholas, this is good. I will not wait the fortnight, but tell you now my will. Remember that you have pledged."

He turned his face to the wall, and gnawed his lip, and began to weep.

"Is it so unpleasing to you, then, that you must wed a dragon?"

"A dragon? But I thought I was to wed you."

She gently turned his face toward her and looked steadily at him, her grey eyes like glass in the candle's light.

"I am a dragon," she said. "This is my childhood, even as the worm-state is childhood to the moth. And in my childhood, I must find a mortal man to get me with child."

"But surely your need is served now! Surely I have got you with child, with dragonets; and I must go back to the village, to . . ."

"Your pledge," she said.

"It will not hold. There were no witnesses, no banns. No man can be held in bond to a dragon; a dragon is a beast, and . . ."

"And what would John the priest say of your lying with such a beast?"

© JANET AUUSIO 1989.

46

GET WITH CHILD A MANDRAKE

Nicholas was silent. All his world crumbled asunder.

"Try and go forth," she taunted. Somewhere below, the dragon roared, loud enough to shake one's bones. Nicholas's puny spell must have expired.

"That was Mother," Alisoun said.

In the end, Nicholas kept his bond, though not at first willingly. It happens that the seed of mortal man is weak beside the womb of a dragon, and so the act must be done again and again, many times, over a cycle of years. Nicholas, not Alisoun, became the captive in the castle. Later, after Alisoun had taught him to hearken to lost treasure in the ground, to catch falling stars fading from white-hot in his hands, to prophecy from clouds, and to will thunder and rain upon the earth, he was glad enough. He grew used to the strange lady Alisoun, with her widow's voice, who never grew withered, though he grew old and stooped. Of course, his sorcery was of no use, since he could never use it for profit among mortal men.

He learned no love potions, and the vast hoarded treasure of Alisoun and her mother were no more than pretty toys to him, who could spend none of it. Sometimes of a holy day he would wear a ring, or a gold brooch wide as the boss on a soldier's shield, or even a heavy crown, all gauded with dark pearls. He learned to catch game and live on it, with only a wild berry or root as relish.

He died before he saw his daughter.

For Alisoun, out of mercy, had not told him all.

For dragons, childhood lasts a thousand years.

⊗

WALPURGIS NIGHT

The warnings come from women crowned with years,
How, on this night, wise travelers halt their way
At some chaste inn until the dawn of May
Redeems the world from its enchanted tears,
For this is when the seeds of primal fears
May grow strange blooms beneath the moon's white ray,
And laughing forms, forbidden to the day,
Dance in the boughs above the bogs and meres.

But if the witches can run unafraid
To their high Sabbath laden with their charms,
Then you and I can also choose this night
To meet by moonlight in the forest glade,
Where none will see you glimmer to my arms,
And, in elopement, take our merry flight.

— **John Phillips Palmer**

MONSTER MOVIES

by David J. Schow

The green ones were Martians. The orange ones were Indians by deferral, since they'd stopped making the red ones. Light brown ones were Mexicans; darker brown, Negroes. Yellow — Chinese. That left green. Martians.

Jason popped the M&Ms before they could smear a rainbow across the warm palm of his hand. Commercials were so full of owlshit.

Oblivious to the classroom natter, he sat, letting the excitement build, as it always did on Fridays. The first thrilling temblor struck early in the week, whenever the new *TV Guide* hit the racks. It oscillated until Friday night at 11:30, when his pent-up anticipation went bang.

Plain M&Ms were the prime taste (Peanut M&Ms were for perverts), followed by Lipton's iced tea and Lay's potato chips. Texture was embodied in a fortress of musty cushions and Jason's ammo stack of magazines, the elder issues furry or lop-eared with handling. The unforgettable aroma was that of the tubes inside the Motorola console firing, scorching off dust.

Nothing good seemed to last; good stuff was forever being stolen, and to Jason the red ones classified. He had always liked them best. Their candy shells seemed hardest, therefore the most fun to chip artfully away with your teeth. They stayed crunchy the longest. And now they were supposed to be bad for you, and had been outlawed. Nobody had warned him, so that he might hoard up a stockpile. His father had mentioned something vague about red meaning Russian and Russian meaning Communist, and thus the *true* reason for doing dumb things like meddling with the colors of candy and disrupting the universe of children.

Jason was not a child. He was nearly twelve, and owned his own bike and radio. And his personally cultivated Friday night ritual was about to commence.

Fairchild tossed back his second Tanqueray martini of happy hour and scoped the catch of the day.

Diffused to soft focus by the neon haze and cigarette smoke of the lounge, all of the women in attendance looked tasty and desirable. He knew from experience that up close, the ratio of physically attractive eligibles would nosedive fifty percent. About half actually were as good as they looked.

Once they opened their mouths, the odds crashed another thirty percent.

Benjy, faithful bar ramrod that he was, had stocked the snack dishes with smokehouse almonds today. Fairchild's fingers dallied in a silver clamshell. Best just to nurture a comfy buzz and cab home. Cable was all titties and gore; the late show, all TV reruns, and most assuredly not what it used to be. Fairchild felt betrayed. Home, then, to an early bed and perhaps a fat, sleep-inducing novel. After one more jolt from Benjy. Weekends sucked.

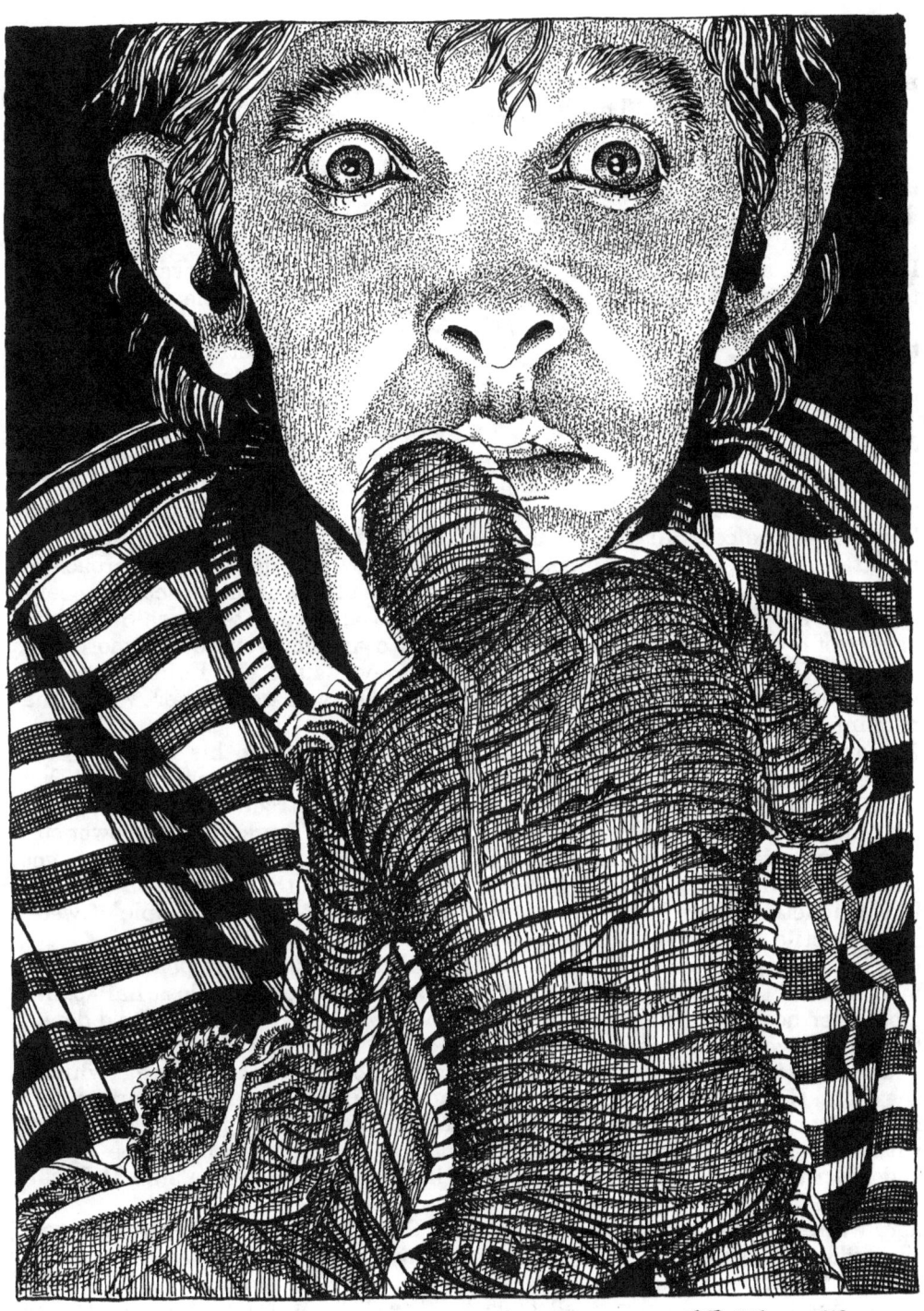

© JANET AULISIO 1989.

Lacquered nails tapped the shoulder of his Verri Uomo suit. "Psst — hey meester. Buy a drink for a real lady?"

"Why, Ms Masterson. Thank whatever gods are left."

She moved in close so he could hear; the din was amping up. "I think it's safe for you to call me Kris; we've been off the company clock since five. Come on, I've secured a booth. You can sit and tell me what in Hell you're doing, cruising this meat rack. Unless you've got to go . . . ?"

From Fairchild's barstool vantage his own apartment was no longer succoring, a shield against the world. It had become a dank trap.

She hailed Benjy, then slid in opposite Fairchild, the swish of her smoky hose lost in the cocktail din. He imagined the sound — silky, sinuous, calculated. What was up?

"Well," she said. "This is the biggest victory of my business day so far."

He raised his eyebrows. Let her call it. Automatically his hands sought the martini glass, the almond dish.

"You didn't say no."

His smile was genuine, and he was pleased. "Are you kidding?" He opened his hands toward her, shrugging, as if her virtues were obvious to any fool. Not beauty, his brain amended. More like magnetism. Her hair looked fulsome, tactile. The lines framing her mouth were pleasantly human; the mouth itself tempting, beneath frosty gloss. Her nose made her face impress too aggressively. She was aware of this and turned it to her advantage when she chose. Her eyes were the best — the irises clear as Zeiss lenses, bordered with green-flecked black rings, so stark and powerful that she kept them damped behind wide executive glasses with spidery white frames. Turn her down, was she kidding? Her posture was charm-school perfect, her legs distracting, her voice commandingly husky. She looked about two inches shorter than him. He

imagined the way a serious kiss would tilt her.

"I was just scrutinizing the male element in this joint. Half of them are tuned to Age-Wave, half to metal rape music . . . and most, to dead air." She was drinking Long Island iced teas.

"Not much room left for anything with a melody."

She saluted his observation with her glass, ruefully. "So clearly, the fields are fallow. I have decided to take bull in hand — or something — and declare that the time has come for you, Mr Fairchild, and me to have a talk about us."

"Us?" Thus far he was being a moron in the banter department.

"Mm-hm. You heard right. You. Me. Us. And the first misconception we need to chuck off the sill is the excuse about how you don't dare approach me because of how it might *look,* me being above you, corporately speaking. I have been dying for you to say more than hello ever since the Fullerton conference. Do you remember when that was?"

He could not. In his mind it reran, overexposed, her image searing hot-white as she strode into the boardroom: attaché case, flunky in tow, power suit, girded shoulders, legs to die for, god, every man in the room must want her. That had been . . . a couple of weeks ago?

"Four months." She pointed, for emphasis. Simple high-gloss nail polish, no silk-wrapped bullshit. She'd done it herself. "You sure know how to hurt a lady. Four months, during which I haven't invited you anywhere, either. I could plead prior commitments. Truth be told, I think we might be equally chicken. Care to grab a stab at Excuse #2?"

"Sure. It's too soon after the divorce." He mimed a tiny violin.

"Yours? Or mine?"

"Yes." That brought on their first shared laughter of the evening. A foundation, in case they cared to build something.

"I guess that makes it time to impose a testing criterion. Always good company procedure. You have to list your faults. I'll go first." She sipped her drink and worked up a mischievous expression. "I don't just wear these glasses to read. I wear flats when I'm not trying to thrill strangers. I don't sleep in the nude. I despise cats. If I drink too much I think I'm too gorgeous, and that my jokes are all hysterical. They aren't. I'm a workaholic. I don't plan on being anybody's mommy. I listen to my answerphone to see who's calling before I pick up. That's not everything, but now you can start."

He duplicated her ritual with the glass. "I wear tinted contacts. I eat too much Italian. I punch elevator and crosswalk buttons more than once. I'm drinking more and enjoying it less. I talk about getting 'back in shape' someday. Except for coffee I always skip breakfast. I think clothes *do* make the man. I terminally adore old monster movies."

"Those things from the Fifties? Giant bugs and UFOs?"

"Yes. Especially the Shock Theatre package." He could see she did not know what that meant. No one did, these days. He shrugged dismissively.

She raised a hand, as if in grade school. "For me it was beach movies, Elvis. In neighborhood theatres. Oh, by the by, congratulations on your promotion."

"Thank you, ma'am." He flipped open a leather wallet and did a bit of prestidigitation. "Check out my new card."

Her eyes narrowed. They were potent at any volume. "You're not thinking of trading that for mine, are you?"

He looked up and fumbled for a response, thinking now that pulling out his card had been artificial, gun-jumping, stupid . . .

"Because every man I've ever met has insisted on giving me his business card. A casebook of shitty and shallow relationships, summed up in a stack of paper rectangles. It's too goddamned easy to collect them." Some past hurt turned her gaze bemused, maybe wistful. She averted her eyes and extracted a cigarette case from a calfskin clutch bag.

He decided to wax Germanic about it, to cover his noise with a louder noise. Rather than stowing the card, he held it over the pebbled orange globe of the table candle. His name, J. ADRIAN FAIRCHILD, browned, smoldered, and then crisped left to right. The card stock was quality, and took its time burning. He offered it to her.

Her eyes approved. "Apology accepted," she said as she held his hand to steady the flame, then leaned in with her filter-tip. They both watched the card eat itself, until it was a curl of black in the ashtray, its stored energy gone forever. The ashtray was identical to the silver nut dish.

"Fire mesmerizes," he said. "Like boiling water or snow on a TV screen. Or a cursor on a computer."

"Pyromania as recreation; now there's a blast from the past. Remember when you were a kid, and set fires to see them burn? Fire was forbidden. Uncontrollable. That's why I liked to watch it."

"Not me. It was oppressive, undiscriminatingly destructive. It turned into a childhood fear I had to get over."

They traded enigmatic looks, instead of cards.

"You did, I see," she said, indicating his own pack of Winstons.

"A subtle acknowledgement of mastery over that old fear. How'd *you* come to smoke?"

"My parents told me not to, the way they told me not to play with fire." Smoke puffed out with her mild laugh. "I always did the opposite of what my parents ordered. They ordered me to pray before bedtime and I retaliated by proclaiming myself an agnostic at the ripe old age of ten . . . just as soon as I found the word in Dad's O.E.D."

"I invented my own private religion," he said. "A congregation of one. Let me tell you about it."

Dusk was bringing on a landmark night.

At the Hilltop Liquors magazine rack, Jason discovered his long-ago fan letter to *Famous Monsters* had proven worthy of print. His legs shook and turned unreliable; this was literally the first time in his short life that anything this enormous had coalesced into printed history around *him*. He ultimately was forced to walk his bike partway home, pausing at every intersection to page back to where his name was writ large in bold black, and savor his own words, inscribed with monkish patience months before, over and over, until what he had to say on his college-ruled paper was purged of the tiniest error. He had signed his name with a modest flourish, then written it again underneath in the same careful block lettering used for the body of the letter, just in case his fancy signature proved illegible.

He reread it a hundred times between the store and his driveway, throat dry, heart thundering, triumphant.

At dinner, his father misunderstood, overpraising Jason for "getting published," as though cracking Uncle Forry's letter column was level with the achievements of Mary Shelley, or Bram Stoker or Gaston Leroux. *They* had created brand new monsters with their pens, monsters with names, monsters that had not existed before the writers thought them up. Jason found himself unexpectedly belittling his own accomplishment, just to press past his father's well-meaning lack of comprehension. His stepmother, who had bought him a copy of *Freckles* which had collected dust for months on his bedroom bookshelf, thought the letter was "nice dear," after wrinkling her nose at the photos

of the Creature from the Black Lagoon throttling an oceanarium worker, and Lon Chaney Jr, as Mary Shelley's monster, carting off Evelyn Ankers. Jason's stepmother looked at the letter, but did not see what Jason saw. To contravene her would be as self-defeating as brushing his teeth with cherry Coke. Parents could be so frustrating; between the two he could neither brag nor be humble.

Still, sundown came and his pulse quickened. Sometimes the best stuff in the world was not for sharing.

In monster movies, sundown usually signalled the start of the good stuff.

One critical factor of Jason's Friday night logistics was adequate provisioning. He picked at dinner, leaving room for the goodies to be raided later. A cursory run-through of homework permitted him to dismiss school from his world for the next forty-eight glorious hours. The triad of upstairs rooms was already empty of his older brother Marcus, who had trotted off to dinner with Monica McMillan and would be spending most of the evening attempting to plumb the mysteries inside Monica's skirt and blouse. She was one of Buddy McMillan's girls . . . and if Marcus and Jason's parents didn't cool it with the embarrassing jokes, Jason might not ever have a future with Laurie, currently the youngest of Buddy's brood.

Two years back, girls would have been unthinkable.

Jason's parents liked to call the third upstairs room the TV room, which was akin to calling *Revenge of the Creature* just another movie. To Jason its purpose was more sanctified. The *TV Guide* for this week had promised potent mojo indeed: *The Mummy's Tomb, The Mummy's Ghost,* and *The Mummy's Curse,* all kicking off half an hour before midnight, with a *Twilight Zone* repeat.

Bulling through the haul from nine to twelve was the toughest; he knew that a triple feature that late at night would knock his body out too soon, and he'd sleep through the crypt cave-in at the climax of the final Mummy film. But he was too agitated to nap. Napping was for little kids. The ability to stay up late was proof of incipient adulthood. Snooze now? No way. He passed the time boning up on Mummy minutiae.

Famous Monsters contained the most of what he sought, augmented by *Castle of Frankenstein* (which he was growing to like better and better; here was a magazine unafraid to say a movie was a stinker from time to time, or to print photos of naked women getting fanged by British bloodsuckers). For a balanced newsview there were the second-string publications — *Mad Monsters, Fantastic Monsters of the Films, Horror Monsters,* and the Mad Magazine approach of *For Monsters Only.* Jason tended his pile of monster mags with the reverence of Egyptian supplicants for the dreaded Scroll of Thoth. He read again what an idiocy it would be to dare to break the Seal of the Seven Jackals, and the aroma and texture of the brittle pages of the older issues made it easy to imagine the smell and feel of Tana leaves.

The *first* Mummy of note was Im-Ho-Tep, Karloff, Thirties. While Jason maintained what he thought to be the accordant degree of respect for what Forry J had dubbed the classics, he favored the more dynamic monsters of the subsequent epoch. Universal Pictures, Forties, *after* they dropped the growling, propellored plane from their logo, when *any* monster in the gang could be depended upon to come lurching back for more. *Kharis* was who Jason preferred to think of when you said *Mummy.* He favored the idea of a monster who could kick butt despite obvious structural disadvantages. Kharis dragged one lame foot; his right arm had curled into a crippled claw and frozen against

his chest; the conflagrant finale of *The Mummy's Hand* had welded his right eye shut forever. Kharis was a handicapped monster, for christsake. You could outrun him, sure, but he'd catch up while you were sleeping, the tortoise beating the hare, and Kharis never gave up or stopped, ever. Jason visualized a business card, gold, bordered in diamond-shaped Cleopatra eyeballs and bird-headed guys wearing skirts. *Vengeance Our Specialty. Slow But Inexorable.*

Kharis was implacable, determined, and mean. He even strangled a German shepherd that barked at him once. The sound of a dog barking in the night could still suggest to Jason that perhaps Kharis had found some excuse to serve him with a personal termination notice, and perhaps he was shuffling silently up the front walk, right now. Jason's stepmother would discover his wide-eyed, almost twelve-year-old corpse at breakfast time. His father would exclaim that, why, those grayish marks on his neck look . . . almost . . . well, like *mold.*

That had been the original justification for the fortress.

An important component of Jason's Friday night setup was raiding the TV-room sofa for cushions with which he constructed a sort of open-ended pill-box, facing the screen. It was superior to a mere monster blanket (not to mention more snug, and certainly more grown up), and the fortress helped enclose Jason and his supplies within the influence of the picture tube and its monochromatic shadow plays. His tradition was to kill the lights and entrench with the sound turned down until the *Twilight Zone* faded in, just him, deliciously alone in the dead of night with his monster movies. Beyond the rearward limits of the fortress there was nothing to see save darkness, a buffer between Jason and a world of retribution.

53

"Put that way, it really does sound like a classical religion," Kris said.

The bar traffic had gridlocked, and two uncollected empty rounds loitered on the table between them. His butted smokes were mingled with hers in the clamshell ashtray. Their tab kept their booth locked down during the lounge's prime trolling time, and they stood secure against assault from all comers. They held, oblivious to the flesh shoppe/slave bazaar ambience, and in spite of the clamor level. An inversion layer of smoke hung stubbornly and rendered all sights beyond three feet of the booth ghostly and nimbused, as though viewed across a moor clogged with swamp gas and St Elmo's Fire. He had begun ordering water chasers to keep from dehydrating.

"Your basic coursework in classic monsters always reminded me of the hierarchies of Greek and Roman gods," he said. "More like the Egyptians, actually, where the roles were separate but equal. No real pecking order; no monster was especially more powerful than another. The focus is on the mythology of genesis and transformation; how they all got to *be* card-carrying monsters in the first place."

Her existence in the corporate megastructure had been defined by ladders, and the idea of equal power equally portioned held a special appeal for her, whether it was among monsters or vice-presidents. "I heard the movie companies just invented a lot of that stuff — about how the Wolf Man only wolfs out during the full moon, or how Dracula can't hack sunlight."

"I thought you weren't allowed to watch those things when you were a kid."

She laughed at something personal. Her smile involved her eyes every time, with an effect more soothing than any cocktail. "I don't know what sort of youngster *you* were, sir, but as I mentioned awhile ago, I generally considered any parental ukase to be a gauntlet cast down. I invented the most elaborate hookup imaginable for reading after curfew. My bed was tucked into a nook below a semi-circle of cupola windows in the second floor of our house — a big, old, rambling coastal thing in Florida. By hanging my comforter between the edge of the bed and clamping it to the wall molding with clothespins, I made a lean-to. I sneaked a 25-watter into my bedside lamp; normally all my parents had to do was look out their window and see if the cupola windows cast any light on the lawn. My weak lightbulb outfoxed 'em. If I heard them coming up the stairs, I could kill the whole outpost in ten seconds flat."

He nodded, mouth full, anxious to reveal his own version of the subterfuge she had just outlined.

"I had one of those rough-hewn wooden treasure chests, the kind you buy in Mexico? It was hasped with a cheesy brass padlock. Guess what I kept in it?"

"Doubloons?" Her lips encompassed a sliver of bar ice. It slid into her mouth. He could feel his own tongue cooling. "Human skulls? Some nasty-ass boy shit I'd rather not know about?"

"Lipton's Instant Iced Tea." He said it with newscaster gravity, as though copping to the sale of bomber specs to the Russkies.

Her glass hesitated midway. "You're not serious. You mean I'm sitting here chatting up a man who *actually* . . ." She pressed back from the table edge. It was like opera, in its way. "Omigod."

"Yeah, I know. Child molesting pales. Necrophilia is more forgivable. But I feel compelled to bare the true ugliness of my soul to you." He clasped hands over heart and sought divine sanction in the direction of the ceiling.

He reminded her of a bargain martyr. "You're starting to drip."

"No doubt. Anyway, I drank tons of Lipton's, more than any soft drink, and my measures in composing a glassful would shame NASA with their precision. If I didn't get my tea, I'd die. I powered it down by the gallon but mixed it one glass at a time. Some procedures you just don't rush."

"Or compromise — like the rules in monster movies."

"Exactly." He pulled the green olive off its pic, thinking of stakes and vampires. "My stepmother — Wicked Stepmom — took a dim view of my guzzling what she called 'caffeine product' on school nights. And water didn't make it — it wasn't a *flavor*. I couldn't sneak tea up to bed, but I could take a glass of water, from that cold jug in the fridge. I made sure she saw me pouring that water and taking it with me upstairs at bedtime."

Child's mischief glinted in her steady return gaze. "You conned her. Because up in your room you had your pirate chest with the instant tea inside."

"That, and sugar, in carefully purloined margarine tubs, plus long-handled spoons I had to keep from the Dairy Queen. Napkins. I couldn't manage your light setup, but I did have candles and matches."

"You little turd. So you were probably up way past the witching hour, grinding your teeth to sleep."

He swatted this serve back. "While you were skulking around with your nose in . . . what? Nancy Drew? *National Velvet*? *Dick and Jane Hit Puberty*?"

"Sherlock Holmes. When I found out the Speckled Band was a snake I nearly wet my bed. No sleep *that* night."

"What, no boogeyman alarms? No tucked-in sheets?

She shook her head vehemently. "I hate that. Still do. I have to poke my feet out or I feel trapped. Another fault for the list. Hospital corners are too confining."

"Gee, I thought I was the only one. We ought to keep this to ourselves. The mob might lynch us by torchlight."

She surveyed the singles on the hoof. "My. Yes. Definite bounce-a-quarter-on-the-blanket types. All the men in here have the same haircut."

It was easy to laugh with her. "It's actually a vinyl skullcap they swap on a timesharing basis. Even some of the women are wearing it. See?"

They mocked the players around them. Kris had a way of holding in cigarette smoke that was terrifically contemplative. When her thoughts were organized and ready for articulation, the smoke would then stream out in gray plumes. "Well, despite all this peer pressure I think I still turned out fairly unimpaired." She executed a stiff little bow. "Thanks for not contradicting me. I really have to visit the Ladies'."

He had always used cigarettes primarily for gesticulation; elucidating some point with an unlit smoke, then pausing to ignite it, almost as punctuation. With no audience, he felt no need to enkindle a fresh Winston. He tapped it back into its hard pack. When she returned, he watched her cut through the lounge's bustle — great legs, to be sure. Traffic jammers. Her eyes favored him with another smile, as though they had shared a secret.

They talked rationales, and another Long Island iced tea was conquered. "My family moved all over the country," she said. "New classmates, virtually every year. Families aren't tied to towns or states or even other family members, anymore. People get divorced so routinely . . ."

He saluted that. "Parents die."

"And there are no constants. Except the bad stuff — the disruptions, the adjustments, the constant restructuring of your life. Tough on a kid. Ultimately there's no one to really depend on, except yourself."

"And the Creature, and the Mummy, and Frankenstein's friendless Monster. They're weird-looking, they're alien-

55

ated, they're picked on, and they're so dependable that when you're a kid it's almost blasphemy to think that *Midnight Frights* won't still be dutifully on the air when you're *aged.*" He said the word with a comic downward twist of mouth. "You know, it's funny. All those monsters in all those movies frightened me. Yet I kept their pictures, cutouts, taped to the wall where I could even see some of them in the dark. They scared me, sure . . . but once the sun was up I couldn't wait to make sure they were still there."

"You didn't really fear them," she pointed out. "You respected them."

He lifted his Winston pack, drew, and fired up. "Is that intuitive, or are you just preternaturally astute?"

"It's both. Plus intellect, style, and great legs. Made me the success-hungry power bitch you see before you today. Your *superior,* I'd say, if it didn't make me want to start giggling." She did anyway; helplessly.

"I think you're right. Them, I respected. Loved, even." He could see the coal of his cigarette bouncing back from the lenses of her glasses, combining with the candleflame already living there, and the sparks of her inspirations, nebulae dancing in her eyes.

Whoa, back off on the gin for awhile! he thought.

"Family and friends might fall apart or move on or betray you, but those monsters were always there for you."

"Not always," he said. "But I agree. I was unusually forgiving where they were concerned. Those movies frequently lost track of their own rules. I compensated. Instead of being offended when the Wolf Man got offed with something other than silver, I made elaborate justifications. Sort of the way TV evangelists can twist a Bible verse to mean anything they want. Creative reinterpretation."

"*Were* you especially religious as a kid? Conventionally, I mean." When she saw the sour expression cross his face, she said, "Oh. I see. Dumb question."

The *Twilight Zone* was the one with the thing on the airplane wing. Good warmup. Jason sank back and let the cushions of his fortress embrace him.

The *Mummy's Tomb* was two Mummy movies in one; its first half consisted almost entirely of flashbacks from Kharis' debut feature, *The Mummy's Hand.* His entire cinematic chronology, therefore, waited for Jason within the palm of a single night, and for once Channel 13 and *Midnight Frights* got the order right.

To all those who violate the tomb of Ananka, a cruel and violent death shall be their fate!

Princess Ananka had been Kharis' girlfriend, back when he wasn't the Mummy yet. They weren't supposed to be fooling around. Then Ananka croaked from some lady disease, so Kharis swiped a tea-chest full of Tana leaves that would bring her back to life. Which was . . . sacrilege! So the Egyptian guys caught him and *cut out his tongue* before wrapping him up and burying him alive to guard Ananka's resting place for eternity. They fed him soup made out of Tana leaves to make him into an immortal sort of night watchman, and everything was cool until a bunch of guys from museums started digging everything up. Ananka began this habit of getting reincarnated as gorgeous women living in small rural towns in the USA, so after Kharis bumped off everybody related to anybody who had bothered her tomb in the first movie, he had to keep chasing her around. Usually the High Priests of Arkhon (swarthy guys wearing medallions and fezzes who knew how strong to make the Tana leaf soup) fell in love with whatever version of Ananka was currently wandering around the woods in a nightgown. And that usually pissed

Kharis off to the point where he'd smear the priest by the end of the movie. Getting shot or set on fire didn't bother Kharis much; that he could go three thousand years without going to the bathroom puzzled Jason more. And the world supply of Tana leaves had to run out eventually, even though that carved coffer always seemed full up. Various High Priests of Arkhon gravely maintained that if one fed Kharis too much Tana leaf soup, he would become — ominous musical sting — "a monster such as the world has never seen." Kind of a Turbo-Kharis.

For that, Jason could hardly wait. He just hoped he was not distantly related to anyone who had ever seen a pyramid.

The WWII vintage of these films permitted Jason invaluable access to the social and courting rituals that had, no doubt, influenced how his parents had turned out. All the women were frail, shrieking things. They fainted a lot, in order to get carried around by either the Mummy or the good guys. Said good guys had pencil moustaches and black hair that gleamed like casket polish. Everybody smoked a lot; it was adult and sophisticated. Jason took mental notes, mimicking the cigarette gesticulations with a toothpick. Secure in his cordon of night, his fortress awash in a silver glow, he could study the behavior of adults in black and white without getting interrogated or yelled at. Or worse.

Sometimes the heroes were foolhardy enough to try taking on the Mummy fistwise. It was the only time their oily skullcaps of hair ever got mussed. But exhibiting bravery by slugging Kharis usually won you the fainting girl . . . unless you got your voicebox imploded in that bandaged vise-grip. Kharis just sort of pinched your neck shut, and you ate pavement faster than a snipped marionette. He had no reservations about choking girls, either. Or dogs. Just GLURK! And dead.

© JANET AULISIO 1989.

After prying potato chip shrapnel from between his teeth, Jason theorized, holding his toothpick, mannered, between his index and middle fingers and jabbing it toward the TV's iridescent eye as though debating a crucial point with the screen. He had read about the transmutation of fossilized dinosaur bones. Maybe beneath Kharis' rags, after thirty centuries, was a skeleton of solid iron. That might account for his invulnerability, and why he did not crumble to ash whenever one of the Basil Rathbone lookalikes clouted him with a club.

During *The Mummy's Ghost,* Jason gobbled up the scene in which Kharis makes the museum security guard go bye-bye forever. As the victim thrashed, he busted a huge plate glass window. *Famous Monsters* had tipped Jason to the fact that Lon Chaney Jr had accidentally gotten wounded during the filming of the scene. Jason fought not to blink, and there it was, by god: two big dots of blood on the Mummy's chin. Real blood. Real *actor's* blood. Unplanned bloodshed, captured on film for all time.

Wow . . .

Against tradition, Kharis, even though he was a monster, usually got the girl by the final reel. In this particular installment, Princess Ananka's reincarnation began to age into the real thing as she was being lugged away, having fainted. She grew this broad streak of white in her hair, then got all wrinkly just in time for her and Kharis to waltz into a bog and leave hardly any bubbles. The End.

Until *The Mummy's Curse,* when the bog gets drained, and guess what happens.

Jason must have drunk several quarts of tea, if what he peed out was any clue. In defiance of his stepmother's admonitions about caffeine product, he dozed off ten minutes into *The Mummy's Curse,* but awakened in time for the

crypt cave-in at the end. Once a monster got mashed, good old Universal Pictures would wrap things up so fast it made your eyeballs throb. He liked the idea of falling asleep during a Mummy marathon, then waking up to find himself still safely within the fortress and the world of Kharis, where the hard and fast operational rules handed down by the High Priests of Arkhon were constant. If you fell for this week's Ananka reincarnation and Kharis found out . . . so much for your fez-wearing status, bub.

Only on Friday nights like this one did rules make any sense to Jason. These rules, he could pace and comprehend. Unlike those of his parents.

"I'd say atheist, if I didn't find the 'theist' part so . . . prejudicial. Godish."

"You're talking to a wobbling agnostic, remember?" She tapped ash. "The conventional stuff was already superfluous for you, even redundant. That's clear. You didn't need a prefab holy writ because you already had one inside those monster magazines. You had your own communion wine and ceremonies. You had your pantheon of deities — Frankenstein, the Wolf Man, Dracula, and especially the Mummy."

"Kharis. Who sprang fullblown from the boxoffice receipts of Im-Ho-Tep."

"See? You even joke about it mythologically. Don't underestimate magnetism like that. Jesus, you even had a fixed time for worship."

Oh, Kris was very good.

"It's tough to convey how *important* that was, once," he said, sucking the water from a template-formed square of cocktail ice. "My generation fell into the interstice between threatricals and videotape. It was a brief span of years in the Sixties during which a kid *had* to depend on *Midnight Frights,* or risk never seeing *I Married a Monster from Outer Space.* It's easy to get homesick

58

for the ritual aspect of camping out Friday nights, waiting for the monster movies to commence. Faithfully."

"One thing you never realize is how fleeting a period like that can be in your life." She tried to head him off. "But a time machine would be useless, you know. Because it would be impossible for you to warn your younger self how fragile some moments in time can be. You couldn't do anything . . . except maybe spoil the fun."

"Like trying to explain to a kid the difference between an agnostic and an atheist, I suspect."

"The nomenclature isn't really cardinal," she said. "The underlying emotions are. I think my parents sensed that. They were fairly noncommittal — or open-minded, to be fair — about their daughter's interface with belief systems. Common sense and thrift and, later, wit were more valuable. I think they were more apprehensive about what species of boy-monster I'd eventually drag into their parlor to soil the throw-rugs. Turns out they were right . . ." She made a face in remembrance of the day she had decided white knights were extinct. "You could arguably call it a learning experience. Vietnam was a learning experience, right?" When the flash-replay of her love life finished behind her eyes, she caught up with the question she'd asked earlier. "So, let me rephrase: Were your parents religious? Was it a problem?"

"My brush with 'conventional' religion," he said, making quotation marks in the air with his fingertips, "was akin to a car getting sideswiped by a bus — the kind of accident where the car gets totaled and the bus drives on with a ding in the bumper. Soon after my dad married Wicked Stepmom, she decided it would be 'spiritually' prudent to inflict me on a Christian Sunday School class." Again the quotes, stirring trails in the smoky air. "Or vice-versa. My brother Marcus was exempt.

Why? He was older. And he, for whatever reason, attended grownup church with Wicked Stepmom, without a fight. Maybe he was doping out religions for future use. Anyway, like Mojo doin' rock 'n' roll, I found myself compelled to *do* the Sunday School *thang.*"

"Trapped like a rodent in a holy Catch-22. Looks like God really wanted your ass."

His laugh came out crooked; more a snort. "Not for long he didn't. He'd already rounded up a kid in the class named Eric Lowrey. I sat in his vacant folding chair. He'd died of leukemia, just like my real mom. *His* mother was teaching the Sunday School class, and she nailed me, my being the new face and all. I got sniggered at for never having read the Bible. So I bit her back; I knew about Eric's death, and remembered what my mom had looked like the last time I'd seen her in the hospital. I was six or seven; they had brought her out in a wheelchair and she was all blotchy. I'd had no concept of death then. By the time I was pushed into the Sunday School class, I'd formulated some pretty definite ideas. Rules for death. And I concluded that if Mrs Lowrey's 'god' had killed my mom, then he or she or it deserved to get run over by a bus. He or She or It spells *horsh'it.* And I said to her, 'You don't *really believe* that Eric is in some place called 'heaven' you can't really *see* . . . do you?' "

"Omigod."

"Yeah. It hit the fan, no lie. Poor woman burst into tears. Bet your ass she filed a full report."

"Oh. Oh, no." She covered her face with one hand, then peeked out between the fingers. "What happened to you?" She spoke softly. Harsh words might leave dents.

"I didn't have to worry about attending Sunday School much after that. I got grounded for three months, two of which were June and July. I got a thorough yelling at." His words came out in a huge exhalation of smoke. "While Wicked Stepmom was bellowing and asking me *just what did you think you were doing,* she finally lost it and backhanded me. She wore this massive emerald ring that split my lip in three places. I stood rooted, unmoving, scared, crying my head off. I thought, goddamnit, I'm almost twelve, I'm nearly a teenager at last . . . and here I am, crying. Baby. I sure didn't cry when my real mom died."

He took a drink, aware it was melodramatic. Kris let it ride — in fact, she sipped her own, to balance, to encourage.

"She hit you."

"Mm. *Pow.*" He swatted air to demonstrate. "Having perpetrated sacrilege, I found myself playing Town Heretic. I had tampered with her religion . . . so she destroyed mine. Burned it down. Funny — just like the lab going up in flames at the end of a Frankenstein movie. Conflagration bashed down monsters better than Raid on roaches. She tornadoed upstairs to my room, and tore all the pictures off the wall, and dumped all my magazines into a trashcan and set fire to it in the back yard. I'll never forget the sound of that trashcan being dragged down the stairs. Clunk, clunk, clunk; worse than blows in any beating. I watched out the window. A line had been drawn, you see; a new rule set up without warning. Now I couldn't leave my room, couldn't even go downstairs for a glass of water. Everything in the can went up in smoke while I stood there watching and doing nothing, and after it was clearly hopeless, I turned away and went into the bathroom. There was blood all over my chin. My lip was swollen and felt novocained." His fingers, remembering, sought scars where there were none.

Kris watched him snub the half-smoked Winston. The twisted wreckage bled tendrils of gray, then gave up for good.

"Next weekend, no monster movies," he said. "I missed *The Thing* and *Frankenstein Meets the Wolf Man.* I tried waiting until my parents hit the sack, then sneaking into the TV-room and watching with the sound and brightness knobs turned way down. Until Marcus ratted on me. *Pow,* again."

"It's almost Shakespearian," she said. "Brother betrays brother. I used to try to read in the dark. When the moon was full and bright, you could. Hell on the eyes, but exciting in its way, when you found out it was possible. Your mom, did she —"

"Stepmom."

"She didn't burn the magazine with your letter in it, did she?"

"She only missed that one because it was in my school pack with my books. I carried it with me everywhere, feeding off it. Eventually I read it until it fell to pieces. Whenever I opened it up I was afraid she'd pounce and take it away. It never took her long to make the stairs when she suspected I was up to no good."

"The barking dog," Kris said, with a hint of a smile.

"What? Oh." He had passed the memory, and now it receded the way a sleeping town dwindles behind a train in the night. His mouth had become quite dry. "You know, contrary to this blather, I'm not a nostalgia nut. It's too rosy. If I was inside the skin of that twelve-year-old, this moment, I wouldn't relive how great those movies seemed to me. What I'd feel again would be the terror, the impotence of what it is to be that age."

"And Wicked Stepmom? Did you ever reach détente? That sort of thing seems to take forever when you're a kid."

"She eventually forgot it or found new things to be angry about. But that didn't bring back my magazines or erase what happened. In fact, *she* erased it; she never mentioned the incident again. She died not long after I left home. Pharyngial tumors. Her throat closed up and she died. Ironic, huh? But you're right — I did respect the Mummy. Kharis was my pal. It was Wicked Stepmom I was afraid of, Freud preserve us."

"I knew you were a boy who loved his mummy."

They cracked up. She had seen how this reverie might turn wet, and she wanted to yank him out of it. It worked.

"Hey," she said. "It's nearly eleven. *You* have to think about leaving soon; *you're* working tomorrow." She held, slyly. Clearly she was not going to dash for an exit herself, just yet. Sip, puff.

"I like this. We've been here for hours that have passed like minutes, talking like old buddies, with hardly any social bullshit." She toasted this sentiment with a modest nod.

"Bullshit makes the world go 'round. It's our day-to-day coin. You'll pardon the residue? Sometimes it's difficult to shut down the alarms in your skin — the ones that order you not to try, not to get involved."

They clinked glasses.

Mischief had sneaked across her countenance again. "Oh — just so you'll know: I fully intend to close this evening with a kiss that deserves immortalization in a book of bests."

He could not stop the arch of his eyebrows, nor blank the pictures her words thrust into his head. It was past the time where the *will she/won't she* game retained any flavor, and she knew it. The struggle toward the easy comfort they now felt in each other's space had been long in arriving for both of them, and to cap the event with a quickie would be sordid and inappropriate; it would vindicate the predatory callousness all around them. To rush matters would be like gulping Veuve Clicquot — no savor, and certainly no latitude for appreciation.

She had foreseen this, and jumped ahead to the perfect answer. Just enough spice. He no longer wondered at her obvious administrative talents.

Her own thought chain would never become public record, but it turned her smile into a cherished, private thing. In the smog of the lounge, her clarity dazzled. "What I'm talking about is my lips, stalking yours," she said. "Most people are lousy at osculation. You'd better not disappoint me, because I'm taking a huge chance here. And no, I'm not normally so flamboyant."

"Blame the booze."

"Actually, I'm a sucker for that little boy."

"I doubt most of the yupsters here even know what osculation means." It was his conversational escape hatch, and he used it to dodge the ripe red blush her bold words had set to creeping up the collar of his Pierre Cardin shirt. "Fish-lip kisses. Yucch."

"How about the car crash of lips, the kind that chips your teeth? I hate those. Or those wormy kisses, where the lips are ashen and cold. French the cadaver."

"Hm. And then we have the Neanderthal oral rape kiss."

"Ow. Yes. The onrushing mouthload of meat. Suddenly a tongue has invaded your face, a quarter-pounder boxing your tonsils. And it reminds you of the last time you woke up face-down in your pillow, and couldn't breathe, except the pillow wasn't soaked in saliva."

They wrung out a bit more fun at the expense of amateur kissers everywhere. Somebody should start a school.

"Not guilty on all counts," he assured her.

"Good. I just wanted you to contemplate this forthcoming kiss for awhile. The kiss with which we shall end this evening. You were beginning to look a touch blue, kiddo." She let her tonguetip test her lip gloss, just a flicker, a tease that brought his dormant blush flooding to the surface. "Aha. Good sign. I did it again."

61

"Evil," he said. He rode it out; there's no way to duck a sneak attack by your own metabolism. He parried. "You have to promise not to faint, though."

He thought about the kiss a lot over the next hour or so. If this was torture, he never wanted it to end.

After midnight it began to rain. Droplets tamped brittle leaves of pulp paper ash into black muck, and the lingering ectoplasm of smoke was beaten down. The trashcan's sides had blued, then scorched and peeled in the hot shimmer of the fire. Its contents grew more insubstantial the wetter they got. The rain made the dross of combustion collapse upon itself. Soon there would be nothing left.

Getting outside took Jason a lifetime. Thousands of heartbeats, pints of paranoid sweat, a triple helping of jumpy stealth, with a veneer of patience that he strained against with each tic. Window to shingles to trellis, the ground a blurry dark void somewhere two stories below, the footing on the roof treacherous, yet irresistibly inviting. To *not* venture out, to remain uncertain for the rest of his life, would be the ultimate horror. His friend, the darkness, was with him, rendering him invisible and keeping from his eyes sights that might have kept him off the roof.

It was cold, and he regretted having to creep out barefoot. But his stepmother might notice wet shoes the following morning, and the surface of the roof was slickly waxed. Hairy.

The can in the middle of the back yard still exuded heat; Jason could feel it from three feet away. He groped for the steel lip and tentatively snaked both hands inside until they collided with the topmost mound of cinerous residue. It fell away at his touch.

Tears were sluiced saltless on his face by the rain as he felt the bones of his magazine stack crumble and puff into soot beneath his fingers. This time he

was not crying, merely running off at the eyeballs — internal emotional pressure seeking the easiest vent. He was in control now, and okay. He was not so successful keeping his teeth from doing a castanet dance in the wet, windy chill.

Logic demanded remains; even cremation left *something*. Dust was enough to recorporate Dracula. Fire could never totally obliterate the good Doktor's namesake monster . . . could it?

The magazine had landed, bent double, on the very bottom of the can. The glossy cover and front and back pages had peeled away a sheet at a time as they had browned and shriveled, heat pounding paper back toward basic carbon. From the edges inward it had tasted flame and succumbed to crawling buglike embers, neon orange, burrowing their feed paths in the darkness. They spat and hissed as the rain killed them. A finger-length of binding glue, still hot enough to sting, clung to a smatter of barbecued pages the size and shape of a round-shouldered paperback. Jason's questing grasp had stumbled across the prize.

One *Famous Monsters* had pulled through. Some of it, at any rate. About a third.

Back inside, he sank his hands into a basin of warm water to shock back feeling. He washed his blackened feet, listening to Marcus snore obliviously in the next bedroom. How could Monica McMillan bear the noise? It sounded like a foghorn with a crawful of snot. Maybe she hadn't actually *slept* with Marcus yet. Yeesh.

The magazine remnant, Jason decided, was fragile as mummy dust itself, and dead. Best not to attempt life support. He unlocked his tea-stash chest, scared up a candle, and struck a Blue Diamond match. The tang of ignition stung his nostrils and caused the bits of pages in his hand to expel a postmortem smell like dirty ashtrays. They weighed nothing. By candlelight he parted the page fragments.

A single picture of the Mummy had survived the inferno. The entire photo had been magical — Kharis hoisting Elyse Knox's (fainted) form onto a crypt slab while an oilslicked Turhan Bey watched, from *The Mummy's Tomb*. The center had pulled through: half of Kharis' profile, truncated by a binder gutter where the magazine had been stapled.

The corona of char made it resemble phonied parchment. Jason flaked it away, and used scissors to trim it to a tight shot. He taped it safely inside the lid of his treasure chest. Other salvaged portions followed.

The pressure of Kris's lips on his had blessed him with a spontaneous erection.

She tilted her head, cradling the nape of his neck with one slim hand, gracile fingers tickling the fine, rising hairs there. Her eyes were slitted to black and wet with the sight of him. He saw them close. The best stuff happened in the head. He heard her inhale nasally, as he had, neither of them daring to break the seal.

His brain got full up, outdistancing him.

Her teeth caught and caressed his lip with the slightest excruciating pressure, and her own mouth proved as generous as his imagination. So commenced the tango of brushing and sampling, tempo accelerating, that divorces adults from all reason.

The pit of his stomach slid giddily into zero gee. Alone in the foyer of her building, she had beckoned and he had RSVPed in kind, both of them in a hurry, hearts like cheetahs wildly battering their cages of ribs, the anticipation of tasting her nearly boiling forth and blowing off his scalp. Their mouthwork grew hotter, more fervent, starving strangers taking what they needed, then waned to a gentle softness, friends now, with time, a calm eddy of passion. So much could be said just with lips, without words.

Their embrace slid and wound and wrapped tight. They fit. In that instant he realized how it would feel to be sheathed inside of her, shed of their workaday business armor, caught in the grip of cunning musculature. This time he could hear her stockings whisper past each other, and the sound flinted sparks behind his eyelids.

She offered her throat, and he began in the delicious hollow where jaw and ear and neck cojoin. By the time he had chewed his way to her shoulder and the arch of trapezius, she was berserk and trembling. She returned a nibble of her own and he felt gooseflesh shoot all the way down to his heels.

He had not been kissed this way nearly enough in his life. Nor could anyone ever be. No matter how fast you ran, some things never stopped stalking you.

The following Friday night was historic, damned near a religious experience.

At Kris's behest, via intercom, the foyer sentry permitted Jason to elevator up to Five. She awaited him, arms folded, chiding stylish tardiness, leaning against the threshold of her open door, just barely inside of a deep-cut evening number that swiped his first few breaths and made promises that knocked his train of snappy patter off the rails.

"Hi, stranger," she said, and kissed him again.

He had been a skinny kid who had turned out a thin adult; something metabolic. No swap of hair on top for gut on bottom. He remained symmetrical. His eyes were brown, almost generic, behind long, almost feminine lashes. These eyes caught and held, their gaze frank, frequently challenging, but open and friendly for those who had the backbone. Right before bidding adieu to his 20s forever, he had asked why some people found his facial package a threat and was told, "It's the 'stache." He lost the goatee but kept the 'stache as his first line of defense. And now he stood awash in mellow amber light, Kris embracing him full-length, and wondered like a fool what had attracted her, thinking that the sum of his outward masque made a difference. Fooled, even in honest romance, by surfaces. His marriage had been a surface thing. Snapshots had boasted the perfection of the union; pictures constituted hard proof of happiness. Photos were important, especially to parents, but he had never cared to prove anything to his parents past the age of eleven. Judging from what Kris had disclosed about her first husband, some samaritan ought to introduce their two exes — united they could live the illusions fostered by their mommies and daddies, and shoot lots of keen pictures to prove what fun their programmed, dead lives were. Hi, Mom!

"Hi, stranger," he returned, unable to stop the grin. Too boyish.

Dinner was catered, and throughout Kris reserved some secret amusement, extra baggage to her usual smile which she declined to illuminate until dessert and digestifs. Crystal and wine and tapers did unforgettable things to her eyes.

"Okay." She cocked a thumb toward the living room, where a sparkling panorama of cityscape waited beyond floor-to-ceiling glass. "Here goes almost nothin'."

She led him toward the sofa group and he made a joke about heeltap. When you tried to get the last drop out of a glass, it coated the glass on the way out and never emerged. Her solution was to refill the glass. Things were at that precise stratum of silliness.

She sat him down and, with very obvious pride, enumerated the items ranked before him on the low coffee table. The arrangement was shrine-like.

"From your left," she said, "Lipton's Instant. Your own personal Tana leaf high-octane liquid fuel input." Next to the jar was a carafe of icewater. "For completeness' sake. I'd prefer you didn't actually switch to this stuff right now because this Moet is bloody good."

He nodded gravely.

She lifted a flat, opaque plastic bag by one corner, holding it gingerly, like undusted murder evidence. "Do you have any conception of what this thing costs in real money?"

"Jesus Christ — *Famous Monsters* . . ."

"In what they call *fair-to-good* condition. I call it criminal. Have you ever *been* to one of those grotty little shoppes? They're full of people who —"

He dropped the foxed magazine open on the table, as though afraid to mangle it. "There's the photo. Almost exactly as I recalled it."

"— yeeucch. I don't want to guess when they bathed last. Anyway, *attendez*. I presume your lightning intellect has by now divined the intent of that stack of videotapes, there. Now hold out your hand and close your eyes."

"Sure you're not going to put a snake in my hand, Sherlock?" He shut up when he heard the rosary-bead click of his palm filling with candy.

"They've been putting the red ones back in for some time now," she said. "Remember you told me they'd banned them way back when because they thought the red dye was carcinogenic? Turns out it was guilt by association; there was never anything bad about the red dye used in M&Ms. But a different red dye cursed *all* red dyes. It took all this time for the dust to settle."

"God." He deposited most into a dish on the table, then popped a single M&M — bright red — thoughtfully, as if sensitized to the possibility they might vanish again at any moment. "This is truly weird, Kris. Incredible. I think I'm nervous."

The Martians had landed, too. He ate one.

She scooted closer and soon her hand was on his neck again. Soothing. He likes to be petted.

"I thought I oughta check out these here Mummy movies in case I was missing something fundamental in life. Backstory from a lost age. Here, I need your help."

They denuded her corner group of cushions and set up for a triple bill.

"I'm notorious for dozing off midway through. I think I mentioned that."

"I guarantee you will not fall asleep."

"Ever think of putting a white streak in your hair?"

She raspberried him.

"Guess not." He toed off his shoes before her big-beam TV screen. Her sofa had offered more building blocks. The fortress was an improvement over the old version. Only the bad stuff had been left behind. Until now the good stuff had not been for sharing.

They had been putting the red ones back for some time now. He had simply failed to notice.

"Peelers," she said. It was what she had called pillows as a child. She settled in, barefoot, legs tucked, achingly at-tractive there in the semi-dark, a champagne flute to her lips. She had fathomed him well, and knew just how much anticipation was good for him.

On the screen, Kharis lurched again, pinching shut the necks of the Banning descendants one by one, shuffling ever onward, for love, the vigilant caretaker of a hopeless and unconsummatable devotion.

"A toast," Kris said. "Here's to dark rooms, things that go bump in the night, staying up past bedtime, and magic shadow shows."

"And being grownup enough to know what to appreciate."

"Humph. So practical." She frowned. They clinked. It was good, old crystal, thin and musical. "Cheers, Mr Fairchild."

"Cheers. I think you can call me by my first name, Ms Kris."

The concrete canyons surrounding her highrise worked acoustically, like cathedral archways, bringing to them from an unknowable distance the sound of a dog barking, shortly past the witching hour. It stopped abruptly. Somewhere, in some other dark bedroom, a child might remain wide-eyed until the predawn, in fear of barking dogs. But not Jason. Not tonight.

⊗

NONSTOP

by Tad Williams

Henry Stankey hated flying. Actually, "hate" was perhaps the wrong word. Hatred implied anger, active resistance; hatred was a type of control. Airplane flight filled Stankey with the kind of helpless despair he sometimes imagined must have poisoned the air of Belsen and Treblinka; he only felt anger when he looked around the boarding area at his complacent fellow passengers, slumped in identical airport chairs like an exhibition of soft sculptures, their faces bored, uncaring, flattened into shadowlessness by the fluorescent lights. As he stared he could feel moisture again between his hand and the chair's plastic arm. He ground his palm on the knees of his corduroys and was miserable. Why hadn't Diana come?

Stankey hated himself for needing his wife this way — not for herself, but as a handholder, a nursemaid. When she had told him that her boss was out sick with strep throat, that they couldn't do without her at the office and that he would have to go to Dallas by himself, he had wanted to reach out and shake her. She knew he couldn't cancel out this late; he'd already paid good money to ship his artwork to the hotel. He'd also used his scant funds to pay convention fees. He *had* to go. Diana knew how much he hated flying, dreaded it, yet she had chosen to stay and help out her boss Muriel rather than him.

The night she told him, he had not slept well. He had dreamed of cattle herded up a ramp — eye-rolling, idiot cattle bumping against each other as

they were prodded into a dark boxcar.

The Thursday afternoon flight out of San Francisco was terrible. He almost took a couple of the Valium hidden deep in his pocket in a twist of Saran Wrap. Only the compelling thought that the plane might catch fire on the runway, that the panicking crew and passengers might leave him behind, immobilized in drugged sleep, prevented him from taking the tranquilizers. Instead, as he always did, he clutched the lucky talisman hidden beneath his shirt — he was ashamed of it, really: a hideous bolo tie Diana had brought back from New Mexico, where her aged parents lived in a trailer camp — clutched it, and willed the aircraft down the runway. Sweaty hand clasped on chest, he forced the plane up off the tarmac through sheer force of mind, dragging it aloft as the other passengers stared unconcernedly out the small windows, or read gaudy paperbacks, or slept (slept!).

Once the jet was in the air he began his terrified drill: smoothing the turbulence, wishing away dangerous crosswinds, tensing his legs so as to put the minimum amount of weight down on the cabin floor and avoid the laboring vibrations of the plane's underpowered, overtaxed engines. Fortunately, the passenger by the window — Henry always got an aisle seat — was one of those nerveless clods who dozed through flights, and did not have his window-blind open. Stankey was spared the additional stress of watching the plane's wings dipping and bucking crazily,

© JANET AULISIO 1989

67

straining to break free from the fuse-lage.

No one who did not feel as he did about flying realized what a strenuous job it was: three hours in the air, head flung back and eyes closed, white-knuckled hand wrapped around the hidden bolo-charm, forcing his mind through an endless circle of airy, buoy-ant thoughts — helium, swan's down, drifting dandelion puffs. At every bump or shudder his heart began to speed even more swiftly; he had to redouble his efforts to smooth interference away, to guide the plane back once more to the path of least resistance.

The landing was the worst part.

As the captain's (infuriatingly bland) voice announced the beginning of de-scent, and the plane nosed downward at a sickening angle, Henry Stankey pulled back on his seat arms until his wrists ached. The pitched whine of the engines mounted to a panicky scream, and he felt himself gradually lifting from the chairseat, gravity in tempo-rary abeyance like that time — the one and only time — he had ridden the old roller coaster at Playland-by-the-Sea. His heart climbed into his chest, his stomach pressed against the bottom of his lungs — but the man across from him was reading a newspaper! Calmly extinguishing a cigarette! Henry closed his eyes again.

The seemingly endless fall ended at last. There was a momentary sensation of leveling out; the wheels touched, lifted, then hit the ground once more with the full weight of the plane upon them. At once an even more terrible squalling started up as the pilot des-perately tried to stop the hurtling plane before it skidded off the end of the run-way into the terminal, to explode in sun-hot flames.

It didn't explode this time, but rather rolled down the Texas tarmac to a final stop. The distorted voice of a woman on the PA system gabbled something at the unheeding customers, who were already up and shouldering their lug-gage down from the overhead compart-ments, laughing and chattering and pushing up the aisle. Stankey hung limply in his chair. His shirt front was creased and sweat-stained where he had clutched his lucky bolo — but it had worked! Again, somehow beyond all hope he had gotten through, kept the plane up, then lowered it once more to the stable earth.

As the panic began to recede he sensed the high-water mark of his fear: although he had struggled to hold it back, the terror seemed to have crept higher than ever before. He felt as though he had been beaten up and left lying on a downtown sidewalk.

Damn Diana for deserting him! Damn her!

After getting into his hotel room and showering the sour odor of perspiration from his body, he slept for an hour — a dark, heavy sleep that nevertheless smoothed some of the cramping from his limbs and back. By the time he got to the conference room where the art show would be, ascertained that his paintings had indeed arrived and began to set them up in his assigned corner, a feeling of mild elation began to well inside him. He had made it by himself, without Diana, and now could look for-ward to tonight, Friday, and Saturday before he would need to begin thinking about the flight back. A tiny smile worked at the corners of his mouth as he tacked his paintings into their frames and fussed with the arrangement; it was good to feel good again.

These conventions were important to him (of course they must be, he went through Hell to get to them); they were a priceless opportunity to have his art-work noticed, to touch bases with peo-ple who could steer jobs his way and help him to break through. He had been just getting by for too long — that was the worst thing about free-lancing: the never-knowing, the waiting . . . waiting for an offer on a cover-bid, waiting for calls back, waiting to see if a project would hold together long enough to get him a guarantee, a kill-fee. . . . He was grateful for the lightening of spirit he was suddenly feeling: it was hard enough to make a living without scaring people away on top of it.

It turned out to be a fairly good convention. Several people praised his work; he sold two small paintings, a large pen and ink, and a few smallish sketches. Roger Norrisert of Lemuria Press dropped some large hints about an upcoming cover-and-illos possibility for a projected special printing of a Manly Wade Wellman book.

Thursday and Friday passed quickly in a blurry montage of handshakes and nametag-squinting and several cheerfully tipsy conversations in the hotel lounge. Both nights he slept deeply, dreamless interludes that did much to restore his normally affable outlook. Eating breakfast at a table splashed with Saturday morning sunlight, he remembered that there were indeed things he liked about conventions.

That night Stankey went with Norrisert and a couple of writers to a Cajun restaurant downtown where they sat up late, swapping stories and drinking beer. Henry got pretty tight, and did not wake until late Sunday morning.

It had not been a pleasant night. He had tossed and twitched, pulling the sheets loose from the mattress. Waking sometime after four in the morning from a dream of choking (faulty oxygen mask, hole in the hose, smoke everywhere), he had found his lucky New Mexico string tie twisted tightly around his neck, bruising his throat. After worrying it loose with sleep-clumsy fingers he had pushed it into the pocket of his jacket, which hung on a chair beside his rumpled bed.

Later, after dawdling around the hotel for a couple of bleak hours watching the Cowboys and the New Orleans Saints play an endless game of exchanged turnovers, and after laboriously packing and labeling his flats, he found himself with nothing to do for an hour and a half until the shuttle bus, like Charon's ferry, would whisk him away to the airport. To the waiting airport.

The hotel bar was almost empty, the last knots of conventioneers clumped around small tables, luggage at their feet. Stankey saw no one that he recognized; he could think of no excuse to introduce himself, to join a conversation and enlist support in his battle against reflection. The prospect of the flight home had risen from its temporary grave and was groping for attention with clammy fingers. Against his better judgment — needle-sharp reflexes were vital in combating the treacherous, gravity-embracing tendencies of airplanes — Henry ordered a vodka tonic and nursed it as he sat in a corner seat trying to read a Ramsey Campbell book.

The drink was a good idea. It soothed the ragged edges of his thoughts; he felt it working like aftershave lotion on a just-shaved face, stripping away the heat, quieting scratchy nerves — well, after all, aftershave was alcohol, too. He thought, a little cavalierly, of just ordering another drink, but he knew that was the lulling effect of the first one at work. He could not afford to be that relaxed: he was needed, even if the other passengers never realized it.

Still, the one drink had been a good idea. The Campbell novel had not. The dank, depressing Liverpool setting and the hopelessly phobic thoughts of the characters made Stankey feel a little sick. He put the book down after thirty pages or so and stared out the window at the hotel parking lot, toying with the slowly melting ice in his glass.

69

The bus came. It took him, tight-lipped and silent, to the airport, and left him there. On the walkway outside the terminal he could already feel the acid gnawing at his stomach, the placating effects of the vodka-tonic evaporated by harsh lights and disembodied, inflectionless voices, by the chill, echoing vastness of the place. He carried his hand-luggage to the boarding area — no massive suitcase in the hold for him: why make the plane any heavier than it had to be? — and stood in line between a Mexican woman with a screaming child and a boy in a baseball cap who, except for his drooping, moron's mouth, could have been a Norman Rockwell character. Some of the other passengers were talking about something he could not quite catch — the flight? — but he would not be distracted. At last he reached the front of the line, put his ticket on the counter, and was told by the female mannequin in the royal blue vest that plane was delayed: it would be an hour and twenty-five minutes late taking off.

She might as well have hit him with a hammer. His defenses were keyed up, he was wound tight as a mountain climber's rope — and now this! He wanted to shout, to screech at this incomprehending woman with her twinkly Rose Parade smile. Turning hurriedly, he lurched to the high window where he leaned against a pillar and willed his heart to slow down.

He-would-be-calm. He-*would*-be-calm.

When he felt a little more in control he went to the payphone to call Diana, to tell her he would be late. No one answered at home. It was hard not to feel betrayed.

So he sat, staring out at the now-darkening sky, trying not to watch the technicians scurrying like parasites beneath the bodies of the big jets. This was the last time, he vowed to himself. Never again. Other artists and writers got by without having to leave home. He could take the train if he really needed to go anywhere, even though it took days. It was ridiculous to scourge himself this way. Nothing in life was worth this kind of sick fear.

An announcement about his flight crackled over the PA system. The message was hard to make out, but he was positive he had heard the words "mechanical difficulties." When he demanded to know what had been said, the woman at the counter — looking a little amused — confirmed that he had indeed heard that numbing phrase, that such in fact was the reason the jet had been delayed in Atlanta. But, she told him, it was in the air now and would arrive soon. Under sharp questioning about the nature of the "difficulties" she professed ignorance, but assured him that everything was being taken care of. This time he went back to his window even more slowly, like a man mounting thirteen steps to the gibbet. The counterwoman favored his retreat with a condescending smile.

Damn the bitch. And damn Diana too, for good measure.

At last the plane arrived. Stankey, squinting suspiciously through the high boarding area windows, could see nothing overtly wrong — but that, of course, meant nothing. He would never see the loose bolts that would vibrate free and drop the engine like a stone, never detect the fault in the landing gear that would snap the wheel off on contact and send the jet sliding to flaming oblivion. He boarded, a stale taste in his mouth, and found his way to seat 21, near the back of the plane. After stowing his shoulder bag he sat down and promptly fastened his seat belt, then reached his hand up to his breastbone to feel for the lucky bolo tie hanging beneath his shirt.

It wasn't there.

He checked the pockets of his jacket, which disgorged keys, wallet, ticket folder, receipts, and matchbooks . . . but no good-luck talisman. In a growing panic he unbuckled his lap-belt and sprang up, nearly knocking over the crew-cutted businessman seating himself across the aisle. Stankey jerked open the overhead compartment and levered out his bag, opening it across his lap to rummage through the carefully folded shirts and socks. The Mexican woman in the seat before his shifted her wet-mouthed baby to look over her shoulder at him as he cursed to himself, emptying the bag with trembling hands. The bolo tie was nowhere inside. Henry could dimly remember taking it off in the night and putting it in the pocket of his jacket — but he was wearing that jacket now. He searched the pockets again, fruitlessly.

As he sat in the wreckage of his meticulous packing a pert-faced stewardess leaned over to ask if he needed any help. Unable to speak, he shook his head and began to stow the clothing back into the bag, dislodging a stack of convention giveaway magazines which slithered to the floor. He excoriated himself and his disability as he crouched on the cabin floor picking them up. A middle-aged woman in a parka waited impatiently for him to finish so she could get past to the window seat. As she slid by he forced the repacked bag into the compartment, then slumped back into his chair.

What could he do? The damned bolo must have fallen out on the hotel floor, must even now be in the pocket of some maid, or lying unnoticed behind the bed. He knew how much he needed it. It had gotten him through every miserable one of the dozen or so flights he had taken in the last five years — even the one to Wisconsin where the turbulence had been so bad the seatbelt sign never went off. It had gotten him through Thursday's flight, the first one he had ever taken without Diana. Now he had neither his wife or his lucky talisman.

He thought seriously for a moment of simply getting up and walking off the plane, but he knew that was a foolish idea. He would still have to get back to San Francisco somehow, the expensive airline ticket would be wasted, and he would miss the Monday afternoon meeting with Janicos from Beltane Books . . . No, he would have to stay on the flight. Again he cursed his poverty, his childish fears, his treacherous wife.

The final passengers had boarded, and the doors were being shut. The compact thump of the vacuum seal sounded like the coffin lid of the Premature Burial. He could see the stewardesses walking down the aisle, checking to make sure the compartment doors were closed — trim, blue-skirted death angels, hair shining in the cabin lights. Henry unbuckled his belt again and scrambled out into the aisle, moving quickly to the lavatory.

In the narrow room, scarcely even a closet, he felt the surge of claustrophobia. Why had he come back here? His face in the small mirror looked pale, haunted; he turned back toward the door. It all felt like a terrible dream, a grinding nightmare which he could not shut off.

He remembered the Valium in his pocket.

Maybe I can take one of these, he thought. . . . No, better yet, take two, take three or four, sleep through the whole damned flight. If it catches fire on takeoff, so what? I'll never know.

But how would the plane stay aloft? He knew, somewhere in his fevered thinking, that planes traveled every day without him on board — lifted off, flew, and landed without Henry Stankey's straining intercession. It could fly while he slept, just this once . . . couldn't it?

Yes, planes did that, but *he* had never been on one that had. He had always worked like a dray-horse to keep them aloft, pulled them along through the turbulent winds that sought to batter them to the ground like badminton birds. Could he relinquish that control?

He had to. Otherwise, he would never make it — he knew that as a certainty. Without Diana it had been nearly impossible; without either wife or talisman it was flatly inconceivable. And if he couldn't manage the strain, wouldn't it be better not to see the last moments coming? To sleep a narcotized sleep through the screeching final seconds? He was disgusted by his own spinelessness, by his desertion of his fellow passengers who (although they didn't know it) would be deprived his valuable assistance in keeping the plane safe and themselves ignorant and happy . . . but there was no alternative he could see. None.

Hands moist with fear-sweat, he unpeeled the plastic-wrapped pills and plucked two out of the jumble. After a moment's consideration he took up another pair, then downed them all with a swallow of water from the tiny sink. Wrapping the remainder, he stumbled back to his seat. The plane was beginning to roll, heading toward the takeoff site. As he wedged himself into place and cinched the belt tightly across his lap, he wondered if the pills would take long to kick in. He knew he would have to get through at least the beginning without help.

The jet gathered speed down the runway, engines howling like late-night-movie Indians bent on massacre, and Stankey's hand rose reflexively to his chest. There was, of course, no charmed bolo tie to grasp. He clutched his lapel instead, crushing the material into a wet, wrinkled knot. Straining, heaving, the plane forced its way upward. By some miracle it broke from the ground's cruel pull and mounted up at a fierce angle to the waiting sky.

Henry Stankey, tendons stretched like violin strings, waited for either the sickening lurch of lost altitude or the now desperately-awaited onset of drowsiness. Drowsiness won. By the time the aircraft had leveled out six miles or so above the earth's hidden surface, he could feel languor beginning to creep over him, as though a warm, woolly blanket was settling over his body. His muscles unknotted. His breathing slowed. The woman sitting by the window a seat away looked at him sharply, questioningly. Henry, growing groggier by the moment, was even able to muster a thin smile. The woman turned away. The drone of the airplane made him feel as though he rode the night in a great, glowing beehive . . .

It seemed that he had to claw his way up from sleep. The tarbaby grip of the Valium held him back, but a part of his mind knew that he was urgently needed: even as he clambered up from unconsciousness he could feel the plane lurching and rocking, the cabin rattling like a toy in a child's fist. He opened his eyes, fighting for wakefulness . . . and knew he had been right. All his fears were now confirmed — he should never have taken those pills, never have relinquished control! He moaned, straining to dislodge the tendrils of sleep.

The faces of his fellow passengers told all. This time no one was reading unconcernedly or chatting with neighbors. Like Stankey, they gripped their seat arms and stared straight ahead as the plane bucked and swerved. Eyes stared darkly from pale faces. The Mexican woman clutched her sobbing baby; Henry could hear her voice moving in the urgent, rhythmic cadences of prayer.

A sudden lurch and the plane plummeted, a drop that seemed to last minutes, like the freefall of an amusement park ride. One woman's voice rose in a brief, muffled shriek. The plane bottomed out, climbed a moment, stabilized. There was none of the usual nervous laughter; the heaving and the battering side-to-side swaying continued. Above the tense muttering of the passengers Stankey heard the voice of the captain on the intercom. Even as he spoke, the stewardesses hurried down the aisle to the back of the plane.

There was another sickening plunge, and a meal tray tumbled out of a passenger's grip to carom down the aisle, scattering food everywhere. The flight attendants did not even look down as they made their way back to their own seats to strap in. To Henry, this was the grimmest proof of all.

Was it too late? He strained outward with his mind, murky thoughts wrestling with the shivering plane and its staggering attempts to defy gravity. For a moment he thought he could do it. The lights blinked on and off, the captain's voice gargled through the cabin: . . . *fasten seat belts, stay calm . . . turbulence . . .* Henry concentrated his will, fighting treacherous sleepiness; the plane seemed to settle a bit, its passage momentarily smoothed. The shuddering became less. Almost without knowing Stankey relaxed — just a little, the most minute concession to the downward drag of the medication — and lost it.

The plane heaved like a gutshot dinosaur and rolled to one side. Several of the overhead compartments burst open, vomiting luggage on the shouting passengers. Suitcases somersaulted down the aisle in slow motion; a blind man's cane, folded in segments, accordioned out from his seat to fly end over end through the cabin like a bizarre albino insect. The airplane hung for a moment on its side: Stankey felt himself dangling across his seat arm, sliding toward the gap-mouthed face of the woman by the window. The glass behind her looked out on black, formless emptiness. The plane nosed down so steeply that it seemed to Henry the passengers near the front of the cabin had

©JANET AULISIO 1989.

fallen down a hole, a hole from which he was being dragged by some fierce power, pulled back against his seat, chest and lungs crushed in a giant's grip. The cabin was suddenly a lively Hell of flailing arms and flying objects. A woman's faint voice screamed: *heads down heads down heads down . . . !* The turbine shriek of the wind buried all other sounds; the mouths that gaped and worked without words joined their last cries to the panicked roar of the plummeting airplane. Sound cutting through his head like a jigsaw, Stankey screamed too — screamed out his despair and terror, screeched out wordless curses at what fate, his wife, his own fear had done to him. He struggled to force himself up against the shocking, smashing pressure of pitched descent. It wasn't fair! He had tried everything! He had to take the pills, couldn't have kept the plane up this time! Why?! Why?! Whywhywhywhywhywhywhy . . .

impact

Time . . . is . . . stopping.

Henry feels himself standing at last . . . a man at last . . . on his feet. He is thrown forward — his flight as inexorable but unhurried as the slide of a black-ice glacier (time now creeping as slowly as eroding stone) — forward like a stop-motion film of a plant growing, unfolding, hurtling forward but barely moving . . . The passengers around him are a frozen flash photograph, eyes bulging . . . suitcases hang in the air like corpuscles in the clear ichor of a god's arteries. The walls of the plane wrinkle, contract around him, surge toward the nose; the seats fold forward like a row of dominoes, the passengers folding with them — slowly, slowly, like a child's pop-up book being carefully closed.

Stankey, unfettered, is passing through them all now, flowing remorselessly for-

ward, sliding through the dividing substance of passengers and objects like a bullet tumbling through a sand castle. The way opens before him, a kaleidoscopic mandala of blood and bone and fabric and torn metal — a succession of slow-blooming, intricate flowers through which he tumbles like a bee in melting amber. His journey to the crystalline heart of the petals takes millennia.

Slower now, slower . . . matter bunching up, molecule on static molecule . . .

Dense.

Denser.

Densest . . .

. . . Until Time itself falls behind his ultimate slowness, until only the remembrance remains, the memory of the light years of waiting before the next tick of atomic decay

and then he is through . . .

The morgue attendant slides the drawer back in. The widow is led out by friends; her shoulders heave.

When she is gone he pulls the drawer out again and stares at the body. He twitches the sheet aside to look at the bruised pelvis, the mottled black and yellow bars where the victim broke the seatbelt across his own body struggling to rise from his seat.

The airline says that the victim had slept through the whole flight until the last descent, when he began to shout and writhe in his sleep, in the depths of an unbreachable dream. Unwaking, he had struggled with the seat, with gravity, with the belt itself until he snapped it loose — the heavy canvas torn by a near-incomprehensible strength — and had stood shouting in the aisle, eyes shut. When the wheels touched the runway, the airline representative said, the man had screamed once and fallen forward, dead.

The attendant looks the body up and down and shakes his head. He slides it back inside on near-silent rollers. A heart attack, they say. Extreme shock and terror, they say.

So, the attendant wonders, why is the corpse smiling?

. . . he has come through — and

Henry Stankey is no more. He is a mote of light passing through a radiant universe, speeding through unending brightness.

And flying is a joy.

AND SOON A WOLF FOR EVERY DOOR

When I called the streets home in my fortieth year,
no vagabond or addict, the days were rich about me,
the times were technological and high electric wizards,
with satellites and dishes, acclaimed a world complete.

When I made the pavement bed and the daily news a sheet,
no derelict or gypsy, no capital gains or fortunate father
to shoulder my needs, I read of racing sloops and summits,
of fashion's latest revelations and detente with the East.

When I combed the trash for sustenance in the fullness
of my age, and scanned tin ladles for a scrap of meat,
I was not the best man nor the worst to ever be deceived
by the sell songs all about me and the promises of thieves.

When I named the curb my only chair and a refuse fire heat,
no surcease from this senseless stone, no anodyne to ease
the pain within my bones, just the deadening of my flesh
as winter sirens howl and the deftly modern city sleeps.

And when I have become a man no more, as hollow and as mean
and as hungry as the streets, on some fey night at your door
you'll hear me start to gnaw, my nails thick, gone to claw,
the decimation of my soul will bare a sad and savage beast.

— **Bruce Boston**

SOFT

by Darrell Schweitzer

Richard never knew why it happened, or how, but, in the end, he thought he understood what it meant. And perhaps that, at the very end, was enough.

The screaming was over. The completely inarticulate fits of obscenities they'd both descended to when they'd run out of real words were gone too, passed like a sudden summer storm.

He felt merely drained. He stood alone in the living room, listening to the ticking of the clock on the mantel, and, beyond that, to the silence of their dishevelled apartment. When at last he made his way to the bedroom, he found, much to his surprise, that his wife had left the door unlocked.

He turned the handle slowly.

"Karen?"

The bedroom was dark.

"Karen?"

She muttered something he could not make out, a single word like a profound sigh.

"What?"

She did not answer.

His only thought had been to slip through the bedroom into the bathroom, then come out again and retrieve his pajamas and a blanket from the closet so he could spend what would very probably be his last night in this apartment on the sofa.

But as his eyes adjusted to the darkness he saw that she had rolled over to one side of the bed, the way she always did. When he was ready, he got into bed beside her, more out of habit than any

76

hope or conviction.

The bedsprings creaked. If he listened very hard, he could still hear the clock over the mantel in the living room.

Karen muttered something again. She was talking in her sleep. It was just like her, it seemed to him then, just like the self-absorbed, overgrown child she had become, or perhaps had always been, to go straight to bed after the domestic war to end all wars and sleep it off like a Saturday night's drunk.

He lay still for a while beside her, staring at the ceiling, his hands joined behind his head.

It was beyond apology now, beyond grovelling, beyond absurd bunches of roses with absurd cards. Everything was decided, and there was some relief in that, a release from all doubt and tension. It was *over*. They were getting divorced as soon as possible.

That was a simple fact he could cling to.

But the fact didn't seem so simple as he lay there. He spent a long, masochistic time rehearsing their early years together in his mind, not dwelling so much on *her,* but on how he had felt, the sensation, the satisfaction of being perfectly in love for just one, perfect day. There had been *one* perfect day, he somehow knew, and everything had declined subtly from it. Yet he couldn't find the day in his memory, for all he was sure there had been "one, brief, shining moment," as the phrase went, and he wept softly for the loss of it.

Then he turned angrily on his side,

his back to Karen, his fists tight against his chest, and he cursed himself for the sort of fool who would go back for punishment again and again and never learn.

He listened to the clock ticking, and to Karen breathing. Once again she babbled something in her sleep. It seemed to be a single word over and over. He still couldn't make it out.

Perhaps he slept briefly. He was aware of some transition, a vague disorientation, as if a few minutes had been clipped from the film-strip of his life. Still he lay in the darkness on the bed, his back to Karen.

He couldn't hear the clock. There was only the silent darkness holding him like a fly suspended in amber.

And a word. He felt it forming on his own lips, and he had to speak it aloud just to know what it was.

"Soft," he said.

What followed was temptation. Part of his mind laughed bitterly and remembered the old Oscar Wilde jibe about the only way to deal with temptation being to give in to it. Part of his mind watched, a disinterested observer, as his body turned toward Karen, as his lips said again, almost soundlessly, "Soft."

She was wearing a sleeveless nightgown. The same compulsion that made him turn, that made him speak, now caused him to reach up, ever so gently, and touch her bare shoulder.

"Soft," he said. He squeezed, and his detached puzzlement grew as he felt that her shoulder was indeed soft, like warm, living clay. His fingers left a deep, firm impression in her flesh, as if she *were* a clay figure and he had just ruined the sculptor's work.

He ran his fingers into the grooves and out again, confirming what he felt.

Then he drew his hand back quickly and lay still, afraid, his heart racing. He stared at the dark shape of his wife on the bed beside him. He thought he could make out just a hint of the disfigurement.

It was impossible, of course, but he couldn't bring himself to *tell* himself that, to say aloud, or firmly in his own mind, *You must be dreaming. People do not turn into Silly-Putty, not in real life.*

Part of him wanted to believe.

The word came to him once more. The urge to reach out to her followed, like a child's uncontrollable desire to pick at a scab, to touch a sore.

"Soft," he said, kneading the whole length of her arm like dough. She didn't seem to feel any pain. Her breathing remained the same regular in-out of deep sleep.

Again she mumbled something, her breath passing through flapping lips almost as if she were trying to imitate a horse.

He touched her. He felt the warm flesh passing between his fingers, never breaking off the way clay would, but losing all shape as he squeezed again and again. He felt the hard joint of her elbow for only a second before it too became flaccid, endlessly plastic.

"Soft," he said, and with horrified fascination he stretched her arm until it reached down past her ankle, then flattened it until it was like the deflated arm of a balloon figure. That was what she was, he decided, an inflato-girl ordered from the back pages of a men's magazine. That was what she deserved to be, he told himself, and his anger suddenly returned. He knelt over her now, astride her, and he touched her flesh again and again, smearing her face out on the pillowcase, crushing her other shoulder, while he thought how much he hated her and could not find the words until he arrived at Poe's perfect phrase, *the thousand injuries of Fortunato.*

"Yes," he whispered as he pressed her, as her flesh flowed and changed and spread across the covers. "Yes. Fortunato. Soft, Fortunato. *Soft.*"

77

© JANET AULISIO 1989

78

And finally, reaching into the ruin of her chest, pushing his hands under the layers of flesh as he might under a heap of old clothes, he held her beating heart between his fingers.

Still she breathed gently, her distended, lumpy body rising and falling as if someone were making a feeble attempt to inflate the inflato-girl.

Then his anger passed, and once again he wept, and lay motionless on the bed, atop her, beside her, her flesh all around him, her steady breathing caressing every part of him. He felt himself becoming sexually aroused, and he was afraid and ashamed.

He listened to the silence of the apartment where he was spending his last night and wondered what precisely he should do. He laughed aloud, bitterly, at the prospect of going into the street now, at whatever late hour it was, approaching a policeman and saying, "Er, excuse me officer, but I've squeezed my wife a little too hard and —"

He imagined the expressions on the faces of the nurses at the hospital emergency room as he brought Karen in draped over himself like a poncho, her face and hands dangling down by the floor.

Her breathing caressed him and he said again and again, "Soft. Soft. For you, my dearest Fortunato, soft forever."

Once more he wept, then laughed aloud hysterically, then hushed himself in sudden, desperate dread, terribly afraid that he might *wake* her.

He lay paralyzed, and swiftly, without the slightest effort on his part, the memory he had been searching for came to him, and he remembered that day ten years ago when they were both twenty-three, about six months before they were married, when he took her on a picnic to some scenic spot up the Hudson, near Tarrytown perhaps, where the towers of Manhattan were like grey shapes of cloud just around a bend in the river.

Nothing much happened, but he remembered lying beside her on the blanket in the warm sun, gently stroking her hair while an orange and brown butterfly flapped around their faces and neither one of them bothered to brush it away.

It was a moment of perfect harmony, perfect agreement, and their futures seemed so certain. It was a relief, a release from all doubt and tension.

She had risen on her elbow, holding her chin in her hand, and smiled down at him.

"I love you," she said. "When they made you, they broke the mold."

"You too," he said.

He awoke with a feeling like a sudden drop, as if he'd stepped off a cliff in a dream.

It was dawn. By the first grey light seeping through the Venetian blinds he could make out the dresser against the far wall and the bathroom door hanging open.

Something stirred on the bed, touching him from many directions at once, caressing him.

He closed his eyes desperately, and groped about in this self-imposed, utter darkness, weeping again, sobbing, "Soft, soft, damn it, one more time, please," as he tried to gather her flesh together, to shape it, to reassembled the ruined form into some semblance of the original.

But he was no sculptor.

By full light of day he had to, at last, open his eyes and behold his attempt.

He screamed.

She opened her eyes.

He felt her flesh closing over his hand, his fingers giving way, mingling with hers.

She spoke out of a gaping wound that might have once been a mouth.

"Soft," she said. ⊗

THE EMPEROR'S RETURN

by Harry Turtledove

29 May, etos kosmou *6961* (A.D. *1453)*

Cannon roared in the distance, each blast like the cry of a creature from Hell. Closer, the air was filled with the clash and clatter of swords and spears; with shrieks and cries in Greek, Italian, Turkish; with the stench of smoke and of despair. The Ottomans were in Constantinople. The Queen of Cities, the New Rome, millennial capital of empire, was falling.

A graying man, bare-headed, dashed into the great cathedral of Hagia Sophia. Priests still gathered there, praying for a deliverance that would not come. One bowed low before the newcomer. "Lord, is there —?" he began. Then he stopped, as if afraid even to put his question into words.

The graying man did it for him. "A chance? None," declared Constantine XI Palaiologos, Emperor and Autocrat of the Romans. "All is lost. I threw aside my crown when I saw we could not check them, and would have thrown myself after it into the brawl, save only that I could not stomach being even a corpse in a Constantinople ruled by Turks."

"Would you flee, then, my lord?" the priest quavered. "Do you know a way through the circle the infidels have cast around us?" He hated himself for the fearful hope he heard in his voice.

But the Emperor said, "This for flight!" and spat on the marble floor, stained with the blood of wounded men who had come to the great church to pray or to die. "By God, by his son Jesus Christ, by the immaculate Virgin who bore

Him, by the holy saints, I should die, and die gladly, sooner than run away."

"What then, my lord?"

Constantine XI sighed heavily. "I know not. I came here to beseech a miracle: for God to let me see this city in Christian hands again. But are there any miracles left for this empire, for this city, for me?"

A mantle of pearly flame suddenly draped the Emperor in glory. The priest cried out. Constantine XI, sword still in hand, sank silently into the floor. For a moment, the priest could see him even so, shining through the marble slab. Then he was — gone.

The priest fell to his knees. *"Kyrie eleison! Christe eleison!"* he quavered, again and again and again. "Lord, have mercy! Christ, have mercy!"

Constantinople fell. The Emperor's body was never found.

*7 June, 2003 (*etos kosmou *7511)*

A machine-gun chattered from atop the breached ruins of Theodosios' wall. Bullets spanged off the Greek MICV, stitched through shrubbery and threw fountains of dirt, a couple of them less than a meter from Yannis Pappas' face. The sergeant hugged the ground as if it were a lover.

The MICV's cannon spoke once, twice, three times. Ancient masonry and pieces of Turks flew through the air. Pappas screamed in animal delight. He scrambled to his feet, clutching his assault rifle.

He and his squad followed the MICV past the fortifications from another age and into the city. A sign leaned drunkenly, a few meters away. It was in unintelligible Turkish, even the alphabet alien to Pappas, but one word he recognized: **ISTANBUL**.

He jerked a thumb at the sign, gestured with extravagant obscenity. "It's Constantinople again now that we're here, you bastards!" he yelled. The men with him screamed themselves hoarse. A private named George Nikolaidis crossed himself. He had tears running down his cheeks, scouring clean lines in the grime there.

Pappas did not say anything to him. His own sight was misty — the Queen of cities, *the* city, Greek again after 550 years! That, by the God he had not believed in since he was a child, was worth crying over.

An F-16 blazoned with the Turks' big red square screamed overhead, just above treetop height. The Greeks threw themselves flat again. The earth jumped under them and a giant boxed their ears with noise as bombs exploded, much too close. A soldier hit by a fragment shrieked.

Another blast, this one overhead — a SAM blotted the fighter-bomber from the sky. Pappas got up. He was sergeant; setting an example was his duty. He could not keep from looking up from under the rim of his helmet, though.

Anastasios Kiapos perfectly understood that glance. "They haven't had many planes to throw at us," the corporal said. "One less, now."

"They haven't had too much of anything to throw at us, Taso," Pappas said, "not with the Russians rolling down on them out of Armenia."

"They won't hold them, either," Kiapos said. He sounded grimly pleased at the prospect: having someone else smash the Turks was only a little less delightful than doing it personally.

"The Russians can wave to us from across the Sea of Marmara tomorrow, and I will wave back," Pappas said.

© JANET AULISIO 1989.

"But Constantinople stays ours." That was part of the price Greece had demanded for turning on her one-time NATO ally, and the Russians had paid it.

More planes thundered by, these out of the west: Greek fighter-bombers, heading probably for the bridge across the Golden Horn and the ones further up the Bosporos. With the bridges down, the Turks would not be able to reinforce the city, assuming they had reinforcements to spare. . . .

"Tomorrow, you said," Kiapos muttered three days later. He had been dirty before. He was filthy now. So was Yannis Pappas. So were both the other men in the squad left alive and unwounded after the endless street fighting. The MICV was no more — a wireguided rocket had made an inferno of it in the park by the mosque of Murat Pasha.

But Constantinople, most of it, was Greek. Pappas' squad was only a couple of hundred meters from the sea. The sergeant, however, found he had no more interest in emulating Xenophon. Just ahead lay Hagia Sophia. One of the ugly minarets the Turks had added to Justinian's great cathedral was half as tall as it should have been — there had been snipers up where the muezzin once called the Muslim faithful to prayer.

Pappas, for his part, had more faith in Marxism than Orthodoxy. But to be the man whose squad freed Hagia Sophia — He grinned. All Greece would want to know of the man who did that. He might even make lieutenant if a TV crew showed up at the right time.

He started up the broad stone steps. "Careful," Kiapos said behind him. Both men had their assault rifles ready. No firing had come from the great church since the top of the minaret crashed down, but caution was never wasted. Hagia Sophia was big enough

to hold a battalion.

The doors that led to the narthex were open. Pappas' boots thumped on polished stone. Echoes came back at him. Though chaos still raved outside, it somehow did not impinge here. For the first time since that dead MICV jounced past the Turkish frontier in Thrace, the sergeant thought of peace.

One by one, his men joined him. "None of the bastards," Pappas said. Even to himself, he sounded amazed.

"Unless they're waiting inside," Kiapos said. He nervously rubbed his chin; whiskers rasped under his fingers.

But Pappas tossed his head in a Hellenic no. "Too quiet for that. Besides, we'd *feel* it if they were there." The squad's survivors nodded. None of them had more than ten days of combat experience, but they knew what he meant.

The sergeant tramped up to the inner doors of the narthex, threw one open. At the same moment, he sprang back and to one side, his rifle swinging up. He was sure the church was empty, but he did not believe in taking chances.

Save for the hollow boom of the door slamming back to hit the wall, nothing happened. Pappas stepped through, wary still, his men close behind.

The last time he'd been inside a church, he hadn't needed to shave. Even restored as a museum, Hagia Sophia kept but a pale shadow of its Byzantine magnificence. Yet the beauty and splendor that remained were enough to make his breath come short.

He looked up and up and up, to the cross in the center of the great dome. The sunbeams that pierced the windows at the base of the dome seemed to leave it floating in space, insubstantial, unconnected to the bulk of the church below.

He saw Kiapos make the sign of the cross — and the corporal, he knew, was no more a believer than he was himself. Behind them, Nikolaidis began to chant the words of the Trisagion hymn, the thrice-holy: "Holy God, holy mighty one, holy undying one, have mercy on us . . ."

The private's voice broke. He fell to his knees, crossed himself again and again. Pappas, who prided himself on cold rationality, was rational enough to see that, to someone who was Orthodox, nothing could be more moving than praying in the newly liberated Hagia Sophia.

He gently slapped Nikolaidis on the shoulder. "They'll have priests here again one day soon, I expect," he said, without adding, as he usually would have, "for those stupid enough to want them." The great church was great enough to instill in him, if not reverence, at least respect.

"Don't need a priest." Caught up in something close to ecstasy, Nikolaidis swayed back and forth. *"Kyrie eleison, Christe eleison, Kyrie —"*

Then Yannis Pappas, good Marxist that he was, signed himself and felt no shame at all. Light glowed within the floor, above the floor, light that reminded him at the same time of the glow from a fluorescent tube and of the uncreated Energies of the God his conscious mind rejected.

Even in the midst of miracle, he was too rational to question his sanity. He clutched his assault rifle; it anchored him to the world he understood.

The light slowly faded. A man took a stumbling step out of it, a man with a sword.

For a moment, Constantine XI Palaiologos did not realize anything had changed; perhaps his ears reached full awareness before his eyes. He knew combat when he heard it: a certain scream belongs only to wounded men. But even so soon, he wondered. Where had the Turks found so many guns? He knew with dreadful certainty they could not belong to his own men.

His own men . . . Where were his own men? Where was that coward of a priest with whom he'd been talking? And who were these four strangers staring at him, white showing all around their eyes as if they were spooked horses?

They were soldiers, he saw at once, even if like no soldiers he had ever known. It was not the helms on their heads that told him; not the likeness of their tunics and trousers, all the same and all in the colors of mud and dirt and grass; not even the unfamiliar weapons three of them carried (another such weapon lay beside the fourth, who was on his knees). No matter how afraid they were, though, they did not break and run. They only waited, to see what he would do. That made them soldiers for certain.

"Whose men are you?" the Emperor demanded. "Are you Turks or Romans?" The soldiers stirred, looked at one another; the one on his knees crossed himself. "Romans!" Constantine said joyfully.

"Yannis Pappas, sergeant, army of Hellas," said one of the strange warriors in an even stranger accent — clipped, hurried, slurred. But it was Greek! "And who the ——" — a word Constantine had not heard before, but one that sounded like a Turkish obscenity he knew — "are you, and where'd you come from?"

Constantine proudly named himself, adding, "Emperor and Autocrat of the Romans in a line stretching continuously back to the first Constantine, the great, whose namesake I am, and through him to Augustus, who ruled the Roman realm when Christ Himself walked the earth."

One of the standing soldiers did break then, shouting wordlessly and dashing out of Hagia Sophia. Pappas and the man at his side yelled after the panicked soldier. The fellow did not stop. Pappas raised his weapon, lowered it with a shrug. "Curse me if I blame

84

Spero," Constantine heard him mutter.

The soldier still on his knees raised his eyes to peer fearfully at Constantine, jerked them down the instant they met the Emperor's. "Christ have mercy on us," he stammered, crossing himself again. "It's the *marmaromenos Basileus,* come among men once more.

"The who? The what?" Constantine and Yannis Pappas asked together. Pappas went on, "Up from your knees, George, and talk, if you know something of this."

"The Emperor who turned to marble," George repeated as he got to his feet. "Didn't your grandmother tell you that one, sergeant? The last Emperor, the one who sank into — well, my grandmother said the wall, but that's wrong — into the floor of Hagia Sophia when the city fell, never to come out until —"

"— Until Constantinople was in Christian hands again. That was my prayer," Constantine broke in. It was his turn to make the sign of the cross, slowly, humbly, in awe of the favor he had been granted. "And God saw fit to hear me. How long have I slept?"

"Five hundred fifty years," George said softly.

"You joke," Constantine said. He checked himself. "No, I see you do not." Now his awe had a chill edge to it. An age had passed away while he slumbered unknowing. No wonder these men looked and sounded strange! He made the sign of the cross again.

"Grandmothers' stories!" Pappas tried to make that a snort of contempt, but found it wasn't easy, not with a Byzantine Emperor practically at his elbow.

"Sergeant, what are we going to *do* with him?" Taso Kiapos asked.

That was the question, all right. "Let me think," Pappas said, which meant he didn't have a good answer. He kept staring over at Constantine Palaiologos, wishing he could pretend the man

was a maniac who just happened to be wearing chainmail, who just happened to have wandered into Hagia Sophia in the middle of the firefight, who just happened to believe he was the rightful Emperor and Autocrat of the Romans . . .

The sergeant shook his head. The odds of all that coming together were slimmer than those for Constantine's being exactly what he said he was.

"Sir —" George Nikolaidis wasn't talking to Pappas, he was talking to the Emperor. "Sir, now that God has restored you to us, what will you do with your second time here on earth?"

"Why, take up my rule again, of course," Constantine said, as if no other thought had entered his mind. Pappas suspected no other thought had. Constantine went on, "Take up my rule again, and proclaim God's glory for preserving me to see this day come. Surely the lord who rules you now will yield his throne to me when he learns of my miraculous return."

Pappas had a picture of the members of the socialist cabinet in Athens prostrating themselves before the restored Byzantine Emperor. He started to laugh, but the laughter froze on his lips. Plenty of his countrymen still longed for the kings now almost two generations gone, and plenty more, like Nikolaidis, were good sons of Orthodoxy. Constantine might get a hearing after all.

That would not be good. Socialist Greece found enough in common with the Soviet Union for them to work together. A Greece convulsed by Constantine's partisans would hardly be so attractive an ally — and might tempt the Russians into coming down "to help restore order." And the Byzantine Emperors, from all Pappas had read, were autocrats indeed, autocrats even more thoroughgoing than the hated colonels.

"We have no one lord," the sergeant told the Emperor. "Greece is a democracy these days."

"Demokratia?" Constantine used the same word as Pappas, but understood it differently: "You have only mob-rule? For how long have you suffered under it?"

"More than thirty-five years," Pappas answered. He had, the Emperor thought, the effrontery to sound proud. Constantine was appalled. Even the Zealots who seized Thessalonike during the civil wars a century before his time only managed to hold it a handful of years. What sort of mob could rule long enough to let a man go from youth to grandfather?

"You will need a strong ruler, after so much anarchy," Constantine declared. "God must have sent me to you, to let me turn you to the right path once more."

"He is right," said George, the soldier who had been on his knees. He turned to Constantine, bowed low. "Lead me, lord, and I and all Greece will follow."

The Emperor swung up his sword in salute. "Follow, then, and announce the miracle to all we meet." Without looking back, he started out toward the narthex of the great church. He heard George's boots clumping along behind him, and smiled. After only moments in this new world, he had his first sure subject. Soon he would have more.

Pappas and Kiapos exchanged a look full of consternation. Once Constantine got outside Hagia Sophia, he might be locked up as a madman. But — and especially *but* in the euphoria of this moment, this avenging of an ancient defeat — he just might be believed. Then euphoria would turn to hysteria.

"Taso, do you really want to live under a medieval king, even one brought back by a miracle or magic or whatever?" Pappas asked quietly.

The corporal stood a moment in thought, rubbing at his drooping black moustache. Finally he dipped his head. "No, sergeant; do you?"

"No." Pappas' mind worked furiously. Whatever he did, he would have to do it fast. Only luck, or maybe a Turkish counterattack somewhere outside, had kept more Greeks from rushing to Hagia Sophia. Until they did, the danger Constantine XI represented was still small. Afterwards, especially with Nikolaidis shooting off his mouth — "Back me?"

"All the way," Taso Kiapos answered.

"Watch George, then. I'll deal with — the Emperor." Pappas raised his voice to a parade-ground roar: "Halt!"

George Nikolaidis automatically clicked to attention. Constantine Palaiologos also stopped. His eyes were wary as he turned. Pappas was glad he was too far away to make that blade he carried any real risk.

Constantine looked back to find out why the soldier had shouted. He could see no reason. What he did see was Pappas' weapon — could guns be made small enough for men to carry them easily? — pointing his way. Of themselves, his fingers tightened on the hilt of his sword. "Turn it aside," he said. "That is not how friend treats with friend."

The weapon stayed steady. "We are not friends, you and I," Pappas said. "Believe me when I tell you I wish it were otherwise, but we are not friends. To me, you are everything Greece — everything the world — has tried to outgrow. Greeks have changed since your time." The latter-day soldier had not forgotten the sword. He gestured with his weapon, not enough to hurt his aim. "Set that down, please, or I will shoot you sooner than I'd have to otherwise."

It *was* a gun, then. Constantine did not drop his blade. If Pappas fired and missed, the Emperor expected to gut him immediately afterwards — he was not even wearing armor to protect himself. Guns, Constantine thought, were all or nothing. He stood on the balls of his feet, waiting.

"Why do you want to shoot me?" he asked, honestly curious. "Do you set yourself above God, Who gave me life again for this very moment?"

"I don't believe in God." Pappas' voice was flat, matter-of-fact; he meant what he said, and saw nothing remarkable in it. For the first time, Constantine thought to wonder by how much the world now was different from the one he'd known.

"Sergeant, you can't!" George said. "It's a miracle — you saw it yourself!"

"There's no room in the world for miracles," Pappas said. "They cause too much trouble."

Constantine knew a death sentence when he heard one. He tensed, ready to throw himself at the man who dared to try to set himself against divine will. George shouted, "No!" and raised his own gun.

The soldier with Pappas had stood so quietly that Constantine hardly noticed him. Now he fired. By some devilish trick, his weapon shot again and again and again, so fast the muzzle flashes nearly blurred together and the reports merged into a quick, stuttering roar.

George spun backwards and crashed to the floor, as if hammered by a giant's fist. His gun spun away. Even as Constantine knelt beside him, he knew he was dead. No man could live with half a dozen great holes in his chest and belly. The twin stinks of blood and dung rose from the body.

"He was your comrade," the Emperor said, not rising.

"He was not of my faction," Pappas said coolly. Constantine's lips quirked. In some ways, the world had not changed after all. Faction was always the besetting curse of the Greeks, whether they called themselves Hellenes or Romans.

"So you killed him. Greeks haven't changed at all." As the Emperor spoke, he sprang at Pappas. He'd fought the Turks with everything he had; he would not tamely yield to death now. And having granted him this new life, would God desert him now?

Yannis Pappas clicked a fresh magazine into his assault rifle. "Let's get out of here, Taso," he said. Kiapos nodded. They stepped over the two bleeding corpses. There was still mopping up to do.

THE SHAFT

by David J. Schow

I made it to the rail just in time to watch Chiquita destroy an aluminum umbrella table, face-first, five stories below the balcony on which I stood. She missed the pool by a good ten feet. Until I saw her brains splatter all over the sun deck I hadn't realized she'd *had* any. Then the shit really started flying, and as Rosie says, when the shit starts flying you gotta be careful you don't inhale none.

That's how I wound up in this sleazoid dump right in the bowel of Chi-fucking-cago, this winner of the Cockroach Club's Tenement of the Year Award, pushing nose candy at high school dips and sweating out centuries waiting for a goddamn phone call from Rosie. That's how I wound up peering down a hole — another five-story drop, easy — and thinking, Jesus, man, somebody could *die* down there.

I remember Rosie's reaction even clearer than Chiquita's swan dive. A textbook of cool in a shitstorm, that dude. He humped across the hotel suite on that bum leg of his, his face milk-white, and hustled me into the nearest vacant bedroom while the other party animals were still puzzling out what had gone down, I mean, besides Chiquita. I'd dared her to jump — but hey, it wasn't *my* fault; it was just the Peruvian flake being mischievous. Rosie made a hurried, whispered phone call. Then he crushed a fist-load of damp Franklin notes into my hand and told me my ass was bound for Chicago.

Why? Because Chiquita was spread all over the poolside terrace on my dare, and she was Emilio's latest squiff, and Emilio would be jacked off enough about this little interruption in his sex life to have my bones broken in alphabetical order if he found me acting casual around the suite when he arrived. You know, nonchalant, a cold Chivas in one hand and a warm tit in the other, sucking up the comp snow and the beam-screen movies? Not cool. He'd bounce me out the window and I'd join Chiquita the way peanut butter joins jelly when you squish the bread together. And if I didn't tear ass out of there pronto, Rosie would help Emilio chuck me over the side, because that's the way the pecking order works. I understood. *No hard feelings, huh kid?* Splat.

Emilio's talent for making his rivals evaporate without even leaving ashes was legendary, and Rosie and I both knew he could probably perform the same trick on anybody who crossed him. I didn't want to find out how it was done. Luckily for me, Rosie had the whole scenario scoped out in seconds. He made his pitch superfast: "Listen, Cruz. I like you. You're a primo runner and I don't want to see you become history. I know this guy in Chi; you can go north and hole with him." Rosie was the only guy I'd ever heard call Chicago *Chi.* He was kind of old-fashioned, but he dealt straight with me and I looked up to him, I guess. "I'll grease Emilio

THE SHAFT

out," he told me. "Couple of months, no heat, I'll bring you back in. Emilio'll cool out once he gets a new bitch. But now you've got to get the fuck out of here, before the shit starts flying."

"Don't wanna inhale none," I said, and he returned a sad kind of grin. I knew he was pleased I'd picked up one of his pet expressions; it made him feel like my mentor. I try not to be a bad guy, you know what I mean?

I caught a cab and left my apartment phone ringing. It might be one of Emilio's bad boys, sniffing already. A few hours later I was freezing my *cojones* off at O'Hare Airport. For the record, O'Hare really sucks the canary. Baggage claim is in the next area code from where you debark. I had no bags to claim, but no idea where to wander. I'd never been a fugitive before.

I finally located Rosie's pal, Bauhaus, tucked inside a cherry-red Corvette that was sitting in the loading zone with the heater running. Man, that car must've had eighty coats of lacquer; it looked as though it had been dipped in blood-colored liquid glass. Bauhaus was large and fleshy-pale. He chuckled at my clothes. Big joke. "We need to *pro-cure* you an overcoat, boy, if you're planning on staying in this distribution zone for a spell."

I grunted because I didn't want this asshole in the Giorgio Armani suit to know my teeth were trying to chatter the beat to that Asexuals classic, "Mister Useless." Once my legs warmed up, I looked at him and said, "So why Chicago?" I'd been dying to ask somebody that. "And don't call me *boy*."

"Sorry," he said, eyes front, no handshake. "Off on the wrong toe. Let's start over." He rummaged around inside his sheepskin coat. "Thai stick?"

I took it from him and fired up. All I'd had since Chiquita's big dive had been a couple of those teeny bottles of Johnny Walker Red and a toot or two in the can, on the plane. I welcomed a draft of sweet smoke. Bauhaus refused my pass and dug out a silver breast pocket flask with a blued dent in the cap. "Got my own insulation," he said, uncapping and swigging and chuckling again. Jolly dude, this Bauhaus.

We zipped past a lit-up welcome sign featuring the mayor's signature in two-foot high script. After a few inbound miles, Bauhaus said, "I'll tell you why-Chicago, my man. I got another boy — man, excuse — a runner by the handle of Nugget Astaire. Nugget is currently in the slam for porking some fourteen-year-old high school squack from Oakdale. They take Ash Wednesday *seriously* down there, dude. It's a dry township. No liquor stores, no sense of humor, and a jailbait offense is the pits there. It doesn't matter that the chick was totally blasted out of her gourd on cokesmoke and Lite beer. She and Nugget did it four times on the coffee table and her parents walked in on the climax of Act Five. She wins a bellyfull of bambino — strictly dark meat, you hear what I'm saying? — and Mommy and Daddy, being staunch local God freaks, don't know what in hell to do except maybe lock her up in a nunnery after she drops. So Nugget's a gone gofer, because even if I could slide him free, I couldn't run him in Oakdale again . . . and the Oakdale High footballers need their dope to go ten-for-ten again this season."

I held in my toke and grimaced affirmatively. Rosie had a way with logistics, making something that was useless in one place real important in some other place. And that is how I came to be subsisting in this scuzz-dump, staring down this particular hole.

The building super told me it was a ventilation shaft. I didn't see how the hell it could ventilate anything, unless maybe you wanted to catch a whiff of your nearest neighbor's potty waft. By standing in the bathtub, you can look

89

out a two-by-one casement window, across the drop, at another sealed-up bathroom window about ten feet away. Staggered above and below are other bathroom windows on all three sides, black and cataracted the way windows next to the shower always get, foggy with mildew and rot and soap-scum. The shaft is lined with rusty corrugated steel. Whenever anyone in the building bathes, you can hear a tinny dripping noise. From my fourth-floor vantage it was impossible to make out the bottom of the shaft, even with a flashlight, but it must've been lousy with mulch and bilge and toilet leakage. It was an iron-pumper's task to pry the damned window open even halfway, and when I did I sucked in a smell kind of like humid fertilizer. It was impossibly dark in there, and suffocatingly close; you couldn't see a bloody thing up or down. The mouth of the shaft, up on the roof, was tarped over because of the snowfall. "Ventilation," right.

From his hairy nose wart to his webbed feet (his wino style Converse All-Stars looked like toe-goo city, if you hear what I'm saying), Freddy the super was a total pusbag. And I was beginning to have revised thoughts about my good pal Bauhaus, who had set me up in less than palatial splendor. A whole week of dead, damned nothing had wasted itself without a peep from Rosie. I was unveiled as the new runner to some of the Oakdale boys (a Yuppified zoo of blond-on-blond *palomitas* with firm handshakes, PR grins and eyes like TV sets tuned to static snow). After that, the only times I saw Bauhaus were to either drop off cash or collect new dope. After ten days, I was getting high off my own supply — a business no-no, and always a depressing state. But my ass was bored fartless.

I first heard the building's ghost moaning one day after I'd powered up on powder and decided to start cleaning

my bathroom like a maniac. Coke makes your senses more acute; it gives you an edge. You fine-tune instead of getting stuporous. I focused my ears and the sound became . . . well, the sort of deep-gut, belly-hugging groan an alley drinker makes after blowing a quart of Thunderbird out of an empty stomach. There was a riot of peripheral noise in Freddy's four-story fire hazard tonight — battling stereos, slamming doors, Hispanic delinquents charging up and down the stairs, the black-and-tan newlyweds next door slapping each other toward court. Some derelict old white motherfucker downstairs was bitching about how the Jews were overrunning the country "like rabid rats, storming a ghetto!" Typical Saturday night action. Yet past all this interference I could still pick out that low, creepy moan. It really started to bug me. And I'm a tolerant guy.

I dug my fingers into my temples, rubbing. Then the phone went off. Instant migraine. I was hoping for Rosie and got Bauhaus: "Say, boy, how's yer hammer hangin'?"

Some righteous coke freaks experience hallucinations with what doctors call a "clear sensorium." Whatever your mind invents for your eyes to see *looks* correct because it's not overtly weird, just like when you do acid and see chartreuse-plaid, Jello-breathing neon dragons. One dude I knew got it into his head that there were tiny spiders crawling all over his skin. Normal tiny spiders, lots of them. It was perfectly believable. When he found he couldn't brush them away, he tried to burn them off his arms and legs with a propane torch. Like I said, I *knew* this guy, past tense. But I also knew the moaning sound was real; my brain had not manufactured it. I know what planet I'm on, and I'm not a drooling drug addict. And the awareness of that subtle, almost subaural distraction began eating into the back of my skull like a runaway dentist's drill. On top of this, I had to suffer Bauhaus: "Well, my Chrysler's all fixed. Even got new keys. How 'bout that?" It was a moronic code — a new stash was in. I'm sure Bauhaus loved playing the Man from B.L.O.W.

Again, that vague hint of a moan, of something in nearly silent agony, like cries for help in the middle of the night no one ever answers. It cut past everything else and locked my head up in a woodworker's vise of pain. "Hang on a second," I said, dumping the phone onto the bed since the cord would not reach to the bathroom. In there was the only window that wasn't iced shut, the one looking out into the air shaft, and I smacked the frame with the heel of my hand until the crookedly-mounted, rotting casement squeaked reluctantly open. Then I shouted out into that tunnel of metal amplification loud enough to hoarsen my tonsils: *"Shut the fuck up!"*

There followed that single beat of dead silence that comes between the time you smash your thumb with a hammer and the time you howl. Then, the whole building responded. The salsa music chugging forth from the floor below was cranked up a good twenty decibels. Babies screamed. The scaly anti-Semite laid into the topic of young, disrespectful, snot-nosed, loudmouthed shitheels. The musclebound black badass next door yelled for me to come on over and make him.

Then my body surprised me by yanking my head back into the bathroom, posthaste. The stench in the shaft was Jesus-Christ-putrid tonight; it had been like sticking my face into the chimney of a crematorium. Something had *died* down there, for sure. Something big, and from the smell, rotting merrily away. I know how dead stuff stinks. I found a dead mouse trapped in the works underneath my fridge once in Miami. Here, the upward-drafting febrile odor was similar, but fifty degrees

riper. My face closed up all ports in a tight pucker. Even my shocked pores snapped shut. I started whacking the window down to choke off the smell, and it skewed in its track and jammed. This was just frustrating enough to kick my brain over into panic-button cocaine overdrive, and I bashed that fucker solid with my fist, pretending it was the anthropoid skull of the lip-moving asshole next door. Bash, bash, paint slivers jumped away and *bash!* the window banged shut, tight as an airlock, with a bloody handprint on top of it.

I was sweating and panting now. The individual pepperonis off my dinner pizza were fighting to grease their way up for an encore. But the moaning had stopped. I could deal with my headache, with that slug Bauhaus, with all the other shit minutiae of my life.

Rats, I thought. *Sure, rats. Maybe they crawled into the sump to eat, and drowned down there.*

But what about the ghost? The phone was still upside-down in a tangle of blankets on the bed. It had a rotary dial; Bauhaus had been too cheap to spring for a touch-tone. With a pointed sigh instead of formalities, I said, "When and where?" I was disgusted now; I ached. Let Emilio pummel the snot out of me. It'd be worth it just to flip Chicago the goodbye birdie. As Bauhaus began to encode his ETA and coordinates, I overrode him. "Wait a sec — you run any girls, Bauhaus?"

He groaned a prissy bitch of a groan. *"Jeeezus,* Cruz! Don't talk shit like that on the *phone,* man, I might be bugged!"

Or a cat. Maybe a cat fell in and the rats bit him to death. A big cat . . .

I knew full well no one was listening to our conversation except the good and bad demons of Bauhaus's impoverished conscience. "Don't dick away my time," I snapped, itchy now. "You're throwing me a bonus tonight, and don't feed me any smoke, because you can afford a party girl. And she'd better not have

91

any diseases whose names are, like, acronyms, you hear what I'm saying? Otherwise, you can pound your stash up your loading dock with a mallet." I hung up.

My ears strained. No ghost. There was nothing now but the drumming of my headache.

Awhile later, Bauhaus made my walking weight heavier by half a kilo of the white stuff — a guaranteed felony bust for dealing, should anyone wearing a badge pat me down. Before I could work up a good invective about his mother, he tossed me the keys to an '83 Camaro with snow tires and 35,000 miles on the odometer. *No hard feelings, huh kid?* My rented date waited for me in the suicide seat, next to a jug of Chivas that Bauhaus had popped for, gratis. Rosie must have told him. Thank God for Rosie.

Downtown Chicago wasn't worth the drive between blizzards. Cruising Oakdale would be like checking out the bondage action at a Bible study meet. I didn't particularly want to get drunk. Tomorrow was a school day for me.

The girl bit me, giggled, and gave her name as Drea. She had a purple streak job, Isis eye paint, a Madonna album's worth of tramped-out rock 'n' roll lace, and fantastic legs. I made her keep her spikes on while we did it. After she had freebased herself up into the ionosphere, she wrapped those legs around yours truly and made vigorous use of an extremely motile pelvis. She was better than any of Emilio's aerobicized bimbos, and she talked about oddball stuff like auras, and tarot cards, and Buddhist chanting in between times. While she went to the john, I checked out her bag. Mixed amid a nightmarish jumble of cosmetics, I found a pinky vial barely dusted with lees of coke, a plastic case of good old Ortho-Novum, and an Illinois state ID that assured me I had not made the same error in judgment as my predecessor, Nugget Astaire. Her

name was really Loretta, and she had turned 22 three weeks ago. The ID mugshot made her look green, like one of the living dead. I refilled her amber cocaine vial from my fresh stock and tucked it back into her bag, to be discovered later as a belated birthday gift. Like I said, I try not to be a bad guy.

Later, as she was dozing on top of me with what was left of my last erection easing out of her, slowly, slowly, I said, "Did you hear that?"

"Mm." She slitted her eyes open. "Hear what?"

"That sound. Kind of a moan." It teased the limits of my perception, and I tried to approximate it for her.

"I don't hear anything except that fucking samba music." She rolled over and lost me. "Oops — sorry."

My slight fix on the ghost noise was erased by the lunatic calliope rhythm and abrasive Latino singing penetrating the floorboards. Drea pushed her ass into my lap, spoon-style, and gave me a place to warm my hands. Outside, past the thick condensation fogging my windows, snowflakes as big as my palm began to meander down from the sky to bury the city.

My first taste of bonafide snow was pretty comical. After four straight weeks of what the imbeciles on the news here called "medium to light flurries," my neighborhood had become a Dantean vision of the Arctic Circle. Lumbering automobiles skidded ass-sideways into each other, providing a lot of employment for Chicago's fender, body, and paint people. Dead black slush, like concentrated air pollution mix, obliterated the curbing while the sidewalks simply vanished beneath a four-foot snowpack that settled into solid ice. Pedestrians pretended it was nothing abnormal. Cursing, they teakettled about and broke their bones. No big deal. Everybody slouched along, muffled into anonymity, necks bowed by

92

the forces of nature, defeated and pissed off, avoiding eye contact and snarling at all comers — the Chicagoan in full wintertime flower. It was positively medieval.

I got the use of Drea three times a week, once for each cash drop. Bauhaus seemed to think this little perk compensated for sticking me with far more dope than I was comfortable holding. There was more snow inside my rathole than out.

Gradually, I became convinced that the moaning noise was actually coming from the airshaft, as though the shaft itself was haunted. When I finally got convinced enough to batter open the bathroom window again, to check, it stopped for good.

For reasons I do not totally understand, I didn't flash on this fact until I was making it with Drea. I actually stopped in mid-stroke to say, "It's gone." The silence in the building flooded full-blast into my skull.

She sucked in a breathy gasp. *"What?"* Her eyes went wide and started scanning around for the police.

"Our ghost. He's gone. Guess he decided to vacate."

Her expression fired up, to hover midway between short-fused anger and utter disbelief. "Jesus *Christ,* Cruz!" She rearranged herself and began a direct assault — the fed-up leading the retarded. "Look — the only thing I want going bump in the night is you."

I pondered the fate of my ghost until Drea started squirming around. Then I forgot it, and did some moaning of my own.

As was her habit by now, Drea recharged her coke vial from the open kilo bag in the second drawer of my dresser. It was part of her preparing-to-leave ritual. By this time she hesitated at the door, and turned back to kiss me. I think I gaped.

"I kinda like you, Cruz," she said in nearly complete innocence. "You're nothing like some of the pigs Bauhaus has made me fuck. I like listening to you talk; you never talk about *normal* shit. You talk about ghosts in the building and how all the geezers tramping around in the snow look like their bulldogs. It's . . . I dunno. Kinda poetical."

This really whacked me. it sounded too much like a roundabout farewell. *It's been fun, hon, but . . .* I grabbed her by the forearms. "What the hell is wrong with you?"

Without even a pause for dramatic effect, she said, "Bauhaus is setting you up." Her matter-of-factness scared up gooseflesh all over my back. "I heard him on the phone. He said, 'Tell him I'm gonna take care of Cruz, tonight.'"

She shrugged. "Somebody in Miami."

I thought of the Lady and the Tiger. If he'd been talking to Rosie, then his remark was innocuous enough, even benevolent. But if that wimp prick had said the same thing to Emilio . . .

"Listen, Drea, I need you to find out for me —"

She shied instantly, eyes glazing with fear. "Too late. I gotta go now, Cruz. I'm sorry." And she pulled away.

"Why? What's gonna go down?"

"I dunno — I just gotta go, *now,* that's all!" She was definitely scared. Now.

Now. I checked the window, scoping out the street below. My Camaro was parked half-under a snowbank thoughtfully provided by some plow pilot with piss-poor aim.

"Sorry, Cruz," I heard her repeat, feebly, before the door closed. Whatever was coming up, she'd pushed herself over the borderline by warning me, and needed to insure her own safety in the approaching shitstorm. I understood that. She didn't want to inhale none. I stayed posted at the window until I saw her crunch hurriedly out into the 2 A.M. snowfall.

Thirty seconds after she rounded the corner, a pair of Metro cop cars crept from opposite ends of the street like stalking wolves, and rendezvoused beside the Camaro. A dark, burly police shape wiped off my license plate and then looked up toward Freddy's building. His line of sight was targeted two windows north of my position.

Thirty-two thousand dollars worth of refined cocaine, more or less, was sitting in a drawer five feet away from me. Screw "street value"; that bullshit is just to make drug busts sound more impressive on the evening news. It all rushed together to make a picture in my head, and my heart fell down and went boom. As I watched three uniformed cops head for the downstairs door, I knew the one place I did not want to be was on television.

If I tried to flush the whole kilo, my ass might really be out to the wind. What about the plastic bag? Could a whole kilo clog the pipes? I couldn't take the chance, and didn't trust Freddy's Cro-Magnon plumbing. If I could successfully ditch the stash, I could make my normal morning rounds and use the cash to buy my way out of town. I could also make a pit-stop at the pawnshop, and buy a piece of large enough caliber to blow Bauhaus's fucking brains all over his cherry-red pussywagon before I went on an extended leave.

There was no time for a passionate review of my options. They were already clumping up the stairs. I scooped the heavy baggie out of the drawer and dumped it into a plastic trashcan liner. I yanked the adhesive strip, sealed it and dumped it inside another, then sealed the whole package into a third. If water gets on coke, you might as well try to peddle cooking fat. I swabbed out Drea's sloppings in the drawer with a handful of moist paper towels. Those I flushed down the toilet along with two fingers of Panama Red from my smokebox. I took the plastic package (which was now watertight, I hoped) and

dropped it (gently, I hoped) down the air shaft. It splashed when it hit bottom, far away, and I prayed there had been nothing sharp waiting down there to jab a hole in it. I heaved the window down and blew away the paint and wood flakes. I made sure the shower curtain was drawn.

The cops outside heard my toilet tank refilling. Sometimes the plunge handle sticks and the damned thing runs and runs until you jiggle it. "Good morning," I said with a smile. My manner told them I'd run around this track plenty of times and knew the drill. But the sound of my toilet tank told they'd missed instead of hit. I could read the expressions they traded. That's why I was smiling.

The only way to get to the bottom of the air shaft at 2:30 in the morning was through the bathroom window.

There was no time to wait until sunrise and visit a hardware store in search of a do-it-yourself fire-escape ladder. By morning, Bauhaus would know I was still loose, and by lunchtime he'd set a better trap into motion.

Likewise, I couldn't go downstairs and start rapping on doors to see if I could crawl through on a lower floor. As far as I knew, the building had no vacancies, and even knocking on an empty apartment door might rouse the curious.

I thought instantly of Freddy the super.

He was not in residence here; I think it was too clean for him. But he maintained a seedy office in the basement near the laundry room. I'd signed a bullshit lease down there. Nobody used the laundry room now; it was like the inside of a glacier, locked solid with ice at the terminus of a frozen tunnel. I recalled a circular power saw that had been sitting on Freddy's desk. If there were power tools among the junk and salvage ferreted away down there, maybe there was something I could use as a rope. Or maybe Freddy had a secret hatch leading into the shaft.

I shrugged into my fatigue jacket, patting the side pocket to make sure my roll of duct tape was still there (Trust me: nobody in the dope trade lacks duct tape; it has a million uses.) The only building noises at this time of night on a weekday were half-hearted — the after-bar-hours domestic punch-outs, TV noise from behind triple-locked doors, the occasional burglary in progress.

I made a crosshatch pattern of tape on the window of Freddy's office door, then planted my elbow sharply into the X, dead center. The tape web sagged quietly into my grasp, laden with fractured glass. In seconds I was in.

Three minutes later, I was out, carrying two figure-eight coils of heavy-duty electrical extension cord, one 25-foot length, and a 50-footer with plug-mold outlets every ten feet. Both were sheathed in that groove-textured, bright orange insulation that made the wire more durable and bulked it out to a diameter of about half an inch. It was the strongest, most practical stuff I could find for my needs down in Freddy's fetid garbage dump lair.

After ditching the 50-footer in my room, I tied one end of the shorter cord to the banister and unreeled it down into the rectangular void separating the stairwells. It uncoiled in snaky twists and turns. I went down two flights, light-footedly so as to keep my business to myself, wound the cord double around my right forearm, and performed a slow pull-up. The anchor banister creaked like the front door of a haunted house (I thought of my missing ghost), the cord went taut and arrow-straight, and my feet met the risers again. I grabbed above the slack and repeated, counting off slowly to thirty while I dangled there. The cord did not stretch under my 155 pounds. I wiggled

around and the only length I gained was due to the insulation taking a firmer bite on the rail, tightening. I stopped before the goddamned banister could come crashing down on me in splinters and chaos. I felt I could trust this stuff to a two-way climb. As if I had a choice.

Back in my room, I knotted the cords together and tied large, pretzel-shaped climbing loops every five feet. I traded my track shoes for a pair of steel-toed, gum-soled boots Drea had advised me to get for hoofing around in the snow. Before pounding my bathroom window open again, I slipped on a pair of yellow leather trucker's gloves (I'd finally learned my lesson after bruising the heel of my hand). It took a bit more violence than usual to chock the window up all the way, and when I'd forced the cramped access full open, I snugged the glove-pulls around my wrists, for climbing.

I peered down into the black nothingness; it was the first time I'd been able to fit my head and shoulders all the way out. Darkness swallowed my breath vapor two feet beyond my nose. I wanted a backup light, in case I did something stupid, like drop my nightstick flashlight into the water I knew was waiting below. I settled on stuffing one of the Army coat's big tub pockets with candles and wooden matches. I secured the baton light to one of my belt loops by threading a shoelace through the ring on its butt. Just call me Tenzing Norgay.

The eagle-claw feet of the bathtub were permanently bolted to the decaying floor tiles, and the tub was heavy and immovable enough to provide a solid, reliable tie-off. I choke-knotted the cord around the closest foot and fed my line out the window a few feet at a time. A cockroach, irate at my intrusion on his under-the-tub domain, decided to make a run for it and I pulped him into the treads of my boot as soon as he

95

skittered into the light.

It was five minutes to three in the morning. With luck, my presence in this dump would be history by four. And now it was time to find out just how far down the cord reached.

I cinched the waist drawstring of the fatigue coat tight, zipping and buttoning the front flap. It was going to be chilly as well as damp in the shaft. I turned up the collar and sealed it with the Velcro strips.

Then I stepped up onto the far lip of the tub, put my right leg out the window, and backed out into the air shaft.

Heights don't scare me. The dark doesn't scare me. The close press of the shaft is no threat, because I know it's an illusion, and I'm not a claustrophobe. This was going to be rather like urban caving, and part of me thrilled to the fact I was capable of such extreme lengths.

Going down would be the easy part. My biceps and the extensor muscles of my forearms were up to the work. I tipped outward, braced my toes against the waffled metal, eased my weight backward on the line. And slipped.

Five feet of cord skinned through my hands before I fisted leather around rubber and lurched to a lung-compressing halt. Momentum banged my face against the corrugated steel, scattering shock lightning across my inner eyelids. My heart totally freaked, punching blood furiously through my brain along with an assortment of nasty thoughts on my own abrupt termination, like defective cars smashing together in a freeway pile-up. I hung. I pendulumed. The orange insulation squeaked against the windowsill, dropping paint flakes into my hair like chaff. I kept my eyes squeezed shut and tried to orient by feel.

The rust-browned steel mashing and scraping my ear was uniformly moistened with some kind of slime — prob-

ably snowmelt and particulate dirt, though it seemed more slippery than plain water. If I was going to play Batman and live, I'd have to step more cautiously. I was going to lose time by being careful. I reestablished my footholds, toeing-in for a solid friction contact with the metal beneath the light coat of lubrication before belaying my full weight backward onto the line again.

My breathing equalized. Calm. Calm. I was okay. I opened my eyes.

I saw I had stopped eight or nine feet below the pale, yellowish light shining out of my bathroom window. In the light, in silhouette, was somebody's head, looking down toward me.

"What the hell are you doing hanging around down there, boy?"

Fear lanced through my lungs, chased by impotent anger. It was Bauhaus. The son of a bitch bastard had come to check up on his foiled bust.

I hung silent. What the fuck could I say?

"Got a little present for you," he went on, as though I was sitting in my easy chair, in the light, and not starting to sweat about doing a Chiquita. "It's a gift from your old boss, Emilio — who don't like people doing sneakery behind his back." A musical clinking noise echoed coldly in the shaft. It was a sound I recognized far too readily, from the past hassles of my life. Bauhaus had just flicked open a Manila Folder — one of those knives with the hinged and ventilated brass handles.

He was out of my reach by two body lengths.

"It took longer to finish off Rosie in this place than we thought," he said. "But tonight you finally get *your* turn."

"What about Rosie?" I husked, my desperation starting to boil over in an unseemly, messy fashion. "Rosie's here?"

"Not no more, boy." Bauhaus grinned. I think. I couldn't really tell in the useless light. Then he sliced through my extension cord. That part I didn't have to see.

The tension on the line vanished. Air rushed past my head, the steel wall tilted madly away, and I fell like a meteor with the wire still fisted up in both hands. My mouth was wide open. I did a complete backward somersault before hitting the bottom of the shaft at full speed. *Splat.*

It was not a nightmare. When I cracked my eyes open, I knew I was not lying in bed. Bed was warm.

Cold. Then pain, ramming up to full volume, maxing-out my consciousness. Then wetness, edged with ice. Blunted perception of my head split open and crammed full of permafrost and spiders and razor cubes of glass. Too much to fit, head bursting, hard, sharp things jammed into my back, pushing me out of shape. Movement a joke. Darkness hurts eyes.

I think something is broken, then I die. Many somethings.

The well-bottom acoustics woke me the second time. The tendons and ligaments tying my head to my trunk felt as if some sadistic surgeon had torn them out, salted and fried them until they shriveled, then stuffed them back in in the wrong order and sutured up the entry cut with a staple gun. All around me was the suffocating, empty blackness, no illusion now, and the sound of dripping gunk.

My pulverized right arm was a dully pulsing firebrand of junk. It did not respond to my brain's commands — it was a total disconnect. It hardly hurt at all.

Left-handed, I pawed clumsily for my flashlight, and found the baton bent into a crooked U-shape around my shattered ribs. Useless. My internal organs felt like a bagful of flattened aluminum cans. It seemed to take an hour of darkness to dig out one of my candles, and I lost a handful of matches when a spasm of pain shuddered the shit out

of me without warning. I thought of my intestines blowing on impact and loading my pants. I couldn't tell anything past wave after wave of stupefying pain, and when I dropped the matches I cried.

Finally, later, I scratched one alight and held it in my teeth while fishing out a candle stub. My pupils recoiled from the sharp dazzle. More new pain. I burnt my lips, top and bottom. But I did it.

I was propped on my back, facing up, submerged from the navel down in two feet of murky, brown bilge water filling a concrete trough afloat with orts of crap that had all festered to unrecognizability. A loop of extension cord lay curled across my chest. I was tilted at about a thirty-degree angle on top of something like a big packing crate, which had broken my fall and I think my spine. I couldn't feel either of my legs — just blistering green pain starting at asshole level and scorching up through the ceiling of my skull. I thought of Drea, entwining her legs around me. I cried again.

A broad spear of split wood slatting jutted up through the torn right sleeve of my jacket. I could see the fresher-colored wood inside the break. It had dried blood on it. I had been tuned out for quite awhile. I was gone. Emilio's long arm had erased me the way I'd squished that poor fucking roach. I felt like a bug under a dropped safe.

On the opposite side of the shaft, just above the waterline, was what might have been a sub-basement window at one time. Now it was blocked up with a riveted steel shutter. Maybe it was Freddy's private entrance. Maybe he crawled down here to geek pigeons or sodomize pre-schoolers.

No rats. No dead cats.

It was pretty clear that any attempt to locomote would turn me face-down into the slime, and I didn't hanker to die *that* way, thanks. I watched my candle stub burn. After the two additional ones in my left pocket, my light was *finito.*

Bobbing next to my dead right arm I saw my miniature life raft of nose candy. It was seaworthy, after all. I think my heart gave a thump of hope, but it felt like something else bursting wetly inside me. I gagged up bright red froth.

My body was clocking out and I had to *do* something.

Gently, I nudged the circlet of wire off my chest to lasso my buoyant package and tow it closer. Every motion caused a dizzying jolt of pain, or threatened to plummet me back into blackout land. I could have manipulated it for a painstaking hour or two, I don't know, but ultimately I captured it and pulled it up one-handed. It weighed two thousand pounds, easy. I tugged down the zipper on my coat and stuffed the parcel where it could not fall back into the water, then I touched the candle flame to an upper corner and watched the four layers of plastic brown and separate, yawning open like a bloodless wound. I stationed the candle on the juncture of zipper teeth, and scooped up a handful of blow, enough to fill Drea's pinky vial to the brim a hundred times. I cupped it into my face and respirated as much as I could before winking out. I needed a clear sensorium.

. . . gotta make sure you don't inhale none . . .

Rosie's voice was only in my head as I slid back from Oz. I made a noise that echoed in the vertical tunnel, a life-asserting grunt of pitiful weakness. It was all I could muster.

My candle had abandoned its post, rolling off and gone under. But like I said, the dark doesn't scare me. So what *was* I afraid of? I feared getting busted, either by iguana-eyed, trigger-happy cops, or by falling four stories and becoming very broken. I'm afraid of be-

trayal. Of getting shafted, ho, ho, ho.

I used my left hand to feel around beneath the surface for my candlestub. It was easier than trying to wrestle out a fresh one. I came up with several shards of busted wood so waterlogged that they sank as soon as I dropped them back. Then my fingers closed around something long and round, with a knoblike bump at one end, too smooth to be another chunk of the crate I'd obliterated with my body. It was hard and light; I laid it across my chest and struck a new match. It was a porous and glistening bone. An ulna — the longer of the two crossed forearm bones. Once upon a time the bump on the end had been somebody's elbow. I stopped breathing.

"Owww — *shit!*" The match that had just blackened my fingertips fell and hissed out in the thick brown water. The darkness gushed back in and afterimages of the bone danced on the air. It was the sick ochre color of diseased eyes, and had tough little strings of meat still clinging to it. I slammed my eyes shut and could still see it, hovering, dissolving to yellow motes at the edges; when I opened them again there was only the plunging, time-elongating void . . . and an ugly catalogue of my friend Rosie's possible fates.

The water moved. It rolled heavily up toward my face, floating the bone free and then receding in a massy, tidal movement, the way a full bathtub shifts when you climb in.

Something big had just changed position in the sump at the far end of the shaft. The deep end of the pool.

I tried to butt past my own pain, and dug for more matches, more light, fast, my breath whimpering out. All I could think of was Rosie, trapped down here with something that made him into a skeleton. Something big.

He might drift in and out of consciousness, moaning. Making weak, pallid sounds nobody could really hear, because nobody paid attention that close. Nobody, at least, who wasn't using a controlled substance to sharpen his senses.

The match sputtered as I touched it to the wick of the second candle. The water was still rippling, and now I could see that the metal shutter across from me was halfway open. It looked like a way out. *Screw it,* I thought, sudden fear engulfing me to the nostrils and encouraging me to be reckless. My imagination was huffing and straining and doing a great job of making me crazy. But if I couldn't haul my dead ass over there on one arm through a measly two feet of sewage, then I didn't deserve to get out, did I?

I perched my candle on the blood-stained spur of wood. And did it.

I figured my legs would be dead weight, more or less like my pulped arm. I figured wrong. Below the knees I didn't have legs anymore. When I sloshed over sideways to kiss the filthy water, one of them broke the surface and I saw that my thigh ended in a coagulate stump.

The kilo gab wormed from my coat, splashed, and sank. White paste corkscrewed around on the oily surface of the water, like powdered creamer dissolving into coffee.

In the flickering candlelight, I hefted my body onto my good arm and looked up into a bullet-shaped, eyeless head that had nosed out of the water between me and the hatchway. It was the girth of a Navy torpedo, and so was the triangular, turd-colored body that uncoiled behind it and sent greasy waves slopping against the walls of the shaft. The shadows lurched as the water lapped against the spur of wood, then disappeared altogether as the candle tumbled and splashed.

Too many drugs scampered around in my head *too many* like a scorpion stinging itself to death in mad circles *too many fucking drugs, Cruz!*

I screamed for help in the wet darkness then, or tried to scream, coughing up mushy chunks of my lungs barely flavored with what was left of my voice. That's when the blunt face darted in to bite me. Twice. Needle punctures stung me in the kidneys. I yelled as best I could as my hand skidded in the muck, submerging my face. I pushed back up immediately . . . and then noticed I could barely feel my left arm, my *good* arm, anymore. All my pain started to blot away behind a pleasing, novocaine numbness that spread gently up toward my eyes to cloud them over.

It could only eat a little bit at a time. I understood that, yeah.

Far above me, miles overhead, a tiny yellow rectangle broke the total blackness as someone hammered up their bathroom window. I tried to shout again, but the numbness caressed my larynx and all that came out was a purring noise. A moan.

"Shut the fuck up!" someone shouted, and the window banged shut again, bringing the real world to an ugly end. None of this was happening, not really, nobody would be that rude because I try not to be a bad guy, you know what I mean?

Maybe it was like the spiders, an illusion. Maybe, if I became the ghost now, I'd be following Rosie's lead and everything would get back to normal again.

The cool water closed over my face so I could not see or hear any more. Normal. The sliding, sinuous weight embraced me. I think I smiled.

⊗

99

KNIGHT OF DARKNESS
KNIGHT OF LIGHT

by Michael Rutherford

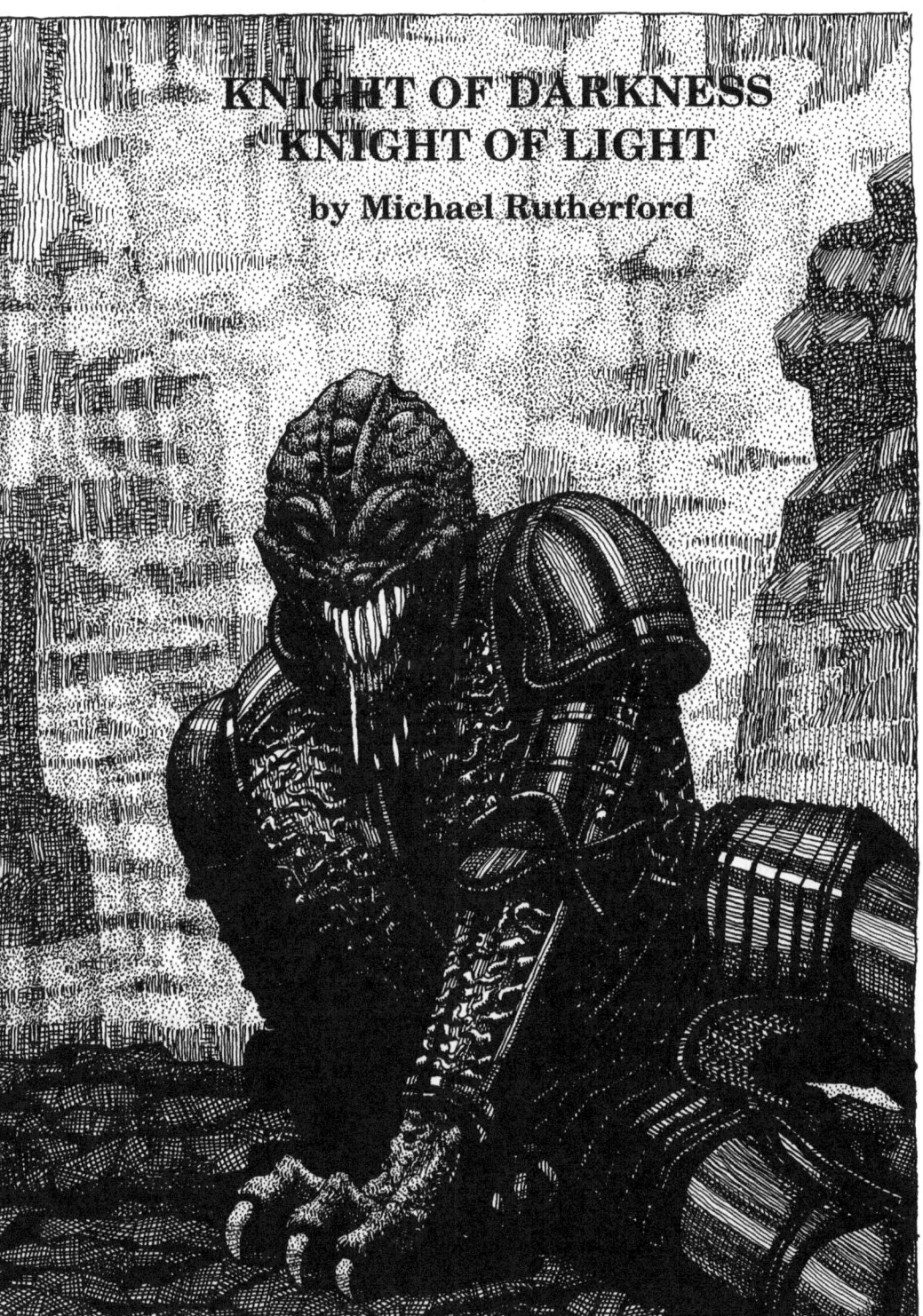

©JANET AULISIO 1989.

Away & Back I

Apollyon, the last Demon Champion, stood in the darkness of the cave. His wife held him without speaking, and only the piping of their children as they pressed against his legs reflected his family's sadness. There was honor in his mission, inevitability in his acceptance. He was submitting his body to a repugnant transformation, his life to a quest as hopeless as it was of desperate necessity. Apollyon bent to his beloved's face, their cold features touched briefly, and he stepped from his family into the circle of the waiting priests.

The sibilant hymns of the Soul-Eaters rose in the high cavern. Bats gave piercing, surprised cries and flapped away. The high priest Druzla raised his arms, the sable vestments of moleskin fell away, and he opened his claws in imprecation: "Oh gods, look with favor upon this noble spirit, the greatest and most generous among us. Give Apollyon luck and wisdom in his painful pilgrimage beneath the odious sun. Look upon us, oh mighty deities of blood, oh wondrous fashioners of spired caverns, oh lords of the enveloping darkness. Grant Apollyon success. Let him bring our dying race its strength again. Look with favor upon this demon's sacrifice."

Then all the circle of mages raised their taloned hands to draw into Apollyon the hoard of magic that the race possessed, the charge of its proud history and the burden of its salvation. The rocks began to sweat and the walls began to crack as power flowed into the circle and wrought Apollyon's transformation.

Finally, the mages of the Soul-Eaters sank to the floor in exhaustion. Only Druzla remained, his robes shielding Apollyon. "It is done," he intoned, and dropped his arms. The champion stood revealed.

Apollyon's wife sobbed against her will. Their children huddled behind her and wept in fear. Where in demon splendor Apollyon had stood, now was a blond man in golden armor. All drew away from him in sadness and disgust.

The Chief Priest handed him a great shield, webbed and pitted with darkness. "To sustain you in the cankered world, we have wrought this shield, graving the history of our race in its surface."

The knight gratefully accepted the boon.

"Remember me as I once was," he said quietly to his wife. The knight bowed to the priests, raised his shield in salute, and strode out the long passage to where a miasma of daylight broke in the mouth of the cave in the Valley of the Bones.

All remembered the nobility that shone through the tragedy of his features.

Away & Back II

Ragnack the warrior, swordmaster, gladiator, bodyguard, weapon instructor, and Terror of the Leather Plains rode his black, raw-boned horse up the narrow trail that creased the saturnine bulk of Desolation Mountain. Heavy rain fell in wind-driven, stinging diagonals. Ragnack cursed his luck, his tongue, and his too quick anger. What had begun as a friendly quarrel with Prince Florimel over the division of spoils from a miserable Glugrud village had ended with the unfortunate decapitation of the Prince. That Ragnack had escaped he owed to the other mercenaries, who saw the Prince's death as a chance to seize the train of Glugrud women Florimel had appropriated for himself.

As the mercenaries of his company fought the dandified regulars of Florimel's house guard, Ragnack took his leave. Ragnack knew that when the quarrel wound down, he would be condemned to the death of the worm pit.

Now as he looked from the mountain's shoulder, Ragnack saw the inevitable pursuit. They were about twenty minutes behind him. Even in the stormy twilight, Ragnack spied the bright livery of the dead Prince's retinue mixed with the raggle-taggle furs and varied equipage of a handful of mercenaries.

Darkness would not fall for an hour. Ragnack's only chance lay in making the pass and then groping down the winding trail into the Valley of Bones thousands of feet below. There, in that ancient battleground of men and demons, among hissing sulphurous rifts and caverns eaten into the greasy rock, Ragnack could hide for a time.

Of such foul repute was the Valley of Bones that Ragnack hoped his pursuers would hesitate to run him to earth once he had reached it. Though it had been centuries since the Soul Eaters had last risen from their sunless world, few ventured to tread past their gate. But Ragnack also knew that the red gold of Prince Florimel's father was a potent charm against superstitious trepidation.

He spurred his horse into the pass. Rain-darkened cliffs rose on either side. Ragnack glanced at the three wide, flat lenses recessed in the rock. Each of the lamps was as broad as a kraken's eye. The lowest was tree-frog green, the middle lens deep orange, and the highest an inevitable blood red.

When the Soul Eaters had swirled out of the rifts of the Valley of Bones to feed on the dreams and loves of both men and elves, the two mutually scornful races had finally pooled the disparate wisdom of their lore. Elven dreamers, glance bandits, and joy thieves had met with the alchemists, vivisectionists,

and wizards from the Six Nations of men. Together they had fashioned the three warning beacons.

In those troubled times, when the energies of men were devoted to rebuilding the disease-decimated cities and the elves fought their terminal neurasthenia, these beacons flashed in ascending intensity to warn of the next wash of the Soul Eaters. Those acidulous vampires were drawn to the fullest, freest spirits of both elven and human-kind. By sheer weight of numbers, the soul leeches drew away the sustenance of memories, substance of beliefs, the dimensions of love, hope, and desire in all but the strongest.

When the blood light at the top shone brightest, warriors of both races marched to reinforce the pass. In those ancient days, these lamps had marshalled the hosts of good, or at least better. But Ragnack noted that the lights had fallen into disrepair long after the last demons had made their cloven-footed way up to the pass. He kicked the flanks of his rack-breathed mount and turned down the trail to the valley's floor, where night coiled like an awakening snake. And so it was, in his haste, that Ragnack did not see the dim lamps flicker to life behind him and cast brilliance into the dust of the road.

Behind him, he heard the clamor of his pursuers, their triumphant cries as they saw him momentarily in silhouette.

And then his horse fell, its front hooves sliding over the edge of the path. With an agility born of terror, Ragnack sprang off and crashed onto the narrow, stony trail. The horse screamed as it vanished into space and plummeted toward the canyon floor.

But Ragnack's hunters also heard the crippled scrabble of his armor as he pushed himself to a stumbling walk. They hobbled their horses in the pass, laughed at the flicker of the archaic lights, and trotted confidently down the

103

bone-strewn path.

As Ragnack heard their taunting hoots, he struggled to regain his senses. The cliff dropped away at his right shoulder. The trail narrowed to a thread of stone. The ragged mercenaries and equally greedy fops of Prince Florimel goaded each other on. Ragnack absently wondered where they would hang his head and how long it would take the jackdaws to reduce it to a bleached skull. He'd dive into the Valley of Bones rather than be taken, he decided. He threw himself down the precipitous, cankered way without regard to his own safety. Finally he spun around a bulge in the cliff and smashed into a shining knight striding up the path.

There was surprise on the blond warrior's handsome face (but no unmanly fear) as he teetered on the edge of the path. He milled his arms, and his gauntlets flew away like lost stars.

To Ragnack's everlasting amazement, with enemies at his back, he found himself reaching out as the knight began to fall, and he caught one of the stranger's bare hands.

Pain boiled up his arm. The world became a cornucopia of darkness, an inkpot of compounded bitterness that made his pursuit casual and wholesome. As Ragnack conjured the knight out of the air, he saw the flesh dissolve from its hand and three dark talons stab into his wrist. With a thew-popping yank, Ragnack heaved the abomination back onto the trail and fell beside it. He stared into the amber flicker that mimicked eyes. What there were of lips drew back in a fanged smile. A scaly limpet of a tongue flicked out once, its tip a sucker rimmed with teeth.

The huzzahs of the ragged band of ruffians rolled down the rocks. They were close enough for Ragnack to smell the pitchy smoke of their torches. The creature cocked its earless head.

"It seems I may repay my debt to you

quite soon," it said. Its tongue seemed to sniff the air, the sucker opening and clenching, the teeth filming with slime. It leaped up, drew its barbed sword, stretched, and turned up the path.

Ragnack weakly stumbled upright to follow. The creature scored Ragnack's breast plate with its talons.

"Stay, friend," it hissed, "I will return for you. Best that you do not see me feed."

That night Ragnack camped with the demon in the Valley of the Bones. The demon had changed back into the form of the knight. Ragnack marveled at the open, honest appearance of his companion. Around them, spasmodic gouts of steam hissed from the rocks, an imitation of the creature's saurian voice. But now, the demon spoke with a voice belled and worthy of its guise.

"You know what I am," the knight told Ragnack, casting another bone into the sputtering fire.

"A woesome, venomous reptile of a creature," Ragnack replied across the flames. He knew that soon he must fight the creature, be sucked dry, and rest with the others here in this dolorous rift.

"A most successful imitation of a man," the knight said, smiling. The face twitched, regained its amiability. "Forgive me. I still cannot quite master this shell."

"Cease your false courtesies," Ragnack told him. He rose and drew his sword. "Better for me to die in hot blood than be soul-shorn."

The knight blandly raised his pale, strong hands, "I am well fed tonight. And I do not violate the bonds of brotherhood."

Ragnack stood bellicose and confused. A familiar stance.

"We shared blood when you pulled me from the air. My nails drank in the pulse of your arm. Any man who lives after we have tasted him, we count kin."

Revulsion crawled on Ragnack's face.

"We are two warriors, separated from our kind," said the knight. "Let us call a truce, talk, and share the beauty of an evening and this place." He smiled with a semblance of sincerity.

Ragnack's eyes washed over the charnel-house floor of the Valley. Things slithered beyond the edge of the fire's illumination in the fractured shale. Raising the sword had renewed the agony of the demon's grasp on his forearm.

"Your wound is almost healed," the knight told him. "Others will see nothing but an honorable scar. There will be no pain, merely a throbbing greeting if we are ever close again."

Ragnack realized the creature had apprehended his thoughts.

"And since we are so close now," Ragnack said bitterly, "will you wander my mind like a stealthy thief in a burgher's house?"

"Though it is painful," the knight answered, "and I would never have wished it, we two have a sympathy that can only be broken by death. We are alone. Let us relax the enmities of our races. Tomorrow, as surely as the wretched sun will rise, we separate to pursue our fates."

"Then you *are* a soul-eater," Ragnack spat, "new-risen to feast on the innocents of the Six Kingdoms, the return of a scourge that ravaged so many centuries ago I thought it legendary."

"We call ourselves the Black Wolves," the knight said with dignity, "and your kind the Blood Sheep. Do you think your pursuers were a host of innocents? The tales I sucked from their hearts made my kind seem generous."

"I am no better than they were," Ragnack said. "My falling-out with that band of pillagers came from my own greed."

"There is more in your blood than you know, solitary knight," his companion told him. "I regret that circumstance has placed you beyond my hunger."

"In the face of such honesty," Ragnack said, "I offer my gratitude."

The moon silvered the floor of the Valley of Bones. Bats flitted over the skeletons and rusted weapons of ancient hosts. The fire itself, feeding on the bones of warriors, brought a truce that sunlight would not tolerate.

Ragnack finally asked, "Why do you bear the form of a man? You seem a worrisome knight, strong, with richly appointed armor; still, I remember the contempt your race has for men."

"I am happy that a warrior perceives me so," the knight said. "I am the repository of my race's magicks, the chief illusion created by a people who once disdained artifice. Our race is dying; I am a scout, a malefactor sent to measure this world and see if we may venture out once more to replenish ourselves. Centuries ago, when we spilled from this valley, devouring all in our path and for decades confounding the armies of elves and men, we took harvest enough, we thought, to hold ourselves these long years. We had so weakened this world that further depredations would bring an end to the flocks we fed on. We retreated deep into our caverns in the semblance of defeat, hoarding our treasure of souls in the glowing mind vats, and resolved only to return when they had been exhausted and this weak world was reborn."

"Then the victories over the Soul Eaters that were sung for generations in the halls of the Six Kingdoms were false," Ragnack blurted.

"Needful illusions," the knight said, nodding. "But the greed and manner of our victory also gave us the illusion of success. As we found, to our sadness, the soul-hoard of our conquest was tainted. We had subdued those principalities too greedy and falsely prideful to unite for the common good against us. True, we possessed souls of power,

105

bravery, and kindness; these are part of every community. But we had driven the souls of quality together, made the wise and great-spirited realize that they must unite against us. And when this host gathered in the last meager corner of the world still free of our terror and turned to march against us, we, satiated, took the treasure we had gathered and hied back to our caverns, to wait for your world to grow sleek and fecund again."

"And you return now," sneered Ragnack, "to survey the numbers of your fleecy sheep."

"I return," the knight said, "to see if I can save my race. There were enough souls of a nourishing tang, that for generations we did not suspect our own gradual decline. Our young must feed on souls, the richness in the hearts of the sun-raised. Though we honor darkness, still we need a measure of light to grow. With each succeeding generation, more and more of our children sickened, withered, and died. Their skin grew pale and pink, the gentle flames of their eyes banked, and their white fangs were thin and loose in their mouths. Finally, with the store of souls low in the vats, we found the brackish, poisoned dregs that stunted the lives of our young. We had taken too great a quantity of diseased souls. In that island of men and elves, where the great-hearted warriors gathered to offer final resistance, where defenseless families from all over the Six Kingdoms had fled to protect their children: there was the reservoir of the spirit that we also needed to give our young."

"Then the Soul Eaters themselves are dying," Ragnack said.

"I may be the last champion of the Black Wolves," the knight said with a grimace. "The final hope that we may still live in darkness."

"How then did you come to your present form?" Ragnack asked with some envy.

"Having grown on the pith of men's dreams, we conceived a form to merit admiration in this world and let me quickly rise to eminence. I appear rich; by your lights, I am fair and strong. I am a fabrication of wizardry and charms. Only if my skin is touched by a man do I briefly revert to my more wholesome self. When I lost my gauntlets and you snatched me from the cliff's edge, our hands met and I became myself. I also wield this blade," the demon raised the black, barbed sword, "a soul-drinker against which no man can stand. And to remind me of my anguished mission, this shield is forged with the rune history of my people." He raised the golden shield: statement and salute. Ragnack saw how the metal drank the light and how darkness welled in its etched surface.

"I walk as a man among men to see if I may somehow force the brave and generous in the sun-scored world into one corner, where my weakened people can feed on them and repopulate the night again. This, my friend, is the mission for which you preserved me. And this one night you have my blessing."

"I too am friendless among men," Ragnack said with a thin smile. "Though foul, you are noble. What difference one demon more or less can make in this wretched world, I cannot imagine. I accept your truce. Weariness conquers my fear. Good night, demon. Sweet sleep, if you do sleep."

"Having taken this form," the knight replied, "I fall prey to its weaknesses. I too must rest. But before we bid good morrow, remember that I have tasted your blood. There is more to your heart than you know. Your rancor is mere loneliness. When you find place and purpose, this ugly world may mean more to you than your own life."

Ragnack grunted at this alien sophistry, laid his bare sword at his side, and slouched to rest. The false knight closed his eyes, lay flat on the greasy rock, and stilled his breath. His shield lay between them; and in the wavering light of the dying fire, Ragnack found that the runes resolved themselves into the long, troubled history of a worthy people.

He first read the curving rim of the shield: scaly warriors of grim and haughty mien hacked down pale ranks of elves and men beneath a squinting sun. Other warriors drove files of captives through long caverns, down to nurseries where newborn ghouls writhed in their worm-beds and mewed hungrily for the milky souls of the sun-dwellers. And Ragnack saw great cities raised in eternal pitchy night, high strong walls built of living rock that joined itself and mortared itself. He saw throngs of demons, Lords and demon Ladies, merchants, singers, servants, and slaves: the variety and teeming activity of a great community. And beyond the walls were farms and fields where the farmers raised the tender fungi. And from the castles issued knights and ladies with the sleek, fierce hunting bats on their wrists, to joyously hunt fireflies. And as Ragnack's eyes moved to the shield's center, he saw the glory of the Black Wolves, the eons when the earth did not turn on its axis and one half of the world was frozen in perpetual night, when demons lived on the world's surface and only the stars and the moon polluted their world with light. And then through foul magicks of elves and men the earth began to slowly turn and the darkness itself was chased around the world, becoming the brief daily respite of night; and the splendor of the demon world was driven beneath the earth by the poisonous beams of the sun. And Ragnack saw the temples raised and the sacrifices initiated and still performed to the demon gods who dwelt in the wild empty expanses between the galaxies, the sacrifices raised that the clawed hands of

divinities would again reach down and still the earth's turning and restore half the earth to the reign of demon-nurturing night. And on this unturning world, Ragnack saw how the frail tribes of men grew beneath the disk of the sun and waited to be harvested by the noble demons. And finally, at the shield's center, Ragnack read the present truth of the Black Wolves: children sickening, a race aging without birth or renewal, the rows of worm-beds half empty of impish babes, those who curled and rolled in their dark cribs sick for the lack of strong souls to feed them. And at end, Ragnack saw the face of the demon's wife and the dear faces of their dying children. And out of a cave, a lone demon warrior, disfigured to the image of a man, strode into a world tainted by light.

Ragnack knew then that he had indeed exchanged blood with the demon. He walked in ebon splendor in deep, fluted caverns, whose great columns had grown with the slow, eternal drip of dark waters; tasted the fulgent draught of a captured soul. . . .

A pale wind blew the ashes of the dead fire onto Ragnack's face and he awakened. Weak morning light fell on the floor of the Valley of Bones. The demon was gone. Ragnack read in the dust that he had taken the path where they had so rudely met.

He stood up, stared briefly at the scorched, clawed clasp of the demon scarred into his flesh and then searched the Valley for another trail. Finally, far down the opposite wall, he spied the faint shadow of a path. At the cliff's top, there was a thin, emerald line of grass. The color seemed to bid him welcome. Ragnack sheathed his sword and strode to regain the day-blessed world.

The Gathering I

Ragnack journeyed for two days after

he climbed out of the Valley of the Bones. The air had heft and flavor; the green roll of the featureless plains was more substantial. He felt hawks wheeling above him and saw patterns where the long grass bent and shifted in the wind. It was more than unity that Ragnack discovered; there was value to the world in its existence. He wondered little whether it was the blood shared with the demon or the recognition that the Soul Eaters waited in shadowed desperation to drink this age empty.

And when night fell and Ragnack nursed a fire of dead brush, he heard the wolves call each to each and understood their voices. He felt them gather beyond the light of the flames, catch his scent, and silently pad away, to hunt a life less in kinship with their own. Then he knew that his deepened knowledge held also a full measure of darkness.

Perhaps it was this that the merchant saw in Ragnack's violet eyes as he stepped onto the muddy road from behind the trunks of the Umbra Forest. The pudgy trader fell off his fat pony, threw his coin-clogged purse at the brigand's feet and ran blindly into the underbrush.

"All I wanted was directions," Ragnack told the pony, as he lengthened the stirrups. He picked up the purse, swung into the saddle, flicked the reins, and let the animal set a slow pace out of the wood.

The giant was gnawing on the drawbridge like a child worrying a stale cookie. The chains on the drawbridge had parted a little, and the slack had given the giant room to try to pull it open. A chorus of woeful cries issued from the terrified warriors peering from the battlement. A few arrows drifted down and bounced off the great cooking pot the giant wore as a helm.

Everything had gone well until they had thrown down the cooked horse. The

108

giant had lumbered out of the Umbra Forest for his weekly feeding, scratched himself, and beat his chest until dust rose from the moldy tent he wore as his only garment.

He squinted his dull, piggy eyes, pointed in the general direction of his cobble-toothed mouth, and bellowed, "Feed me! Knuxor hungers."

The routine was familiar; there was even a certain pride in Castle Melchior at having a tame giant. Lord Melchior made a handsome profit selling spaces on the battlement to the serfs who thronged to watch Knuxor eat.

But this time there had been a woeful mistake. Rather than toss out the usual bloody parts, the new cook had decided to cook the horse.

"Horse BURNT!" Knuxor roared, after biting trustingly into his offering. He stared with dim wrath at Melchior, who trembled in growing fear.

The giant paused to think for a half-minute eternity, "Knuxor eat mean little people, like Knuxor should have from start." He smacked his lips in anticipation and started toward the closed drawbridge.

Melchior was perhaps the only one who fully understood the disrepair of his shabby castle, "A mere misunderstanding, friend giant!" he yelled frantically. "The cook readies a fresh raw colt for Knuxor this moment."

But Knuxor was already at the drawbridge, pulling at the tongue of wood. The rusted links of the chains holding it closed began to part. The picnickers on the walls shrieked as they suddenly realized they had become prey. The giant yanked viciously, a chain snapped, and the drawbridge jerked open four feet. Knuxor slavered, chewing the rotten wood.

And Ragnack rode out of the Umbra Forest.

He had never seen such a ramshackle castle. The towers were so out of plumb they taunted gravity. Moss mortared the walls. And the thirty-foot tall giant made it appear to be a pile of grubby blocks assembled by an imaginative, if clumsy, child.

Ragnack drove his heels into the blubbery sides of his pony. The bootless cries and ineffectual shocks of arrows testified to the need of those quailing on the walls.

When Ragnack had ridden close enough to be enveloped in the unsavory reek of giant sweat, Knuxor ceased pawing the gate and turned. His round, dishonest face brightened.

"FOOD!" Knuxor roared and stumped towards Ragnack, staring greedily at the fat horse.

Ragnack stepped wearily from his saddle, wrapped the reins tight about his fist, and drew his sword. As the giant raised his horny, split-nailed foot to crush him, Ragnack sighed with the ease of it all and drove his sword into

©JANET AULISIO 1989.

109

the flat arch of the brute.

Knuxor wailed with monstrous, sharp surprise and collapsed in a stinking heap. Four blocks of granite tumbled from the north turret. The giant rolled on the ground, clutched his wounded foot, and blubbered at the unfairness of it all.

Ragnack slipped his sword lightly into Knuxor's right ear. Knuxor suddenly stopped his tears and lay very still. He rolled his muddy eyes to stare at Ragnack.

"Greetings, friend giant," Ragnack said in a neutral voice.

"Greetings, kind knight," Knuxor answered. He sniffed, stifled a sob, and smiled at the hateful little wasp.

"Why do you trouble these innocents," Ragnack asked, gesturing to the silent faces peering from the castle.

"I came to eat," the sword quivered in his ear, "to eat my horse," the giant amended.

"And do you often pick your teeth with the beams of the drawbridge?" Ragnack asked.

Knuxor breathed ponderously for a minute, struggling for an explanation. His stomach rumbled the partial truth of his replies. Ragnack's blade tickled his ear canal in encouragement.

"Ah, ahem," a voice quavered from the castle wall, "a word, if I may."

Ragnack looked up and saw a frail, white-bearded man waving to him.

"You know," the old man continued, "we're really quite proud of our giant."

"Knuxor GOOD giant," the behemoth said with ponderous sincerity.

"And who are you?" Ragnack asked in incredulity.

"Lord Melchior, master of this staunch fort."

Ragnack snorted.

"Perhaps we could forgive Knuxor this time," wheedled Lord Melchior. "He does bring in a lot of income."

"Knuxor even eat burnt horse next time," the giant promised.

110

Ragnack drew his sword from Knuxor's ear in disgust. The serfs on the wall cheered. The giant tottered erect, balanced gingerly on one foot. Smiling, he looked down at Ragnack. With a sorrowful expression, he rubbed the round tub of his belly.

"Could I still eat horse?" he asked.

Ragnack waved his sword at Knuxor. The giant hopped off toward the Umbra Wood, whining and sniffling. Trees flew up as he crashed away.

As the audience filed off the battlements, Ragnack sheathed his sword and mounted his butterball charger. As he prepared to ride away, a now familiar voice called to him.

"Ho, worthy knight, where are you bound?"

Ragnack glared at the old fool. "Away," he replied decisively.

"A champion as worthy as yourself must be the chief paladin of a great court," Melchior said.

"Yes," Ragnack spat. He opened his arms to display his soiled armor. "I serve King Rust and Queen Hunger."

"Perhaps you could be convinced to ornament another court?" Melchior offered.

Wrath showed in Ragnack's face. Wordless and with hesitation, he turned his horse onto the castle road. He glared his disgust at Melchior. The Lord of the castle flinched, then drew himself up to accept this rude fealty. The tooth-scarred drawbridge thudded open; and Ragnack entered, to join the bumpkin chivalry of Castle Melchior.

The Gathering II

By default, Ragnack became the marshal of the hosts of Castle Melchior. The 24 knights were actually the sons of merchants: the only people in Melchior's tiny principality who could afford armor. All were silent when the Prince presented Ragnack in the Great

Hall that evening.

"Ahemm, a little attention here, milords," Melchior said, tapping his wine goblet with his dagger, "I think you all are familiar with the qualities of the knight beside me. We've been lucky enough to gain his services here at our humble court. In recognition of his recent handling of the small problem we had with our giant Knuxor," there were a few hurrahs from those more deeply into their wine, "I've imposed on our new friend to take over commanding our modest forces. Ragnack, would you do us the pleasure of a few words?"

As Ragnack rose to speak, the only sounds were the low growls of the dogs under the table, worrying the joints thrown during dinner. He surveyed the resentful faces. Only the Lady Celine smiled at him, her dark eyes full and inviting.

"I am merely a homeless warrior, fellow knights; and only at our beloved Melchior's insistence do I accept this position. I know there are many of you full worthy as I and offer any and all of you the courtesy of trial by combat if you feel my appointment undeserved."

Even the dogs seemed to have abandoned their bones. All the knights shook their heads in brotherly denial of jealousy.

"I am honored to be so accepted by such a company," Ragnack continued. "As you all know, my responsibilities will include dealing with distractions such as Knuxor, ravening beasts, troublesome brigands, and unwholesome wizardries. As much as I am able, I will do these simple tasks myself, saving your stalwart selves as our last line of defense."

The knights applauded his discretion. Ragnack bowed and sat down.

"Another round of wine to toast Ragnack," Melchior called to the servants. Lady Celine placed her perfumed hand on Ragnack's demon-scarred arm. "You have charmed us all tonight."

"I am pleased you take it so," he said, venturing a brief smile. There was a faint throb in his forearm where the claws of the Soul-Eater had seared.

As the evening descended to vinuous camaraderie, Ragnack studied each face. He would try to steel these reluctant warriors, repair the decrepit castle, and bring a measure of safety to this helpless kingdom. With woeful certitude, he felt darkness gathering. Almost like a father, he watched the cheerful, ignorant revelries of Melchior's court. He would ready them, lead them, and when the black moment came, fight at their head. He could do no less. And, he realized, with awful premonition, not much more.

The Gathering III

In the following weeks, Ragnack immersed himself in an assessment of the resources and blatant inadequacies of Castle Melchior. Ostensibly, Melchior paid tribute to the heavy-handed Lord Lavlog of Ventnor. But Melchior's domain of Holbine was so modest, so off the beaten track, that the few conflicts that threatened the Six Kingdoms had reached Melchior's fastness as mere rumor. The land was steeped in an oblivious sloth. Its armory was stocked with cobwebs, weeds flourished in the jousting lists, and the practice field was untrodden.

But Knuxor had awakened Melchior to his vulnerability. The fields around the castle were fertile; and while exacting modest tribute from his serfs, the old prince had quietly accumulated a most weighty store of gold. He opened his purse; and Ragnack hired blacksmiths, masons, squires, and all the others that he would need to bring the land to readiness.

Scaffolding hugged the tipsy walls,

111

the clang of hammers rang from the forges, serfs scythed the tournament fields, and Ragnack finally allowed himself some relaxation. He called the suety knights to the exercise yard for calisthenics and weapons practice. Bare chested, he led them in mock combat using staves in place of swords. All noted the cross-hatching of scars on his chest, and their absence on his back.

"Now swing with BOTH hands, Lavon, your sword requires a double grip. On him, Endor, such clumsiness should be rewarded."

All his students wore padded jerkins and cushioned helms. They flailed like boys pillow-fighting. Ragnack buffeted and crowned each with his massive quarterstaff as he demonstrated. Sweat ran down his corded arms; his shoulders burned. Routines and responsibilities vanished, and Ragnack fell into the simple clarity of battle.

"Forgive me, the blood fever rose within me," Ragnack said as he pulled three glassy-eyed men to their feet. The rest stood around him in panting awe.

"I needed all my skills to avoid injury this morning," Ragnack told them. "Return an hour after noon to hone your prodigious skills."

With this balm of praise, Ragnack's charges stumbled off to the ministrations of their ladies. And with his senses heightened by his exertions, Ragnack felt himself watched. He looked up and saw the Lady Celine observing him from the balcony of her chambers.

"Forgive my appearance, Lady," Ragnack said as he stood in the dust of the castle yard. "I will move our training outside the walls so we will not disturb you."

"I find it all most engrossing, Ragnack," she said, smiling, her dark eyes taking in the play of his muscles as he shifted uncomfortably. "Please continue your practice here and allow me the womanly curiosity of watching what is so unfamiliar."

"Your Ladyship is most kind," Ragnack said. He turned and walked toward the armory. There was a prickliness on his bare back that was not the drying of sweat.

The Gathering IV

Melchior handed the heavy ring of keys to Ragnack as the festive but determined knights rode out of the castle. After months of dogged practice and conditioning, they were anxious to test their new prowess in the annual Third Kingdom tournament. For years they had been the butt of jokes and the recipients of blows. Now they sensed they might inflict some painful surprise.

"I am sorry to ask you to stay," Melchior told his seneschal. "You must be eager to bring further honor to your name. But I feel easier knowing you are here. And with Lady Celine indisposed, I travel less heavy-hearted knowing she is in your hands."

Ragnack bowed in acquiescence. He had little tolerance for tournaments and less respect for those who fought only in staged contests.

"Perhaps another year I may bring renown to your name, my Lord. Until then, your wishes are my pleasant duties." He took the keys with a certain hesitation. Both men left unspoken that the Prince had temporarily given Ragnack possession of the principality.

Melchior waved once, then rode to the head of the procession. Ragnack mounted the battlements and joined the cheering serfs and retainers in wishing them martial success.

For a moment, the knights stood fast in their shining column, then at Melchior's thin shout, they spurred their gaily bedecked horses and set out. Behind them, side-saddled on ponies and palfreys, rode the bright-wimpled ladies of the court. At the end the minstrels followed on donkeys, beating drums and shrieking on fifes.

Flags waved from the walls, huzzahs rained down; and in such carefree leave-taking, the chivalry of Castle Melchior rode away.

It was after midnight when Ragnack finally ventured to rest from the over-zealous execution of his duties. As he climbed the twisting stairs, a satisfaction came over him, a sense that he had found a place where he was both trusted and necessary.

But despite his weariness, he never forgave himself for falling into the ambush.

He stood before his iron-strapped door, absently fumbling for his key in the pitchy twilight of the torches of the hallway. As was appropriate for one who might be the last desperate guardian of his Lord's family, Ragnack's room was at the head of the corridor that ended with the chambers of Prince Melchior and Lady Celine.

As the tongue of the lock drew back, Ragnack smelled a troubling scent of mandragora. He stood in surprise. The Lady Celine stepped from a darkness between torches. Her lips parted slightly, and her breasts shone like apples of ivory through the thin fabric of her gown.

"What of your illness, my Lady?" Ragnack asked in confusion. "You were sick abed, I thought."

"You shall heal me this night," Celine whispered and brushed against him. Her hands made their light way up his arms. "I have sent the night servants from my quarters."

"But Lord Melchior," Ragnack protested.

"How long would you have me lay beside that dotard?" she asked feverishly, "Can a woman find love in a marriage made as part of a treaty? Many days have I stood in my room and watched you exercise my husband's rabble from my shaded window. I want

© JANET AULISIO 1989.

you in my bed, not a trembling creature with age-tufted ears."

"But I am my Lord's servant," Ragnack said, in rare fear.

"And mine too," Celine told him. She slipped her hands from his arms, passed them over her body. The gown hissed to the floor.

With violent ambivalence, Ragnack pushed her away, shouldered the great door to his room open, slammed it, locked it.

The Lady Celine lay naked on the cold stones of the floor, her face a mask of incredulity. Then tears burst from her. On her knees she gathered up her dress, rose to her feet. Shoulders clenched with sobs, she made her way back to her bed.

By morning, the smoke of the torches had subdued the scent of mandragora.

Three days later, Prince Melchior returned at the head of his warriors. Success flushed his papery cheeks. The armor of the knights was hacked and dented, but only three were so badly knocked about that they were borne in litters. There was a new but harmless arrogance in their faces. The ladies of the court waved charms, banners, and pennants that their champions had won. Flowers showered from the walls. Astonished cheers echoed from Melchior's populace. And in the van, the musicians made drunken joyful dissonance from a haywagon.

Ragnack stood before the open drawbridge. As Melchior rode up, he returned to his Lord the castle's heavy ring of keys.

"A most wondrous success," the Prince said, still beaming at the welcome. "And all of it we owe to you, our most trusted and martial adviser. We unhorsed them in the lists, scourged them in the melee, and won 'most improved court' overall." He looked closely at Ragnack for the first time. "Has anything gone wrong?"

"No, my Lord," Ragnack quickly answered.

"Well then, stop making this long face. You will be honored in our celebration tonight as the agent of our renown." With a gesture that surprised himself, Melchior reached down and tousled the grizzled hair of his friend.

"Forgive me, Prince," Ragnack said in a low voice, "by nature I am prey to moodiness. Already your triumph dispels my heavy spirits."

"Well then, and the Lady Celine," Melchior asked with concern, "how goes the progress of her illness?"

"She still lies abed. Your Lord's eagerly awaited return will help restore her to herself."

"I must go to her now," the old man said simply.

Ragnack took the horse's bridle and helped the travel-stiffened Prince dismount, gave him his arm, and led Melchior to the shaded, incense-heavy chamber of Lady Celine.

The Gathering V

The sun was coaxing the dew to mist when the riders came across the sea of low grass. When the one closest spied the knight, he gave a sharp, brief cry. The scouts turned, wheeled toward the blond giant, and with deceptive ease began to circle the solitary figure. Two drew ropes of plaited leather from their saddles, twirled them above their heads in a whistling arc.

The knight drew his black, barbed sword. The sun paled for a moment, the wind in the grasses sighed, the horses shied and were reined again to obedience. All these signs the riders dismissed in the simple, compelling task of the knight's murder.

The lariats shot out, coiled above him, fell around his gleaming armor. And burned away with the sizzle of spit on coals. Blue flame raced up the ropes, engulfed the two riders, flared, and vanished. The two horses stood unharmed. The knight knew these men would appreciate that.

The remaining horsemen drew up silently in front of the blond knight. Their flat yellow faces held a curious respect but no fear. Having drunk two of their souls, the knight weighed their race. They were admirably suited to his purposes.

"Gobo," said the knight.

The leader nodded. He gestured to the knight to take one of the riderless horses. The knight shrugged. He knew no horse would ever tolerate him. The riders turned to the east, set off at the speed of a walking man.

His armor oiled with silence, the knight ran past them. The barbarians broke to a slow gallop. The knight sped tirelessly in their midst as they devoured the leagues to Gobo's camp.

The Gathering VI

Gobo rose in the East with a slowness that lulled the Six Kingdoms into a fatal belated recognition.

His army first appeared one sweltering summer day on the wide steppes of Ventnor. The sentries looked out from Prince Lavlog's castle and saw, over half a mile away, a thousand bulbous tents sprung up with the suddenness of mushrooms after a rain. Smoke placidly rose through their fire vents. There was surprise, but no initial panic. Word was sent down to Prince Levlog, who struggled out of bed and sullenly mounted the battlements. The mid-year festival had ended the night before, and Levlog was surly with the aftereffects of the fertility celebrations. Most of his knights lay besotted from the exercise of their religious duties. We must view what happened in that light.

Levlog squinted sullenly as he stared out at this rude city, newly sprung up in his fields. "What sorry crowd of gypsies has settled on us?" he muttered. He scratched his red beard, glared with rising anger at the tents.

"The last watch reported no sign of them," a nervous sentry told him. "Apparently they encamped at night, during the castle festivities. None of us heard them. They came as silent as rats."

"I'll deal with them after I've slept," said Levlog venomously. He drew his green velvet robe tight, stumped back to his chambers, drained a skin of yellow feast wine, and dreamt most fiercely of carnage.

About mid-day, a small body of black-bearded horsemen approached the castle. They rode their stocky mounts smoothly. Slung across their shoulders were short, dark horn bows. Arrows rattled in leather quivers on their backs. Curved swords hung from their belts. They wore padded jackets of quilted cotton. Their tallow-greased hair glistened. It was a people unknown to any on the walls. The four barbarians stopped a hundred feet from the battlements. One cantered closer. He raised a flat, yellow face and smiled a vulpine smile.

"Greetings, rock dwellers," he called insolently, "Oh womanish warriors who hide behind walls. The great Lord Gobo, Gobo the Ravisher, the Scourge of the Pale-Skinned, Eater of Hearts, asks if you will surrender to his mercy or be consumed by the People of the Plains?"

The few who watched from the castle gasped at this effrontery. An archer notched an arrow, shot it down at the scruffy thug. But the horsemen wheeled away, and the shaft went wide. Out of bowshot, they slowed and rode back to their camp in a leisurely swirl of dust. Their laughter drifted back.

This insult was enough to rouse even Lavlog from his heavy slumbers. His face filled with blood as he heard the sentries' tale.

"Surrender!" he called. "To the Great Gobo! Gob, more likely. A hawky snot of spit, a fornicator of horses, a dung-burning, grease-headed master of thieves."

He little knew how accurate his words were. Lavlog smoldered on the edge of his bed, and the sanguine veins of his bulging eyes reddened further.

"Drag the knights from their beds. In an hour, we torch the grimy tents of this host of mange." He smacked his lips, clapped his hands, and the men at arms rushed away to muster the might of Castle Ventnor.

In two hours, Prince Lavlog strode clanking to the battlements, his armor sun-dogged and shimmering.

"By the wounds of the gods, the sun is heavy today," he snarled.

Sweat ran in rivulets down his flushed face. He and his captains stared out into the high-grassed plain. The barbarian camp sat complacently where it had first been discovered. In the courtyard below, one hundred and twenty-five knights milled on their chargers, their heads throbbing with celebration pain that the day's heat redoubled. All wanted to give short shrift to the heathen dogs who brought such discomfort. This is the only way that we can explain the fatal improvidence that guided them.

"Shall we send out scouts?" Gavin, Lavlog's steward asked.

"For poxy vermin such as these?" Lavlog laughed. "We will smash this camp of yellow leaves and harvest its foul fruit with the edge of our swords. And then return to celebrate our brief labors."

All nodded in a fog of acceptance and clattered down the steps to resolve this chafing inconvenience.

The drawbridge thudded down. Lavlog and the flower of the chivalry of Ventnor rumbled out of the castle. The populace lined the walls, waved handkerchiefs, called out good-natured ad-

vice. There was an air of festive expectation.

"Assume formation before the vagabond camp." Lavlog called to the knights behind him.

His squire unfurled the battle standard. On a blue field, the Yellow Rose of Ventnor flapped languidly at the head of the straggling column. A few of the knights unsheathed their swords and hacked at the high grass in preparation.

A throng of horsemen had finally appeared before the tents. Lavlog smiled; he preferred a semblance of resistance before they slaughtered the rabble. Abruptly, a measured, deep resonance of kettledrums throbbed from the barbarian camp. A pole with a rail at its top rose before the horsemen. Ox-tails swayed from the rail and bones on rawhide strips rattled together dryly. With no apparent command, the horsemen formed into a battle line. The pulse of the drums quickened. The narrow line lengthened swiftly, until the camp was hidden behind a silent wall of mounted men.

Lavlog felt the timbre of the drums hum ominously within his helmet. There was a disconcerting precision in the barbarian response. He had his first, short-lived doubts.

Lavlog wheeled splendidly to face his knights, drew his sword, raised it. Sunlight gashed its fatal edge. "Form in battle ranks," he roared, "We smash these . . ."

The archers of Gobo's host rose silently from the high grass. They were ranked on either side of the attenuated column of knights. The arrows flew with a hawk's shriek and smashed through the horses' armor. Knights careened from their chargers and lay stunned in the wind-winnowed grasses. Those left mounted, drew together in confusion and slashed madly at the earth. Other devils crept to them and, with long saw-toothed lances, hamstrung the surviving stallions. Within two minutes, all but eight of the knights of Ventnor were unhorsed. They wandered the plain like stricken, glittering beetles. And then, as the drums rose triumphantly, Gobo's horse-warriors screamed, spurred, and fell on them like a wave of acid.

Thank the gods for the knight, Lavlog thought as he lay bound in the wagon jouncing toward the castle. Surprisingly few of his men had been killed. Most followed the wagon, arms tied behind their backs, heads bowed.

Lavlog had been prodded at spearpoint into a large tent painted with a repugnance of detail. As Lavlog's eyes adjusted to the shadows, he found he stood before two grossly disparate figures. One, apparently the leader of the host, was a toad of a man, who stared expressionlessly at his defeated adversary. But the other spoke in a voice filled with palpable sympathy.

"You cannot understand my pleasure at seeing a man of parts before me," the handsome knight told Lavlog. "Though an outcast, I was raised in far more honorable company than this."

"You have my advantage," Lavlog said in some confusion.

"I am driven by circumstance to throw my lot in with these ignorant people," the blond knight said, his face clouded by some sad remembrance. "An adviser to Lord Gobo," he nodded to the toad, "a translator for him as he ventures out to steal horses and return to his wide, windy domains."

"This fat thief cannot understand our words, then," Lavlog said.

The knight smiled.

"These simple folk understand nothing other than horses and the weight of gold in their purses. Though exiled —" here the knight sighed — "still I honor the code of knights and men who bathe. This chance gathering of herdsmen cannot overthrow your castle. I

think that I can convince Gobo," he nodded at his unblinking companion, "to ransom you and your knights for a mere pile of gold and the culling of your flocks and herds."

"There will be a private bounty for you, gracious sir, if this can happen," Lavlog said quickly. "And whatever your deeds, a place of honor among my retinue."

The knight smiled with a gratitude that Lavlog almost found pathetic, except that he keenly felt the thongs biting into his arms.

There followed a brief, heated exchange between the knight and the reptilian leader. Finally, relief on his face, the knight turned to Lavlog.

"Gobo consents, though he wants you to understand it is healthy greed and no faint sense of mercy. He agrees that spoils are more useful than dead men. Only, as he has pointed out, we need your complicity. Will those in the castle submit to these terms?"

"Are you and I not men?" Lavlog pressed. "As honorable knights, we cement this compact." Lavlog extended his hand and the two made a mailed handshake.

As the wagon lumbered to a halt before Castle Ventnor, the knight who had befriended Lavlog dismounted lightly, sliced the bonds of the defeated man with his barbed sword, and helped him to his feet. The dusty line of Castle warriors stood in a sullen mass behind them. Their captors lounged on their saddles and took census of their lice. Seemingly bored, Gobo rested in a shaded litter and watched a slave ready the scales to weigh the ransom geld.

As the blond knight gestured for Lavlog to speak, Lavlog wondered idly why the man did not sweat in the cauldron of the day's heat. Tight, suspicious faces peered down.

"Fortunately, we have made a compact with these poxy horse-lovers that will guarantee our lives. We are to be ransomed for 20,000 pieces of Ventno-rian gold."

Lavlog's voice had regained its air of command. "Gavin, you tight-fisted steward, bring the gold out in half an hour, or we die here before your eyes. Do you obey?"

"Yes, my lord," Gavin finally replied.

Twenty minutes later, the draw-bridge fell open. Gavin drove out the groaning cart.

"I owe you my life," Lavlog said, turning to the knight.

"In truth you do," the knight replied, and touched the barbs of his sword to Lavlog's neck. The master of Ventnor Castle withered to a stinking husk as his soul was sucked away.

The horde of Gobo swept into the castle. The pillage was easy, but not swift.

Gobo sat on Gavin's body in the treasure wagon, splashed the bloody gold over himself. He looked over to his partner, who stood with his barbed sword in his hand, staring into the wide world beyond the burning castle.

"A fine and profitable partnership we've made," Gobo told him.

"A beginning," the knight said. There was an awful vacancy in his eyes; his features slackened and seemed abandoned. He was the only living being who gave Gobo the humanity of fear.

The lathered horse in the gold wagon's traces whinnied. Gobo slid off his gold, walked to it, stroked it calm. His knife was so sharp, the horse never felt him sever the vein. Gobo pressed his face against its neck, swallowed to surfeit.

The two men looked at each other and then laughed.

The Gathering VII

The horde spread out to Datal and rode down the farms that dotted the low hills. Wherever they struck, Gobo let some escape to bear terror before them.

Gobo's host multiplied, its savagery deepened in the reports its fleeing victims blurted.

Gobo himself rode in a great, leather roofed wagon drawn by twelve horses and slept on a mound of gold heaped on its floor. There was a whimsicality to his temper: at one sacked village all that remained was a circle of children's toys: dolls, wagons, and little tools, within which lay the corpses of the villagers. At Ventnor, he left a forest of men impaled on high poles, a wood whose birds were carrion pickers.

Gobo and the People of the Plains cared for none other than their own race. The nations of the Six Kingdoms were merely regarded as providers of horses. And as the horde conquered, the great herds of booty swelled and trailed behind it like a vision of avarice and delight.

They followed a simple religion: a pantheon of carnivorous horse gods. When a warrior fell in battle, he awoke riding across an endless plain, a stallion beneath him, around him the ranks of the valiant dead, and before him an endless host of pale infidels to slay. The gods ate the cowardly. The Six Kingdoms never understood that their opponents had embarked upon this flood of conquest for the wanton pleasure of it: the People of the Plains regarded their invasion as a horse raid on larger and more ornate villages.

Perhaps Gobo alone of the grim and joyful riders, as he sat like a lump of poisoned suet on the trove of his gold, thought of ruling the world. And no one knew the thoughts of the Golden Knight who drove Gobo's wagon; and with impassive face, beneath skulls wavering on tall wands that rose from the sides of the massive wagon, led the rapacious warriors from town to trembling town and counseled the horde on how to wreak victory.

The Gathering VIII

Two weeks after the tournament, Ragnack asked Melchior's permission to thin the herds of wild boars terrorizing the northern reaches of the Umbra Forest. They had grown so numerous that they had forsaken their regular diet of acorns and ravaged the crops. Serfs feared to gather their harvests; and what the wild boars did not eat, rotted on the vine or fell to earth. If the beasts were not contained, the vassals would starve and the castle itself run the risk of famine.

Ragnack also wanted to take himself beyond Lady Celine. Drawn and pale, she emerged from her chambers a week after Melchior's return. As far as Ragnack could tell, she no longer watched him secretly from the shaded windows of her bedroom. Nevertheless, Ragnack found reason to move his instruction of Melchior's knights outside the castle walls to the jousting field a quarter mile away. But, as his Prince's boon companion, Ragnack supped with the court each evening. In brief jagged moments between conversations at table he found her eyes on him, a wistful hunger that he felt transparent to all. When, inevitably, they conversed, it was with a formality that Melchior laughingly chided them for.

And so, Ragnack found the boars a welcome excuse. He hoped distance and the passage of days would dilute Celine's longing.

"You're quite correct," Melchior told him with some reluctance, "the fall harvests are winter's succor. If the brutes are not contained we lose the faith of our people and our own nourishment."

"I've sent scouts out beyond your domain, and there is not the whisper of danger or any treachery," Ragnack said. "I only leave with that assurance."

"But is it wise to go alone? At least I can offer you the company of beaters and woodsmen."

"Allow me my sport," Ragnack told him. "I will find willing assistance from the farmers. They need only one to steel them to the task. Your newly blooded knights now are mickle protection. Should any trouble arise, I am only a day's ride away."

"You have given me an appetite for bacon." He sighed. "Be off. The sooner you leave, the quicker the return."

The two men embraced, and then Ragnack went to the armory. He clothed himself in an uncured leather doublet and trousers, jammed a simple padded cap of steel on his head, bundled together eight hunting spears. The shaggy horse with its plain saddle was waiting outside the stables. As he rode away, a shadow passed in Celine's window. He turned to the northern road, and the wind met his face. For the first time in weeks, his heart lightened.

The Gathering IX

Ragnack found the vassals terrified of the woods. In a week of hunting, the lines of beaters drove eighteen beasts to him to be killed. But they refused to venture into the Umbra Forest to flush the swine. At night, as the spitted sows dripped grease into the cooking fires, Ragnack listened to the usual tales of little people, malignant spirits, and hideous beasts. Every vanished animal, lost child, and blighted crop was attributed to evil welling from the unknown depths of the Umbra Forest.

Ragnack knew that he alone would have to stalk the great boars who lived beyond the timid range of the peasants. If he could kill some of the surly brutes, the herds themselves would be stunted.

And for Ragnack, the Umbra Forest held no superstitious dread. He had spent years as a woodsman, growing to manhood with others like himself who lived beyond lord and law. He ached to slip through green shadows and stalk

119

worthy prey before he had to go back to Melchior and Celine. He knew that the forest was sanctuary, not iniquity, and that rumors of foul magic were often generated by those who would remain untroubled within it.

"My Lord, my sons and I will go with you into the deeps of the Umbra Forest," Wheatshaft told Ragnack. Fear was in him, but as village headman he made the offer.

Ragnack declined. "Let an old woodsman enjoy his sport."

Wheatshaft's relief was genuine. "The service you have done us will forever live in our legends," he said with the proper hyperbole. He fell to his knees, "Our daughters await the honor of your knightly seed."

Ragnack lifted the man by his matted hair. "I will tell Lord Melchior of the hospitality of his people. But I would not weaken my hunting ardor."

"Thank you for letting us all eat meat," the peasant told him with less servility. "Letting us keep two in three of the pigs killed was unhoped generosity."

"Lord Melchior did not look unduly thin when I left," Ragnack said. "Once I am in the woods, send word that I will return in a week. I would rather be on my adventure before Melchior knows of it. He might restrict the scope of my entertainments."

"Someone from the village will wait here for your return," Wheatshaft said, nodding. "Beware the imps, the trolls, the mossy magic of the wood witches, the cannibal dwarves . . ."

"Thanks, good Wheatshaft." Ragnack rattled the spears on his shoulder. "My companions and I go to hunt."

The elder shuddered as Ragnack strode into the Umbra Forest. The trees seemed to close behind him.

Within two days, Ragnack was able to move through the forest without silencing birds. He followed the trails that the swine beat down, saw the

120

ground beneath the oak trees uprooted where the wild pigs searched for truffles after they had filled themselves with acorns.

For four days, Ragnack watched from blinds high in the branches. To his surprise, there really was a King of the Pigs: a massive, dagger-tusked boar whose small eyes glinted with belligerent intelligence. In the scars on his snout and thick shoulders, Ragnack read the death of all challengers to his supremacy. Every day the King of Pigs ran nimbly beneath Ragnack, leading a train of heavy-dugged sows, most of whom ran with a host of piglets nuzzling their bellies. His great snout twitched for scent of danger, his little ears cocked for the sound of a padded, cautious footfall.

In the hunger for battle that seethed in the small, hard eyes, Ragnack knew that if he killed the boar, the herds would cease their growth and lack the confidence that made them despoil the fields of the serfs. The King of Pigs was a worthy opponent. The only certainty was that one of them would die. He sat content in his oak-leaf bower and sharpened the heads of his spears, the whetstone whispering like light wind. When the moon rose and its beams shone on the steel of the spears, Ragnack thought of Lady Celine. He almost hoped that he and the pig would kill each other.

The Gathering XX

Whatever Ragnack's feelings about Celine, he was loyal to Melchior, to the knights, and to the vulnerable, landbonded people of the kingdom. This hunt was his last personal indulgence, before he returned to ready his small world to face the formless dread whose premonition was the pain in his demonscarred arm.

After four days of simplifying his

thoughts so he saw the forest through piggy eyes, Ragnack gathered himself. He tied the spears to his back, their heads moss-cushioned for silence, and crept from his blind. The trees of the Umbra Forest grew so closely together that Ragnack could follow the pigs' regular trails without setting foot on the ground and leaving his scent. He started off at dawn; by mid-afternoon he had reached the bedding place of the herd. He eased along the massive limbs of the oak that sheltered the glade. Beneath him, in the underbrush, a fat young sow nursed a swarm of newborn piglets. A brown path curved through the grasses and ended in a series of trampled circles in the bushes where each pig slept. The odor of pig dung crawled up Ragnack's nose. Noiselessly, he took the spears from his back, drew the moss from their thirsty heads.

From his stalking, Ragnack knew that the King led his subjects on a daily circuit of the forest, stopping to root and feed. The herd ranged slightly, according to what the great boar had a taste for. But they returned to this haven each night, where the ancient oak sheltered them from rain, dropped showers of acorns, and grew succulent fungus on its roots for them to snuffle out.

Led by the King Pig, the herd of wild boar ran with diminutive thunder into the glade. Ragnack fell from the great oak like a crazed ape. He screamed a battle cry and shook his spears. The King Pig wheeled in instant, murderous reaction. The sows squealed away. Only he attacks, Ragnack thought, with small gratitude. Bristles rose like a dark fish's spine on the boar's back, a mad froth streaked his muzzle. He rushed toward the man like a clot of wrath. Ragnack threw two spears faster than a wasp stings. They flew into the King Pig's mountainous shoulders, struck, shook there with as much effect as if Ragnack had thrown darts. In the second and a half left, Ragnack planted

the base of his last spear against the great tree, steadied the shaft with tremorless hands, and watched the King Pig spring upon him, turning its head to work the great, dripping tusks. Ragnack saw the implacable sear in the animal's tiny eyes as the head of the spear slid deep in its chest.

So torrential was the beast's rush that the spear drove totally through him. The King Pig smashed Ragnack flat against the tree, fell dead upon him.

"Would that I were as brave," Ragnack thought as the boar crushed consciousness from him.

As if the oak's knotty roots came alive, seven tiny men rose from the long grasses. They stood in voiceless contemplation of the pig and the man. Then, with their small spears, they rolled the boar off the still figure. They bound the shafts of their weapons together, gently lifted Ragnack onto the improvised stretcher, and bore him off into the forest.

The Gathering XI

Napthinia lay like a lioness on the plains of Nazar. Its alabaster walls glowed in the afternoon sun. Azure sparrows dipped in the shadows of its high towers and sang homage to the wind. Four broad pennants fluttered above its walls. Three were red, green, blue; above them, like the shadow of a swimming snake, a bituminous banner twisted and straightened. The gleaming knight walked swiftly down the road winding out of the Chitronella Hills until he stood beneath the huge tree in the meadow before the castle. His expressionless face surveyed the ranks of shields that hung from its limbs. These were the tokens of knights who had challenged the Lords of Castle Napthinia in single combat. Few survived the first defender; none had defeated the three champions to meet the Black Lord of Napthinia, the strongest knight of this realm. But of such notorious impossibility was the besting of these four champions that many came to measure themselves against them.

The knight raised the heavy hammer that rested against the trunk and struck the challenge bell four times so that its tone rang down the avenues of Napthinia and the shields shook and rattled in the grim tree.

By the time the summons of the bell had dissolved, a paladin in green armor rode out of the castle. He cantered up to the gleaming knight with a confident manner.

"You are without a charger, sir," the green knight observed.

"An accident on the road," the blond knight replied.

"I prefer not to taint my victory," said the champion. He dismounted and tied his stallion to a low branch on the tree of fallen warriors. "We will fight on equal terms."

The handsome challenger smiled. The knight from the castle drew his sword, twirled the heavy blade about his head, and nodded toward the open ground beyond the shadow of the tree. In unspoken agreement the two walked into the field. And the green knight fell on him like a rain of metal.

The golden stranger's defense was marvelous. He caught the shock of each weighty blow on his knobbed shield. The green knight swore that the surface of the shield crawled beneath his sword. He gathered his strength, cascaded blows on the knight. And then, with the green knight momentarily spent, his glittering opponent drew his great barbed black sword and hacked him deep through his side.

The first champion of Castle Napthinia rocked for a moment, uttered a moan of despair and fell to earth, a fistful of smoking ashes within clattering armor. His raiment was like the host

of the grass.

And then with an angry bellow from within his scab-colored helm, the red knight, the second champion, was almost upon him. No courtesy now to the horseless victor. The knight in scarlet twirled his rusted mace and bent down from his charger to brain the knight of gold. But faster than a flame shifts form, the challenger slashed with his black sword and beheaded the horse. Unbalanced, the red knight slid from his saddle and lay stunned in the fountain of the horse's blood. The black sword flayed out and took the man's head from his shoulders. A glistening dawn seeped through the grasses.

Of somber gait was the tread of the third champion's horse. His armor was the azure twilight that bridges the evening sky and the darker setting of the stars. The sweat of his black horse was a spray of jet beads on its cord-muscled haunches. The sparks of its hooves on the roadway were corn-flower. The knight's eyes burned in sapphire wrath through the slits of his helm. And as he lowered his lance to impale the stranger, the horseless knight struck its head into the earth with the flat of his sword. Such was the violence of the blue knight's charge that when the lance buried its head deep in the sward, the blue knight was lifted and headlong swung at the end of the lance, bashing his blue helm into the earth, and shattering his spine.

A great sigh went up from within the white walls of Napthinia, as the blue pennant followed its brothers and slid down its pole. As the shadows lengthened like letters run back to ink, the drawbridge fell open again. For the first time in four generations, the black knight rode out to face a champion who had defeated his three battle-renowned attendants.

He came on in armor so dark that the darkening sky itself seemed to lighten. He was an emissary of the night's potency, of summer clouds coiling to ever-deepening tiers of thunder and shattering lightning. His horse was a fanged shadow forced from a tortured wizard's curse. Its red eyes gaped like wounds. It sprang across the wide meadow, and the grass withered beneath its hooves. The Black Lord of Napthinia reined it to rest and sat silently looking down on the golden warrior. Then words fell hollowly from the black helm.

"It saddens me to slay a man so skillful and fearless. My brother knights were the victors in trials to determine the guardians of our city. But I am of such omnipotent might that none dared challenge my selection. Will you yield to me, live, and serve as my vassal? Or will my demon steed feed on your flesh after I have slain you?"

"I seek my fate as light and darkness allow," the golden knight replied. He drew the black, barbed sword.

The sun fell beneath the horizon as they prepared to fight, and the fortress of Napthinia was lit with the brief, false illumination that surrenders to night.

The Black Lord raked his charger with the dagger-honed pentagram spurs, swung his sword like a pinwheel of razors, and then leaped at the gleaming knight. The golden knight stood motionless, then rushed toward the great, magic-sinewed horse. With a sizzle of brimstone and oily smoke he sank into its body. The horse screamed and its skin curled like leather thrown into a forge. From within the tormented animal's body, the knight drove his barbed sword through the mail of the Black Lord's groin. The horse dissolved in a gibberish of thwarted spells. As the smoke spun away, his armor awash with blood, the golden knight held the body of the Black Lord twitching above his head.

The black pennant above the walls of Napthinia burst into flames and fell like phoenix feathers. With a monstrous throb of drums, the host of Gobo swarmed down from the Chitronella Hills to surround the fortress of Napthinia.

The Gathering XII

Gobo's horde invested the plains around the castle of Napthinia. The tents of the People of the Plains lay comfortably beyond bowshot, but the roads to the beautiful fortress were taken, the harbor beach on the river Borsop behind the castle occupied, the staunch walls encircled. The siege was joined.

Wails and anguished curses rose into the night as the people of Napthinia mourned their champions. Though the walls were mortared with magic, though the larders held half a year's food, and a pure and copious spring bubbled in the court yard; still Gobo and his warriors sensed, as feral dogs will smell the terror in a herd of sheep, that the inhabitants were dispirited and vulnerable. So plenipotent had the four knights been that their fall made the castle itself seem less substantial.

The golden knight raised his tent a distance from Gobo's braying host under the tree of warriors. The bleached leather shone beneath the moon like bare bone. In the tree, the armor of the four dead champions creaked as it rocked in the night wind and scraped the shields of knights they had once conquered. Dust seeped through the mail boots of the red knight and fell softly. The golden knight sat before his tent, his back to the moon, his face bathing in the darkness, a blackness only faintly spoiled by stars. He sighed; and in his weariness, his disguise loosened and his hated human face melted and writhed. He was weakened by constant commerce with men, from holding his hunger from even the simple spirits of Gobo's men. But this day he knew he

123

had furthered his quest, and resolve returned. The flaccid burble of his false face reformed into the waxy beauty he offered to men's eyes.

The knight stood, grasped his barbed sword, and walked beneath the tree. With its black tines, he touched the breastplates of each of the four dead knights and stilled their gentle motion. Then he drew his hand down the blade four times. With each passing along the sword, a flower swelled at its point and fell at his feet. He sheathed his sword, bent down, and gathered the flowers from the cold grass. Four roses: one emerald, one blue, one red, and one black.

Then he raised his left hand and blew into his palm. A wheel of darkest blood spun there; and from the spill of his demon heart, a tiny figure grew solid. The imp unfurled its bat wings, joyfully stamped its obsidian feet, and drew grey lips back from its fangs. Master and servant smiled in lightless understanding. The knight handed his familiar the four roses, then tossed it gently into the night. The creature keened once mournfully, then flew swiftly over the mourning city of Napthinia toward the Valley of the Bones. Four flowers that heralded the unleashing of the Soul Eaters; a taste of things to come.

As the imp flew over Napthinia, sap fell from the gashed stalks, fell as a small rain of blood onto the grey slate of the roofs of tower, castle, and turret.

The Gathering XIII

The two guards at the opening of the main cavern in the Valley of Bones cried out in joyful surprise as the small black figure flapped out of the night and glided into the passage. One demon raised his fist and Apollyon's familiar settled on it like a returning falcon. The warrior stroked its scaly head and set out for the sacred grottoes where the

124

priests, mages, and witches of the Black Wolves prayed for Apollyon.

The guardian stopped in the entrance of the great Chapel of Shadow. Only Druzla, the Chief Priest, raised his face as the chants rose from the kneeling guardians of the faith. The imp cackled triumphantly and flew to Druzla's shoulder. The familiar bent its tiny black face to the Chief Priest's ear hole, whispered, then with a fanged smile, handed Druzla the four flowers. Druzla pulled a petal from the black rose, placed it on the tip of his limpet tongue, sighed. He sprang to his bird-clawed feet.

"Rise, reverent brothers and sisters," he cried. "Sample the first fruits of Apollyon's quest."

And he passed to them the roses that were the spirits of the four champions of Napthinia. Each gently took a petal, and hope revived with their tasting. The imp capered on Druzla's shoulders. Finally the flowers returned to the Chief Priest's claws. The clotted buds still swelled with petals. Druzla raised the blooms above them all.

"Apollyon confounds the world of men. Even now affrighted peoples gather to face the army he has raised. When they rank themselves against this challenge, we will fall on them and savage their souls that our young may grow and our race swell to strength again. With the promise of these roses as token, let us gather a fatal demon host to restore our waning darkness."

Druzla took the imp from his shoulder, blessed it as it stood in his clawed hand. The creature leaped into the air, and the spirit of Apollyon's breath flapped back through the night to the demon champion. Then the priests, mages, and witches divided into four parties; and each bearing a rose as sample and summons, hurried through the leagues of caverns to marshal the thin ranks of the Black Wolves.

© JANET AULISIO 1989.

The Gathering XIV

Ragnack struggled to rise from the bed, but the woman's hands softly pushed him back.

"Too soon, fearless hunter. Sleep on," she ordered, placing cool fingers on his forehead.

A healing lassitude emanated from her. He lay back and stared at the low ceiling. The fireplace crackled. Ungainly little men poked a piece of meat hanging over the flames and grease dribbled onto the coals.

Ragnack gasped in realization, "O gods, I am captive of the cannibal dwarves."

The squatty figures before the fire laughed. "There, there," the woman said. Her white hair drifted over him. As she turned away, the light fell on her face, and Ragnack for the first time saw her beauty. Then, as sleep overwhelmed his confusion, she turned back to him, smiled reassurance. Her silver eyes had the gelid brilliance of the moon just risen free of the horizon.

Four days later, Ragnack sat propped before the fire, quietly eating a pork chop as he listened to the blind woman.

"The elves are a lost race," Snow Rose said sadly, "Once they roamed as shepherds of the wilderness and protectors of beasts, quietly weaving the clouds, crafting the winds. They were the refiners of the myths and superstitions that grace the Six Kingdoms. Now in their shining homes of metal, they sit before flickering images that rise from the shrines of false gods, as their kinship with the world fades in a drugged sleep. No more do they invisibly walk the treetops, bending the high branches as if a breeze passes, nor do they tune the songs of birds, or secretly plant the seeds of new stories. They once lived in noble isolation and now huddle together in tragic enfeeblement.

"I was a young story-teller," the woman said, smiling, "with the ignorant singleness of purpose of the novice. All of us in the Guild of Story-Tellers knew of the elves' decline and recognized the measure of loss. Have you noticed the slow change in the taste of kisses, the coarsening of the varieties of rain? These are just two responsibilities that elves abandoned. No more elves sat before the sacred molten wells deep within the earth, filling with the light that is the very pulse of the world. And no elves came to splatter our sleep or our musings with the holy illumination they had absorbed.

"So I decided to do what no one dared: to sit before one of the elven wells and take the light in through my human eyes. I would fill myself with the burning essence and return to spill it out for my Guild before it ate through me like molten lead.

"In distant Assuria, where the mountains are as studded with caves as a barn with swallows' nests, I found one of the last practicing elves. He was old, abstracted. I followed him to the mouth of a cavern deep in the Colchan Mountains, where there was a path worn down like parted lips by the passing of thousands of pilgrims. When the elf at last emerged that night, reeling, his footprints glowed, then slowly faded. I knew I had found my goal. When his steps had vanished and the path stood bare beneath the stars, I lit my torch and walked into the cave. The way fell down steep faces of rock, soared on thin bridges over pitchy gulfs, wound between dribbled pillars of rock, through chill filled with blind fish. Finally, as my torch sputtered out, I saw the radiance of the wells reflected on the cavern walls. I cast the spent torch aside, fell to my knees, groped along the worn rock of the path. I crawled until my arms cast shadows like ebony staves, until the heat was like the hands of volcano sprites. Finally, with the skin of my hands searing, I could crawl no farther. I knelt, lifted my face, and committed my eyes to the wells of light.

"The folly of my quest broke over me. The elves had been vessels of inspiration. Men and women were shot through with angers, ambitions, and jealousies; we could only tolerate so much light before it ate away the darkness that was so much of our being. And now, this pitiless light, undiluted by elven love and judgment, burst through me like the arrows of the stars.

"The tears scalded back from my lashes and crawled burning across my face. I felt the color drawn out of my hair. The pettiness in me stood revealed in scorching relief for one awful moment before the light incinerated it.

"After consciousness returned, I made my tortuous way out of the cave, almost grateful for my new blindness. Perhaps I had wanted to bring the lost elven power back to the Guild of Story-Tellers, but now I had also seen that I desired knowledge through one bold act, rather than earning it through time and trials. I had not been punished, I had been judged.

"When the night air soothed my face and I knew I had returned to the world, I discovered that my blindness had compensation. I could understand the bats. I could see the auras of men: their emotions and their measure. And I could tell stories. But it was some time before I realized my gifts."

"Tell him about you reception upon your return," one of the dwarves at the fire snickered.

"Yes, Carver, that would clarify our own lives for our guest," the woman said. "At last I made my clumsy way to a village. I heard the creak of ox carts, smelled food being prepared, heard the voices of other men and women. I stumbled crying onto the road and came into the town. And all about me, I saw throbbing balls of radiance. What I later came to know as the soul of each person. As I walked among them, heard the muttering voices, the balls began to deepen and shift their hues. Soon they were like black flickering beards, beards flecked with crawling red lice. Their voices rose in denunciation as the first stones hit me. . . ."

"We found her half-dead outside of the town," Carver said. His knife flicked out, and a sliver of meat curled off the roast into his hand, "Snow Rose had been left for the scavengers."

"In her silvered blindness, they took her for one cursed by the gods," another dwarf added. "One like ourselves."

"We brought her here to our secret home," Carver said. "Like us, she was an outcast. And her beauty moved us."

"This is a haven," Snow Rose said, "for those in the Six Kingdoms whom men despise."

"We whom fate has twisted in the womb," the third dwarf continued, "live here together in tolerance and safety, guarded by the superstitious fear of the woods."

"And my elven sight has shown me that their souls are as great as those of straight-limbed men," Snow Rose told Ragnack.

Ragnack broached the question that had been troubling him. "Why did you rescue me, gentle dwarves?"

Carver spoke for the others. "The great boar and his herd had troubled us and laid waste to our crops too. Though we are fierce hunters, some of us would have died killing the pig lord. We are indebted to you." The dwarf paused, grew almost shy. "You are a worthy man. Though she is too kind to speak, we know Snow Rose is lonely. We brought you here as a gift."

The Gathering XV

Snow Rose knew the village, and Ragnack abandoned his inclination to direct the blind woman and hobbled stiffly at her side. Around them was the

127

bustle of a healthy village. The children's play had a joyous, often cruel democracy that ignored physical disparity. All this Ragnack noted as he walked with Snow Rose out the gate of the log-walled village into the Umbra Forest. He also saw the pits lined with pointed sticks, the deep ditch before the walls. But some of his hunter's violence was soothed by the forest's beauty. He gave the white-haired woman his arm.

"Even though we keep to ourselves, still we guard our home," Snow Rose said. "We call the town Dwarf Jaw, the place of the fatal bite. Among those ill-favored to the world's taste, the town is a haven. All are desperate warriors here because the town offers hopes most had forsaken: anonymity, lovers, and the possibility of children."

"And no one ventures beyond the forest?" Ragnack asked, wondering if he must escape to return to Melchior's castle.

"We are lacking in discrimination." The woman laughed. "All come and go as they please. Most remain here. But the dwarves and I walk beyond the woods. There are supplies and medicinals we must possess. With my storytelling, I am welcomed generously. The dwarves accompany me as jesters, acrobats, and guardians. In truth, some courts seek out the services of the dwarves before mine."

"They are mirthful creatures," Ragnack agreed, "but certainly not equal to your enchantment."

"The dwarves are matchless jesters," she said, smiling, "and stealthy, skillful nocturnal murtherers."

A movement to the side of the path drew Ragnack's eye, but when he glanced into the weave of vines there was nothing. The woman felt his arm tense beneath her long fingers.

"Leave your worry," she told him. "The dwarves always watch over me in the forest."

"Am I a threat to you?" Ragnack asked. There was a rustle around them.

"They are only anxious," Snow Rose said soothingly, "that you please me." And she reached softly to Ragnack and drew his face to hers. The forest seemed to sigh. If she had meant to set his mind at rest, Ragnack thought, she had failed.

When they walked through the forest the next day, Ragnack sensed that they were alone. The wood smelled of autumn's arrival; auburn and gold flared in the trees. Their steps rustled in fallen leaves.

"You will be well enough to return in a week," Snow Rose said quietly. "The dwarves called to your friends and told them you had killed the great boar and almost died and that the spirits of the forest were restoring you."

"And they will let me go?" Ragnack asked.

"We hold no one against their will."

There came over him a strange melancholy as he looked down at this woman. He found her beautiful, her blind silver eyes, the scars of her tears on her eyelids, her hair like a silent cascade. And inextricable from her beauty was the valor in her attempt to gain the elven vision and her tenderness as she had nursed him. All lay unspeakable and unspoken in his heart.

"I wish you could see the forest turn the color of blood and sunlight," Ragnack told her instead.

"I drink the world with different senses," she replied. "I hear squirrels chuckling over their caches of nuts, the badger grumbling as he shoulders his way into his burrow to sleep winter away; I hear the orisons of the flocks as they fly down to the southern lands. And I see the temper of light that wreathes all living things."

"I had forgotten your gifts, Lady," Ragnack said.

"Not gifts, but bartered visions," she said. And then her voice hardened. "You are a warrior, Ragnack, a man known to us by rumor even here. Tell me. What curdles the sweetness of the world?"

"I — I have some confusion," Ragnack stumbled. "Of what do you speak?"

She stopped, and they stood beneath the autumnal glory of the trees, as the wind shook this last beauty before the branches became empty.

"Perhaps you do not know what you know," she said finally. "The birds tell me of catastrophe and rapine. Vultures croak their glut from austere heights. The animals of the forest are nervous with the thunder of hooves and the smell of distant fires."

"But surely this is the nature of the world," Ragnack told her.

"I am well aware of the common cruelty of our times. There is something deeper here than ordinary hardship. Nights I have stood while all slept and I could concentrate my sight.

"I watched a slow, sickly light gather and grow in the east, that I knew was the distant reflection of thousands of murderous souls. I have watched it waver and shift until it gathered itself and slowly flowed toward us. Finally I saw what I had only glimpsed a taint of before. A darkness so profound that it pulsates its hunger and hatred for even the wanton minions it commands. Approaching us is not a mere army, but a hunger so evil and complete that it has its own nobility. It comes not to conquer, but to devour us joy by joy down to the final scrap of each one of us: child, father, mother, noble, serf, bent, and straight."

Ragnack still hesitated. "True, I have heard rumors of a barbarian host." Pain crawled in the cankered scars of his arm.

"In my years of vision, I have witnessed the spectrum of mankind," the woman said evenly. "I have seen souls drip with the putrescence of violence, quaver with infidelities and betrayals, watched the young bruised to lesser wisdom. In all whose beauty and weakness shone for me, I had never before seen the utter wrath that rages at the core of that host, a being so foreign to our lives that it seems crawled from the bowels of the netherworld. And then, to my amazement and trepidation, I saw this nocturnal taint in a man."

"Tell me. Say it," Ragnack replied with despair.

"When they carried you here, your life flickering weakly about you, between the beams of radiance throbbed this same darkness that laps on the edge of the wood. It defined your molten grace like the molds of a goldsmith hold the poured ore and shape its final design."

"I am demon-cursed," Ragnack made woeful admission. "Bonded by fate with the foulness your fey sight perceives. A demon ensorceled to the image of a man walks our world."

Whether it was the black blood that moved in his veins or no, Ragnack still acknowledged the mission that drove the solitary imp to save its race. He realized that the seer's hand with its light, succoring warmth still rested against his skin.

"Think what you will," the woman told him. "You are no more and no less than a man, one who against his will has gained an awareness of the shadows that haunt all of us."

And they continued through the forest, the sun a bit dearer for the man, the wind chiller for the woman. As they returned, Ragnack saw a body of brown robed, hooded figures limp into the farthest gate of the gnarled fortress.

"I have not seen any here shy to display themselves," Ragnack said, as the cowled figures crept in.

"I can read their souls from here," Snow Rose said. "Hearts cleansed of vanity, grateful for each day, greedy only for breath. They are ones even you in your grievous sadness might not wish to trade places with."

"Who are these ones for whom you

©JANET AULISIO 1989.

131

make such blithe judgments?" Ragnack spat.

"Lepers," Snow Rose told him.

The Gathering XVI

The great fields of Roxolani were aflame. The west wind drove the waves of fire across the leagues of heavy-headed wheat. The blasted earth stretched from the edges of Gobo's camp and slowly spread like a lengthening shadow.

The month before the harvest had been dry. Packs of riders from the ravaging horde had driven the serfs from their scything and, the high wind at their backs, had thrown oily torches into the wheat.

The golden knight and Gobo stood on the bench of Gobo's treasure wagon and watched the flames comb away the winter reserves of Roxolani.

"This is mighty destruction," Gobo admitted, "but I prefer the screams of women and the reek of men's flesh burning in the embers of a plundered village."

"Patience, my friend," the knight said. "We drive the fearful peoples of this soft world into a corner. You will soon have your fill of baubles and slaughter."

Two grinning horsemen rode up. At the end of their lariats, they pulled a steaming lump. Wisps of smoke rose from the corpse's hair.

"This plant-eater desired an audience with Gobo the Merciful," the first rider said.

Laughing, they spurred away to search for other sport.

Gobo stepped heavily from the wagon and rolled the dead man onto his back. His fat fingers pried open the heat-stiffened pouch that hung from its belt.

"Wretched thieves," he cried, staring at the three tiny silver coins in his hand. "They've taken this peasant's one

gold piece and left nits of silver to taunt me."

Without thinking, Gobo threw the coins. One flew wide and struck the handsome knight. There was a sizzle, and the knight cried out as he clutched his face. As he drew his hands back, in amazement Gobo saw the coin's image burned into his forehead.

The knight sprang from the wagon and squeezed Gobo's blubbery throat in his mailed hands. Gobo had never smelled the knight's breath before.

"If I find that you ever speak of this moment," the knight said softly, "I will suck all the pleasure out of your fetid body and leave you so nerved with pain that even a hair's weight will be an agony on your poxy skin."

As Gobo watched, the cicatrix on the knight's face shrank and vanished. But deep was Gobo's knowledge of what darkling creatures silver harms. The knight smiled down on his shaken partner. He led Gobo to the back of the great wagon, tore the locked door open, and gestured at the auric hoard of Gobo's heart.

"I would hate to end such a fruitful friendship," the knight said.

"I too," Gobo said hoarsely. "We have plundered so much and stolen so many beautiful horses."

So the leaders of the host were reconciled and once more turned their energies to the ruination of the Six Kingdoms.

The Gathering XVII

After the fields of Roxalani lay desolate, Apollyon directed Gobo's horde to the borders of the Umbra Forest at the edge of Melchior's kingdom. He waited for the imp to return and signal the culmination of his designs. The barbarians set fires in the forest, chased the antelope across the plains, broke the many horses in the train of their booty. After months of activity, they welcomed a loosening of discipline. The first cool winds came from the west, a reminder that soon the seasons themselves would end the wonderful carnage.

The second evening of the lull in campaigning, Apollyon stood outside his tent in thickening twilight. The imp flapped down from the sky like a fragment of night. Apollyon opened his hand, and his familiar danced in his palm before it spoke.

"Druzla gathers the Black Wolves. In a week, during the sun's eclipse, they will harvest the souls of this day-rotted world. You have done well, my master."

"And what of the lands that Gobo and I have savaged?"

"All of the Six Kingdoms make their hasty passage here as rats scamper to a ledge when the spring floods rise in a cavern."

Apollyon hissed his satisfaction. The familiar dissolved to tarry vapor and passed between his master's lips.

The pungent smoke of the dung-fire brazier rolled out of Gobo's wagon when Apollyon opened its door.

"I have consulted the oracles; they speak of one last battle, where men scream your name in fear, where swift horses swell your herds and gold rains into your wagons. We move tomorrow to wreak our will."

The toad-like figure shifted on the mound of his treasure, took the skull-cup from his mouth, wiped away the froth of mare's blood.

"It is good," Gobo said thickly. "Even with the bounty of horses, my men long to return to the free sweep of the plains before snows trap us here. Even my hunger is almost satiated." Gobo smiled. "Almost. A last battle to trample down this scum and we ride home, sleek and storied forever in the songs of our children."

The handsome knight bowed, closed the door of the wagon. He cast his branching sight into the heavens, felt the moon and sun drawing inexorably together, knew that events rushed to unavoidable resolution.

The Gathering XVIII

In the confusion of the smoke-obscured dawn, Ragnack emerged from Snow Rose's cottage and felt a weight on his arm. It was a leper, face hidden in the cowl of his grey robes. Ragnack flinched despite himself. The bent figure spoke haltingly.

"We will not endanger the reception at Lord Melchior's of the community of Dwarf Jaw by including ourselves. . . ."

The scar on Ragnack's arm felt like a warlock's fingernail was tracing letters on his skin.

". . . in the request for sanctuary. The fear of us makes men bereft of tolerance. We would not rob the others of safety."

Smoke from the burning forest churned over the village. Wood thrushes and sparrows flew over them and dropped broken songs. Families huddled with sacks of their belongings. In Ragnack's veins, the demon blood sang of the world's dissolution. And then in unasked apposition, images rose within him: battles fought, Melchior's generosity, his home and station within the castle, the stupid giant Knuxor, Snow Rose's white-scarred eyelids, the great boar's rage, Lady Celine's love, the smell of the pig roasting in the hearth in the dwarves' hall. Ragnack finally embraced the world, the bitter and the sweet, the cruel and the kind, as if it were a matter of being or being undone.

"My skin crawls at your voice," Ragnack told the leper. "But destruction rolls over all of us. We go together to Melchior's. Soon enough we will all probably die without discrimination."

In gratitude, the leper raised his

133

right arm to touch Ragnack, but held back, bowed, and limped away.

Snow Rose had come out of her cottage. How long she had listened he did not know. Her black cloak was a sheath for the whiteness of her hair, her pale face, and the silver foil of her eyes.

"It is wondrous to see you war against the darkness your heart is bonded to. To hear a man subdue the fears within himself is doubly rare."

Instead of the roughly polished knights of Melchior, the last host that Ragnack led was the chivalry of Dwarf Jaw. The feeble-minded and foolish scoured the land as sharply observant as any elves. Disfigured men patrolled as outriders. And, as disciplined as any troops Ragnack had ever commanded, the dwarves marched in close ranks as the rear guard, where if any of the invaders threatened, battle would be joined. The dwarves' drums thudded in stalwart rhythm, their spears bristled like a wolf's muzzle. And within the wall of defenders walked grim-faced women armed with knives and bows, a second wall about the children, the old, and the crippled. On his pony, Ragnack wordlessly honed the boar spears he had borne into the Umbra Forest weeks before. Behind them Dwarf Jaw blazed, fired by those who had raised it.

Elk, deer, and bears fled before the choking smoke, as the despoilers advanced behind the flames of the Umbra Forest. Snow Rose stilled their maddened flight long enough to learn that they were brief hours ahead of the horde.

When they broke from the woods, they found the thatched huts of the farmers abandoned, flocks driven away, the fertile pastures untenanted. Ragnack swung the inhabitants of Dwarf Jaw onto the Eastern Road and drove them mercilessly. Finally, near noon of the second day of flight, Ragnack saw

the distant turrets of Melchior's hold. Before it, a city of tents and smutty campfires stretched on either side into the forest's shadows. As they drew near, Ragnack saw above the vast, confused aggregation, the banners and pennants of many nations and peoples drawn in terror together.

At last they approached the castle, and as Ragnack led the people of Dwarf Jaw to the walls, he spied Melchior and Lady Celine on the battlements. The old, long-bearded man called out his name and raised his arms in relief. The drawbridge fell open to admit them.

Ragnack turned to the silver-eyed woman beside him and said, "Praise the gods, Melchior welcomes us.

"The woman's aura boiled about her as she watched us," Snow Rose replied.

"It is past," Ragnack said.

Together they led the displaced of Dwarf Jaw into the tenuous safety of Castle Melchior.

The Abattoir I

"Things are not as they seem," Zenith, the Elven wizard-king said.

"And when have they ever been?" snorted Ganglion, the new Black Lord of Napthinia.

The leaders of the shards of the Six Kingdoms sat in Melchior's sooty hall and stared at each other across the broad oaken table. That all found themselves exiles in this tawdry principality made the air heavy with rancor.

"I for one am simply glad that my battle master has returned," Melchior said, nodding to Ragnack. Ragnack's eyes surveyed the factions with a murderous blankness. On his lap, hidden from sight, his demon-clutched right arm twitched. He looked back to the stained tapestried wall, where Snow Rose, Carver, and the Council of Dwarf Jaw silently listened.

"At least we can clear our council of

women and diseased and misshapen folk. It is ill-luck to have them here," said Fido of Roxalani. There were low murmurs of approval. Lady Celine's face flushed.

Ragnack spoke for the first time, "We are happy that you are so comfortable with our hospitality that you are open with your thoughts. Lady Celine is the confidant of Prince Melchior and his equal in our councils. These guests against the wall are also worthy folk. And," Ragnack continued with menace, "they are under my protection."

They all sat in prickly silence. Then Zenith said, "The blind woman is touched by elven wisdom."

"Touched indeed." Ganglion laughed.

"My friends," Melchior begged, "let us direct our wrath at our enemies."

"Prince Melchior speaks truly," rumbled Cosimo of Datal, "the barbarian scum are almost upon us. We must join our forces or else find ourselves wiped away like spittle from a plate."

"But more than the hard fact of this host disturbs me," Zenith said. The weak beauty of his features twisted. "As the elves fled here, all of us were seized with the sense of a malignancy swelling within the horde."

"And what is worse than starvation, slaughter, and loss of ancestral lands?" Fido of Roxalani asked.

Snow Rose stirred outside the council circle, prepared to speak, hesitated.

"There is some fell purpose here beyond mere death," Zenith continued. "The scattered tribes of elves were simultaneously attacked, our shrines defiled, the wells where we seek wisdom polluted, the silver-leafed oaks that hold the magic of our people felled, and the direction of our flight closed to all but this quarter. How did the rest of you come to gather here?"

"We woke one morning to find our fields aflame," Fido of Roxalani said. "We fled east ahead of the fire and because we knew Melchior was generous

and his kingdom fertile."

"After the golden knight had slain our champions, the bloody locusts put Napthinia under siege," Ganglion said. "Prodigious spells loosened our walls, and we thought ourselves carrion. Then a miraculous storm arose one night and under the cover of rain, we opened the steel-banded water gates and escaped in barges down the swift river Anthrax. We were borne to Melchior's borders and invoked the ancient treaties of friendship."

"Knights, serfs, and freemen, we are all who broke free of the horde as they sacked Ventnor after Prince Lavlog fell," confessed Lavlog's son and heir, the stripling Melmoth in his pristine armor. "We were driven before the horde, scavenging until we at last reached Melchior's kingdom."

"There was not even the satisfaction of a battle for Datal," Cosimo said. "A handful of greasy horsemen appeared outside our walls, The curs shot a few rag-fletched arrows that scored the facings of our buildings, slid off our roofs. We laughed. Within three days, knobbed plague raged within our walls. With thousands dead, thousands dying, we who remained healthy fled down the Southern Way. When at last we reached Melchior's domains, we had been free of the disease a fortnight. I swear we are clean," Cosimo pleaded.

There was the flickering hiss of rats passing through the rushes strewn on the floor; the wind rose and fell, drew high, weird notes as it passed the windows like air forced through the pipes of a stone organ.

"Each of us seems to have been driven here," Zenith said.

"We have been herded," Fido blurted.

"But why here?" Melmoth wondered.

"What lies beyond our kingdom?" Lady Celine asked them.

"The barren reaches of the Obdurate Mountains," said Ragnack.

"And at their end, the storm-combed Saurian Ocean," Zenith said.

"Exactly," Celine said. "There is no further place for any of us to go."

"We are trapped," said Melmoth.

"No," Ragnack snarled, "it is here we must fight."

In travail and necessity, they labored until dawn was two hours away, arranging the hasty deployment of their warriors. The drums of Gobo's host thudded dully and unceasing behind their deliberations, like the threats of a cantiff whose words are slurred with distance.

The Abattoir II

Ragnack leaned against Snow Rose as they climbed the stairs to Ragnack's chamber.

"In the face of oblivion, these men bicker over the ancient enmities of fallen nations. And worse," Ragnack said, " I let you and the others of Dwarf Jaw sit in quiet exclusion."

"We have never been asked to this world's councils," Snow Rose replied without bitterness. She took the hand of his demon-branded arm. "There is dissension enough without you forcing them to grudge our advice."

Ragnack thought he heard a faint creak of hinges. He looked down the hall, then turned to Snow Rose.

"The dwarves and I are leaving to-night . . ." she said.

"You are under my protection," Ragnack told her fiercely, "you are welcome here."

". . . to scout the mystery of this black-souled host," she went on.

Ragnack stared at her in desolation. His hand twitched and seemed to fall to talons that clutched her long fingers.

"Story-tellers and jesters are welcome visitors even among the most cruel peoples," Snow Rose said. "We will slip back tomorrow night with

136

knowledge of the nature of our enemies."

And such was his love, that there was no question of refusing her. But she had stopped speech in his throat.

"This is our world too. We will fight for it as we are able," she said. "And that you may survive."

Ragnack held her for a moment. His tears fell into her white hair, ran down the scars of her eyelids.

"The dwarves await me in the castle scullery," she told him at last. "Will you take me there?" With slow steps, Ragnack led her down into the bowels of Castle Melchior.

And when they had started down the steps, Lady Celine drew the narrow crack of her doorway closed in bitter silence.

After the young and the frail were housed in the stables of Castle Melchior, the men and women of Dwarf Jaw quietly moved to the far left wing of the battle line. There, where it stretched into the forest, they made camp and drew up their strategy.

The four dwarves dressed in motley waited at the service doorway of the kitchen, which opened out the back of the castle. Carver polished a dagger, while the others practiced juggling. Ragnack brought Snow Rose to them, and the dwarves stood with reverent attention.

"Is there any chance that this masquerade will succeed?" Ragnack asked Carver dully.

"We are but four jesters and a story-teller," the dwarf said. Stubble smiled vacantly and cartwheeled across the stone floor, "five vagabonds welcomed in the camps of jaded warriors. Harmless folk, the camp-followers of even foul conquerors like these."

"We have often used this guise," Snow Rose assured, "to see if danger threatened Dwarf Jaw. And always been ornaments of the most pagan courts. I sing the songs of battle, valor, and pillage that are the common coin of men."

"Once a horse-thief fallen on hard times came upon a farmer who had two beautiful daughters," Gnat began.

Ragnack raised his hands in submission. "Return tomorrow," he begged Carver, glancing to Snow Rose.

"I will bring you two together again," the grim jester promised. "We must leave now so we can reach the camp near first light and not appear to have issued from the castle."

"Tomorrow you will learn from us the baneful anatomy of our enemies," Snow Rose told Ragnack.

Her fingers groped to Ragnack's face. Then she pulled the hood forward, shadowed her great silver eyes. Carver gently took her hand, and the five slipped out into the night.

Lady Celine parted the curtain of the west window of her chamber, quietly unlatched the leaded window and swung it open. The creature flapped down onto the stone frame. Its black face twisted with pleasure as Celine whispered into the whorled leather of its ears. Her barbed words done, Celine stroked the cold, ridged back of the imp, then sent it back to its master waiting in the host of Gobo.

The Abattoir III

Ragnack and Zenith stood on the battlements and surveyed the morning without speaking. A steady, cold wind blew from the West and brought the smell of ashes from the Umbra Forest. The bulbous tents of the invading army stretched in daunting profusion across the plains. Waves of riders wheeled in the yellowed autumn grasses before their camp.

The sky was the distant indigo that heralds snow. No birds flew. The breath of the two warriors plumed in the long-shadowed air. From the courtyard and the fields before the castle rose the jiggle and clank of armor.

Zenith finally said, "How many warriors do we have to defend our peoples?"

"Many less than those horse gleaners," Ragnack said. "Perhaps five thousand, if we can ever bring them to fight as a body."

"I smell winter in the air," the elf said. "They cannot feed their horses on frozen tundra."

"If we had time, you would be right," Ragnack said, "but look around us."

He gestured to the meadows beside the castle, to the forest stretching into the wastes of the Obdurate Mountains. Thousands huddled around weak fires. Songs of distant homelands rose like blanched prayers; the cries of frightened children lifted and fell. Beneath the bare trees, the leaf-speckled ground swarmed with figures moving to keep warm.

"Before the ribs of our enemies' horses will show, these suffering here in refuge will starve. Over fifty thousand tremble beneath our shields, exhausting the winter food reserves of Melchior. We must face down these ravagers quickly and let all return to find the meager reserves buried against famine. Many will die if we win, but all of us will wither away, gnawing on each other, if we remain cornered here. We are forced to do battle."

"I have also wondered at the campaign of these crude horse reivers," Zenith said. "Though our communion with the world's nature has grown enfeebled, the elven folk have tasted bitterness in the winds, felt a lessening in the sun's weight on the grasses, heard mocking laughter drop from the night sky. Even the birds will not fly above the earth this host has trodden."

"Speak more clearly," said Ragnack.

Zenith turned to him. "If the woman blinded by our wells can see souls, even more clearly can I. You are demontouched, you must know the evil that

137

faces us?"

"I am cursed, you mean, a traitor," snarled Ragnack, "a dissembler in our own councils."

"Fool, I am not going to denounce you. That the blind woman loves you shows your quality. You have insight that is denied even to me." Zenith stared in haughty dudgeon at the silver wagons topped with antlers that held the last of the elven race.

"In apathy and ennui, the elves fade from the earth. Yet we still have an abiding love for this life. And a bemused affection for the fecund, clumsy races of mankind. Millennia ago, when elves and humans were guardians of the world, menace boiled out of the earth's bowels."

"The Soul Eaters, the Black Wolves."

Zenith continued, "This greedy massing of slayers has a stench that slinks down from that last demon torrent. If death was all that faced us, I would comfortably slay and be slain. Nations might be shattered, but still men and women would succumb to love and people again the desolate lands. It is what might happen after death that haunts me."

"A tainted pulse sings within me," said Ragnack. "I was blood-bonded months ago to a demon. But he also confessed that the Black Wolves had wasted to negation; that he passed into our world in the guise of a man as the last hope of his people. What damage can a single demon work?"

"Are the Six Kingdoms here in mighty array?" the elf asked, gesturing to the throng pressed against the roots of Melchior's castle. "If we faced four times the number of these horse caressers, I would not worry. But the sun's eclipse falls tomorrow."

"Eclipses pass," said Ragnack with a shrug.

Zenith drew the scintillation of his elven sword, pointed at the filigree of silver that ran its length. "So terrible

138

was the Soul-Eaters' last invasion that to this day, our weapons masters work the demon-biting silver into our blades. That last, devouring rush of ghouls came during the sun's eclipse two thousand years ago, when the Black Wolves fell on the Six Kingdoms while darkness reigned."

"How do we lay our fears before the others?" Ragnack asked.

Zenith laughed. "Do you feel they would believe us? If they barely wage battle in unison before this earth-torching host, they will give little belief to a nightmare. These princes struggle enough to see the surface of things."

"There is a fruitful harvest of souls here to draw the ghouls," Zenith told him.

"Many of the strong warriors of our age will wield their swords here," Ragnack agreed. The elven king looked at Ragnack in momentary disbelief. "If they come, the Soul Eaters will scorn the warriors. Their hearts are flat with pride and vainglory. No, if they fall from the sun-drained sky, the Soul Eaters will rend the children scattered through these woods, the fathers and mothers, whose cares make their hearts bountiful. Only those who rejoice in the simple beauty of these lands will be soul-shorn. Most knights will be safe."

"If the Soul-Eaters come, they will leave the earth even more brutish than it is," said Ragnack.

And as Snow Rose's face rose in his mind, a cry went up from before the castle and drew him back. A cart issued from the enemy camp. The donkey that pulled it slowly plodded across the bleached grass that separated the enemies. Ragnack saw a cap of motley wavering atop a pole tied to the wagon, and then recognized the tiny, still figure that lay in the straw. Blood dripped slowly between the rough-hewn boards.

The Abattoir IV

All who came forward to divine what was in the wagon, turned away in revulsion. But such was the vile artistry of Gobo, that the dwarf still lived. Ragnack gently lifted Carver and heard the halting words.

". . . and we were," the dwarf whispered, "in the monster Gobo's tent, the savages frozen with wonder as Snow Rose spoke, when a knight in gold armor strode in and ordered us seized as spies . . . we killed many, but they hold Snow Rose . . . the knight challenges you to combat or they will burn her before their tents . . . I failed . . ."

So died Carver, the first and final chief of Dwarf Jaw. Like a father whose child has died in his arms, Ragnack laid the small body gently down, and in his face was the awful indifference of one whose care for his own life has melted away. Before Gobo's camp, gangs of men dragged forth the last fire-blackened limbs of the Umbra Forest and heaped them about a stake. None who saw his expression questioned Ragnack as he strode into Castle Melchior to gird himself for combat.

Ragnack knelt in fealty one last time before Prince Melchior. He wore the stained and rusted armor that he had the day he had come upon the giant Knuxor assailing Melchior's castle, a time distanced by love and the workings of fate.

"As I arrived, so I leave. My gratitude to you, my munificent lord, my friend. I go to trial by combat for the woman Snow Rose's life. If this champion beats me to earth, heed the elven King's advice."

Melchior stared down into Ragnack's violet eyes and offered him his blessing. The warriors of the host raised a great ringing cry. Lady Celine sobbed into Melchior's emerald velvet robe. The drums of Gobo pounded like the pulse of a monster.

As he passed out of Castle Melchior,

Ragnack stared toward Gobo's camp, where a limp figure with argent hair slumped against a post. Smoke rose near the heaped faggots. In the sun's benediction, a golden knight strode forth, and stood before the horde. The knight gleamed there for a moment, then walked toward the armies of the Six Kingdoms.

As Ragnack pushed through the crush of knights, Zenith seized his arm. Ragnack raised his mailed fist, then recognized the elf.

"Take my sword," Zenith told him, and offered the beryl-headed pommel to Ragnack. The runes of silver glowed with their lunar wisdom. Ragnack clutched the blade in blood-hunger, forced himself clear, and stood at last alone in the dead meadow facing Apollyon. With steps like nails driven into the earth, they slowly approached each other.

The Abattoir V

If this were fable, then silence would have hung like heavy purple curtains over the plain. But the massed warriors of Gobo's legions screamed and made ululating taunt of Ragnack. The knights arrayed before Melchior's castle beat on their shields. The homeless drew away from their fires and shouted for vengeance.

But all Ragnack saw was the high stake and the still figure bound to it, the only sound he heard was the crackle of the torches in the hands of the men beside the pyre. Ragnack stared at the golden apparition who stood between him and Snow Rose.

"Greetings, brother," said the knight. His fair face was drawn, but satisfaction shown in it.

"What must I do to free the woman?" Ragnack demanded. "Do we fight or must I hostage myself to you? Whatever preserves her."

"I care not for the blind bitch," Apollyon said. "She is bait to draw you out. You alone of these Kingdoms know what I am about. Through my wiles, I know you have not shared with others the delicacy of my quest. I cannot afford even your single voice the chance of steeling this rabble."

"The sheep await the butcher," scorned Ragnack. "For myself, I am a tough, stringy ram and little like being driven," and he drew the elvish blade. "I will hack my way through you."

"As you wish, my brother," the demon replied, and the black, barbed sword hissed from its scabbard. He raised his golden shield, and it drank the hope from the sunlight.

As Ragnack caught the blow on his buckler and hewed with Zenith's sword, the scar on his sword arm was a lattice of agony. Like gods spilling stars at a universe's creation, their blows showered sparks. No man in either host could have equaled Ragnack. But as they fought on through the afternoon, Ragnack bloodied, the knight oozing the semblance of blood, the demon at last grew stronger as shadows lengthened. With two great strokes of the barbed sword, the golden knight ripped the buckler from Ragnack's grasp and forced him to the earth.

"No man has ever brought greater pain to a Black Wolf," Apollyon rasped. "but at last you yield."

"No," Ragnack answered, "I am beaten."

The golden knight stood silently over him in the failing light.

A flame danced up, caught, and engulfed the oil-spattered faggots heaped about Snow Rose.

Ragnack bellowed. Apollyon looked back, saw the fire lick at the woman.

"Little pleasure in killing me," Ragnack cursed. "You must also torture love for your satisfaction."

"Treachery," the knight whispered. "Villainy that I will answer, brother."

Apollyon crashed the flat of the black sword against Ragnack's helm. The demon lifted the body onto his shoulder and strode like gilt doom toward's Gobo's camp.

But four horsemen broke from the camp. Each held the corner of a broad, pale cloth. As they galloped past Apollyon, the links of the silver net rippled over the demon, curled him in pain, and robbed him of his strength. Back the riders came, grabbed again the corners of the net, and dragged Ragnack and Apollyon in subjugation back to the horde.

Lady Celine watched from the window of her chamber as the stake finally toppled into the embers hours into the night. She took the golden pins from her dark fragrant hair and opened the veins of her arms.

The Abattoir VI

As night failed, the sun spilled bitter ochre into the Valley of Bones. The Black Wolves felt the jaws of the dragon moon gape. The eclipse yawned.

Druzla and his holy attendants led out the long-headed, leather-winged wind riders, the artifacts of the early world, when scaled monsters had dominion. Their yellow eyes stared unblinking, the toothless gums rasped as the warriors sprang upon their backs and took the reins of supple man-leather. At the beasts' sides hung spell-strong bladders that the demons would fill with the essence torn from their soft prey and pour into the soul vats for the nourishment of the worm-young.

Buffets rocked the cavern as the steeds stretched their wings. Druzla stood before the small company until the wind-cleavers were calmed.

"One final boon to you to shield from the cankered day. We will weave a cloud of massy shadow to shelter you from day's cursed star as you journey.

Then you must fall upon the pale races while they battle, distracted, during the eclipse."

Spilling blood gathered from the ritual wounds of the priests, Druzla emptied a lazulite bowl onto the fractured floor of the cavern. Noxious tendrils swam up, coalesced, and joined, until the host was hidden to all but ghoulish eyes.

Rocks rolled away from the wide mouth of the cave, and the berserk fighters goaded their steeds. With dolorous, dry wing beats, the final hope of the Black Wolves rose. And if any traveler had looked into the Valley of Bones, they would have seen an ebony cloud ascend and pass like the dreams of the night itself toward the Kingdom of Holbine and the domain of Melchior the Frail.

The Abattoir VII

Ragnack awakened in a low tent, spread-eagled and bound to four stakes, rawhide cutting into his ankles and wrists. He looked up and saw a hand's span of stars through the smoke hole in the roof. The din of revelry surged through the thin walls.

"Our destinies are still intertwined," a low voice said.

Ragnack saw the golden sollerets of the knight across the low, smudgy fire. Silver chains bound him to stakes.

"We lie as equals," Ragnack replied.

"Understand me, brother," Apollyon said. "I wanted the woman to draw you to me. I intended to subdue you and then shelter you both when my people came to feed. The bloated horse-lover betrayed me."

They lay and listened to the rude, ceaseless celebration.

"The People of the Plains celebrate this final victory and their horse-rich return to their uncharted domains," the demon said. "They know the confusion

in the ranks before them. Oh, that I could live to see our warriors fall from the eclipsed sky. But it is enough that I have wrought these events, brought my people to the edge of re-birth."

"I care little, knowing her dead," Ragnack replied. Her name was beyond his speaking. "Praise the death your allies will bring me."

"I drugged her," the demon lied. "She felt no suffering. She was a portion of my partner's treachery. There is evil enough in men to satisfy even a ghoul. Would that I might seize him once in my true form. But before Gobo's horde falls on the Kingdoms, they will sacrifice me to their gods for victory boon. Gobo desires my humiliation. As I thought I molded him, he used me. My torments will afford him smug pleasure. You, my brother, are to be spared for later tortures. In the anarchy my race will wreak, you may even survive."

"All I wish," Ragnack said, "is that I could have the chance of slaying Gobo before they slew me."

They again listened to the jubilation that swarmed through the camp. Then Ragnack felt a trembling softness against his skin, heard the small, busy sound of gnawing. The rawhide that bound him loosened. He sat up slowly, rubbed the numbness from his limbs, saw tiny forms slip away.

"I sense the woman," Apollyon said, "your lover. The animals that she befriended free you." His voice held stark hope.

Ragnack crawled to him, loosened the silver chains at his feet, moved to his hands. And stopped. The raw sockets gaped at him, the humors of the knight's eyes stained his cheeks.

"I see that you have discovered my blindness." The demon laughed emptily.

Gently Ragnack freed Apollyon.

"Another figure in the sum that Gobo will pay," Ragnack vowed. The desire for death bound his thoughts like a

141

crown of black ice.

The mailed gauntlet fell on his shoulder, the eyeless face turned to him. "You do not know the camp, the way, or the look of Gobo. You will die before you even close with the brute."

"Little matters beside the attempt," Ragnack told him. "My life drifted away in the smoke that plumed above the stake. And despite your race's coming, I myself would relieve my world of one of its own evils."

"The world will survive our feeding," the demon answered. "The wise farmer culls his flock, not slaughters it. In my people's desperation, I raised up Gobo. Now he has served his purpose. For the woman's murder alone, I owe you his death."

"Is there possibility of vengeance? I am yours, however you would use me," Ragnack implored.

"It is I that will be brought before Gobo," Apollyon said slowly. "I that he would abuse with his own hands. I that will be within an arm's span of him."

He hesitated, turned his wounded face away.

"How can I help you?" Ragnack demanded.

"Give me your eyes," the demon told him.

The Abattoir VIII

The five jeering men dragged the limp figure of the golden knight out of the tent at mid-day and ignored Ragnack, except to kick him. But so commanding was the knight despite the depth of his fall, that none ventured to steal the demon's sword as it lay against the far wall of the tent.

The People of the Plains were already drawn up facing Castle Melchior, stretching so wide that they merely had to advance on the armies of the Six Kingdoms to turn their flanks. They awaited the final command that would

142

follow Gobo's propitious sacrifice.

Bound in silver chains, Apollyon was dragged into Gobo's great tent, cast in the dust before Gobo's throne of gold bars. He clenched his eyelids shut. He heard the torturers push their white-hot instruments deeper into the heart of the fire.

"I would thank you for your guidance in the procession of our success," Gobo taunted.

The battle chieftains clustered behind him aped his scorn. The golden knight lay motionless.

"You thought to use us for your foul ends, whatever they were," the fat leader told him. "But it is you who have served us. In gratitude, we will offer you to our gods so that our final victory will be all the more bountiful."

Gobo gestured and the guards raised the last demon champion to his knees, prodded him with their silver-headed spears.

"Before our priests and their servants sever our friendship," Gobo lorded, "I would say farewell."

He waddled off his throne; bent his face to the demon's; and, gloating, kissed the knight's lips. And with this touch of the flesh of man, as he had when Ragnack rescued him, at his end Apollyon returned to the fell, savage shape of his true nature and burst the silver chains asunder.

The final, curdled memory that Gobo had before the black claws rent him was the vulpine stare of Ragnack's purple eyes in the hideous transport of the demon's face.

Before the guards at last impaled Apollyon, the flower of the People of the Plains was dispatched to ride forever the wide plains of the netherworld.

The screams from Gobo's tent rang long and loud enough to reach the host poised to annihilate the Six Kingdoms. Minutes passed without explanation or command. The warriors shifted uneasily in their saddles; the horses sensed their apprehension and pawed at the earth. Then at the same moment as a small, strangely isolated storm cloud ground across the sky, the sun itself began to fail as a shadow gnawed its blazing face.

Cries of superstitious dread rose from the People of the Plains.

From the far left wing of the disjointed forces around Castle Melchior, a small company broke toward the great horde. Dwarves marched in its center, spears in their hard hands, broad axes swinging from their belts. Figures on crutches lurched forward. Women strode forth, bows strung, arrows nocked. Mad figures juggled knives. And at their head hobbled a band clad in grey robes. As they neared the horde, the cowls fell back and they raised their arms.

In terror, the riders perceived the disease-eaten lineaments, the knobbed limbs of the lepers of Dwarf Jaw. In disarray and valor-drained, the host of Gobo stuttered to the attack. And from the vortex of darkness absorbing the sun, on nightmare steeds, the warriors of the Black Wolves careened from the sky for the spoils of souls.

Against the assurances given in the war council the night before, the forces of the Six Kingdoms were gathered in no particular order. Each Lord hoarded his forces, so his command would not be diluted. The two men capable of reason and leadership were helpless. Zenith's warnings had been reckoned as elvish weakness, his prophecy of the eclipse derided. Melchior had fallen into sudden dotage in his grief at the death of Lady Celine.

Now the legions watched in confusion as the chivalry of Dwarf Jaw closed with the People of the Plains, the sun failed, and a stygian cloud plummeted from the heavens as battle was joined. The sepulchral laughter and keening exultation were the diapason of no combat the Six Kingdoms had ever heard.

© JANET AULISIO 1989.

143

Deep the Black Wolves drank, myriads they drained in the sun's brief demise, swollen stretched the soul sacks as they filled with the swirling essences. And full satisfied was the company of ghouls when at last they ceased their plunder. With the moon's shadow relinquishing the sun, they hied back to the Valley of Bones on leather wings in the camouflage of the thunderhead.

Despite Zenith's fears, they had not plundered children. Those they found in combat were fulsome enough. They had harvested well: from the free-riding martial hearts of the People of the Plains and from the great-spirited warriors of Dwarf Jaw: the dwarves, lepers, and other scorned heroes who fought without vainglory for the world's salvation.

The ghouls sought no souls from the contentious ranks of the Six Kingdoms. The spirits of knights they had taken centuries ago were those who had tainted the milk of their young.

With the sun's return, the knights before Melchior's castle saw the smoke, the bodies steaming in death, the fragments of Gobo's host wandering the plains in shock. Flailing at each other for precedence, they attacked the barbarians in a cacophonous tumult.

Groping in the tent, Ragnack touched Apollyon's abandoned sword. As a dog will nuzzle the hand of a long-absent master, so the hilt of the barbed sword sought his hand. Gifted by his demon's blood in his blindness, Ragnack felt the souls of Gobo's riders flicker close before him. He slashed free of the tent. In Snow Rose's memory, he fell on them, hewed, thrust, and slew.

The few surviving dwarves found him face down in the carnage of the field. As they had once before in the Umbra Forest, they carried the broken man away to heal him.

So died the last demon champion.

So was his quest fulfilled.

So were the People of the Plains overthrown.

So were the Six Kingdoms saved.

So was Ragnack hero and vanquished.

⊗

BOOKS! BOOKS!

Add to your Weird Library!

Fiction by Weird Tales® authors!

THE ADVENTURES OF LUCIUS LEFFING by Joseph Payne Brennan. $30.00.
More tales of this great psychic sleuth. Signed by the author.
SIXTY SELECTED POEMS by Joseph Payne Brennan. $15.00 (hc). Brennan's
eighth book of poems, and a must for all fans of dark poetry.
AUTHOR'S CHOICE MONTHLY: KARL EDWARD WAGNER. 120 pp. $25.00 (hc).
Five of Wagner's best, plus new introduction.
THE BOOK OF KANE by Karl Edward Wagner. $20.00. Five stupendous
"acid gothic" sword-&-sorcery tales. Illustrated by Jeff Jones.
THE WHITE ISLE by Darrell Schweitzer. $18.95 (hc). An epic fantasy
of strange terrors and hostile gods by the author of The
Shattered Goddess and We Are All Legends. Now ready. Also
available in a signed/limited edition of 50 copies: $50.00.
TOM O'BEDLAM'S NIGHT OUT by Darrell Schweitzer. $22.00 (hc). Short
stories by one of WT's editor/authors. Art by Stephen Fabian.
THE BOOK OF IAN WATSON by Ian Watson. $18.95 (hc). The best short
stories of one of the most talented British fantasists.
FREE LIVE FREE by Gene Wolfe. $45.00 (hc). First edition and only
complete text. Signed by Wolfe (featured author in WT #290) and
signed by artist Carl Lundgren (Featured Artist in WT #292).

Cthulhu Mythos fiction by Brian Lumley:

HERO OF DREAMS. $22.00 (hc).   **ELYSIA.** $26.00 (hc).
MAD MOON OF DREAMS. $22.00 (hc).   **THE COMPLETE CROW.** $22.00 (hc).
SHIP OF DREAMS. $22.00 (hc).   **BURROWERS BENEATH.** $23.50 (hc).

Books by Robert E. Howard:

KULL. $25.00 (deluxe hardcover). A gorgeous edition of all the
stories of King Kull, Howard's first great barbarian adventurer.
POST OAKS AND SAND ROUGHS. $25.00. Never before published autobio-
graphical novel of the young, struggling Howard.
SHADOWS OF DREAMS. $25.00. Hitherto unpublished poetry.

Deluxe hardcover editions of Howard's Conan series:

POOL OF THE BLACK ONE. $25.00.   **BLACK COLOSSUS.** $20.00.
JEWELS OF GWAHLUR. $20.00.   **QUEEN OF THE BLACK COAST.** $20.00.
THE DEVIL IN IRON. $20.00.   **ROGUES IN THE HOUSE.** $20.00.
HOUR OF THE DRAGON. $30.00.   ...Complete set: $155.00.

Exciting fiction:

THE DEVIL'S AUCTION by Robert Weinberg. $18.95 (hc). First in the
Weird Tales Library series...an exciting occult horror/mystery!
A DREAMER'S TALES by Lord Dunsany. $17.00 (hc). Dunsany's greatest
stories, the finest fantasies available in English.
TALES OF 3 HEMISPHERES by Lord Dunsany. $13.95 (hc). 15 classics.
THE GHOSTS OF THE HEAVISIDE LAYER by Lord Dunsany. $20.00 (hc).
Uncollected Dunsany material. 14 stories, 19 essays, and 2 plays.
PULPTIME by Peter Cannon. $15.00 (hc). H.P. Lovecraft teams with
Sherlock Holmes to solve a mystery in 1925 New York. Great fun!
BOOK OF THE DEAD edited by John Skipp & Craig Spector. $22.00 (hc).
Sixteen original stories in the mode of George Romero's Night of
the Living Dead. Authors: King, McCammon, Schow, and many more.
THE MAN WHOSE TEETH WERE ALL EXACTLY ALIKE by Phillip K. Dick. $9.95
(trade pb). Previously unpublished mainsteam novel.
PULPHOUSE: ISSUES #3, #4, #5. $20.00 each, (hc). Something unique --
a magazine published in a 1000-copy edition at affordable prices.

<u>Rave Reviews</u>: "Highly recommended for the discriminating reader."
Pulphouse does four issues per year, one fantasy, one science
fiction, one horror, and one "speculative fiction." The first two
are **Out of Print**. #3 is a <u>fantasy issue</u>, with Ellison, Bishop,
Davidson, de Lint, and 19 others. #4 is <u>science fiction</u>, with
Knight, Budrys, Williamson, and 16 more. #5 is <u>horror</u>, with
Effinger, Bryant, Friesner, Nina Kiriki Hoffman, and 18 others.
WESTLIN WIND by Charles de Lint. 100pp. $35.00 (hc). Companion piece
to <u>Ascian in Rose</u>, using characters from <u>Moonheart</u>. **Signed**.
APARTHIED, SUPERSTRINGS, AND MORDECAI THUBANA by Michael Bishop.
100pp. $35.00 (hc). A new novella by this award-winning author,
concerning everything in the title...a vivid, disturbing story.
AUTHOR'S CHOICE MONTHLY: GEORGE ALEC EFFINGER. 120pp. $25.00 (hc). A
30,000-word single-author collection. 7 humorous stories (one
original) plus new introduction. See also the Wagner volume.
THE LAST COIN by James Blaylock. $60.00 (hc). Beautiful first
edition, limited to 750 copies. Introduction by Lucius Shepard.
Signed by Blaylock, Shepard, and artist Dennis Loftner.

<u>The Best in Non-Fiction:</u>

SPIRITS, STARS, AND SPELLS by L. Sprague and Catherine Crook de
Camp. $17.00 (hc). Definitive work on the Black Arts.
THE DARK HAIRED GIRL by Phillip K. Dick. $19.95 (hc). Essays and
other non-fiction by this cult classic author.
CITIES & SCENES FROM THE ANCIENT WORLD by Roy G. Krenkel. $25.00
(hc). Coffeetable-sized collection of Krenkel's fantastic art.
PATHWAYS TO ELFLAND: THE WRITINGS OF LORD DUNSANY by Darrell
Schweitzer. $25.00 (hc). The first complete study of Lord
Dunsany's writings, with extensive bibliography.
ON WRITING SCIENCE FICTION: THE EDITORS STRIKE BACK! by George H.
Scithers, Darrell Schweitzer, and John M. Ford. $19.50 (hc). A
complete "how-to" guide for novice science fiction and fantasy
writers. By the founding editors of <u>Isaac Asimov's SF Magazine</u>.
THE RAGGED EDGE OF SCIENCE by L. Sprague de Camp. 255pp. $16.00
(hc). Articles on such diverse subjects as "The Mayan Elepants"
("...feathered elephants, as you know, are extremely rare.").
TO SERVE MAN: A COOKBOOK FOR PEOPLE by Karl Wurf. 104pp. $10.00
(hc). <u>Science Fiction Review</u> wrote: "Yes, it's a 'cookbook for
people'...but don't show it to people who are bigger, stronger,
more numerous than you, and haven't been fed recently." Humor.

Enclosed is $_____, by check or money order (in Pennsylvania,
add 6% sales tax), for the titles listed below:

_____   Name:_____

_____   Address:_____

_____   City:_____

_____   State/Zip:_____

_____   <u>or</u> Bill my [ ]Mastercard [ ]Visa card

_____   Card number _ _ _ _ _ _ _ _ _ _ _ _

_____   exp date: _ _ _ _

_____   Signature

Use the form above, or copy the information.
Order from: <u>Weird Tales</u>® P.O. Box 13418, Philadelphia, PA 19101.

www.ingramcontent.com/pod-product-compliance
Lightning Source LLC
Chambersburg PA
CBHW070556180626
46817CB00005B/1872

* 9 7 8 0 8 0 9 5 3 2 1 2 4 *